Death l...

"Fast and breezy, *D...* ...sant mystery . . . Organi... ...ffer little reminders on how to make our lives more organized to have more time to read mysteries." —*The Mystery Reader*

"A carefully crafted mystery with enough red herrings to be truly satisfying and enough cliché poking to be wickedly humorous as well." —ReviewingTheEvidence.com

"This is a fun book . . . [A] pleasant way to spend a lazy afternoon." —*Gumshoe Review*

The Cluttered Corpse

"Talented author Mary Jane Maffini has crafted a clever and fun tale . . . Red herrings and surprises await the reader [and] complexities of the plot make for a worthwhile read." —*New Mystery Reader*

"Charlotte is feisty, funny, and determined to help people, whether it's organizing their mud room or clearing them of a murder charge . . . Delightful." —*I Love A Mystery*

"Amusing . . . enjoyable." —*The Mystery Reader*

"We all should have a Charlotte Adams in our lives." —ReviewingTheEvidence.com

Organize Your Corpses

"A comedic, murderous romp . . . Maffini is a relaxed, accomplished, and wickedly funny writer." —*The Montreal Gazette*

"Maffini provides a first-rate, well-organized whodunit . . . A new series that is fun to read." —*Midwest Book Review*

Berkley Prime Crime titles by Mary Jane Maffini

ORGANIZE YOUR CORPSES
THE CLUTTERED CORPSE
DEATH LOVES A MESSY DESK
CLOSET CONFIDENTIAL

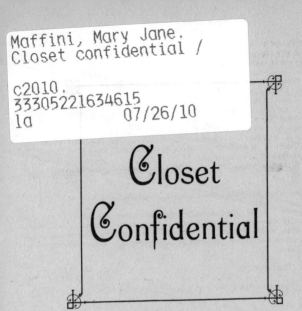

Closet Confidential

Mary Jane Maffini

BERKLEY PRIME CRIME, NEW YORK

THE BERKLEY PUBLISHING GROUP
Published by the Penguin Group
Penguin Group (USA) Inc.
375 Hudson Street, New York, New York 10014, USA

Penguin Group (Canada), 90 Eglinton Avenue East, Suite 700, Toronto, Ontario M4P 2Y3, Canada
(a division of Pearson Penguin Canada Inc.)
Penguin Books Ltd., 80 Strand, London WC2R 0RL, England
Penguin Group Ireland, 25 St. Stephen's Green, Dublin 2, Ireland (a division of Penguin Books Ltd.)
Penguin Group (Australia), 250 Camberwell Road, Camberwell, Victoria 3124, Australia
(a division of Pearson Australia Group Pty. Ltd.)
Penguin Books India Pvt. Ltd., 11 Community Centre, Panchsheel Park, New Delhi—110 017, India
Penguin Group (NZ), 67 Apollo Drive, Rosedale, North Shore 0632, New Zealand
(a division of Pearson New Zealand Ltd.)
Penguin Books (South Africa) (Pty.) Ltd., 24 Sturdee Avenue, Rosebank, Johannesburg 2196,
South Africa

Penguin Books Ltd., Registered Offices: 80 Strand, London WC2R 0RL, England

CLOSET CONFIDENTIAL

A Berkley Prime Crime Book / published by arrangement with the author

PRINTING HISTORY
Berkley Prime Crime mass-market edition / July 2010

Copyright © 2010 by Mary Jane Maffini.
Cover illustration by Stephen Gardner.
Cover design by George Long.
Interior text design by Laura K. Corless.

ISBN: 978-0-425-23564-5

BERKLEY® PRIME CRIME
Berkley Prime Crime Books are published by The Berkley Publishing Group,
a division of Penguin Group (USA) Inc.,
375 Hudson Street, New York, New York 10014.
BERKLEY® PRIME CRIME and the PRIME CRIME logo are trademarks of Penguin Group
(USA) Inc.

PRINTED IN THE UNITED STATES OF AMERICA

10 9 8 7 6 5 4 3 2 1

For my parents, who believed in the magic of books

Acknowledgments

I owe thanks to the capable and generous community of organizers—a truly helping profession for our cluttered era and one which has led me to choose that as a career for Charlotte Adams, the lucky girl. As always, I am very grateful to Mary MacKay-Smith, Linda Wiken, and Victoria Maffini who made time to offer valuable insights on the manuscript for *Closet Confidential*. I must also thank my sons-in-law, Barry Findlay and Stephan Dirnburger, for knowing the most amazing things and not being afraid to share them. No one else can bring much-needed humor to the darkest moment the way my husband, Giulio, can. My friend Chris Myers was very helpful as usual, and I would be lost without his time and expertise.

Once again, Tom Colgan, Niti Bagchi, and Megan Swartz of Berkley Prime Crime and my agent, Kim Lionetti, did a terrific job of smoothing the process and soothing the author. Closer to home, I'm also indebted to Ottawa Therapy Dogs for allowing my spoiled princess dachshunds to bring joy to others. Let's hope they can inspire Truffle and Sweet Marie.

Last but not least, hats off to the legions of cozy fans and authors who make this such an entertaining genre to write and to read.

You cannot hide from me.

I will know everything about you as soon as your closet door swings open and I peer in.

If you are having an affair, I will see the signs.

Terrified of getting old? I'll know in a minute.

Going broke? Ditto.

Letting the people in your life walk over you? Won't take me long to figure that out.

Every closet disaster masks some hitch in life—minor or major—even if it's simply being overscheduled. I'm a professional organizer and when I do my job well, my clients feel better able to tackle whatever else is troubling them. At best, they change their lives to feel happier. At worst, the results are murder.

—Charlotte Adams

Show me your closets and you show me your secrets.

1

Lorelei Beauchamp would not react well to the suggestion that anything in her beautiful life and her spectacular home was less than perfect. I took care not to let the phrase "closet makeover" slip past my Dior lipstick.

Lorelei issued a languid, silvery laugh. "Charlotte dear, you are most certainly not your mother's daughter."

Whatever that meant, it would be the first of many digs. Lorelei and my mother went all the way back to high school when the competition for homecoming queen transformed their friendship. The passage of nearly forty years hadn't changed their status as fabulous frenemies. Their air kisses on the rare occasions they met had all the genuine warmth of dry ice.

I reminded myself that Lorelei had seven closets, jammed with designer clothing and accessories, and I intended to keep our minds on them rather than the rivalry between her and my mother as we sifted through her pricey clutter. Lorelei might also have more money than God, but I wasn't planning to crawl over broken glass to earn my fee.

I produced a smile that my mother would have been proud of. "No, I am myself."

If Lorelei had not lost her only daughter, Anabel, several months back, I might not have been in her home on a cool but sunny Sunday afternoon in June. But Anabel Beauchamp had drowned on a Woodbridge construction site, a freakish accident that left her friends, co-workers, and the young people she worked with badly shaken. I had liked and admired Anabel, and after all, our families had a shared history. I still felt guilty that I'd been in Europe and unable to attend the funeral. All to say, I was prepared to cut her grieving mother some slack.

Lorelei's husband, Harry, shot me a sympathetic glance. He was the only soft, comforting element in the vast glass, stone, and steel living room. Harry and I would probably both be glad when this ritual was over. And Lorelei would be happy when she'd put my mother—who hadn't even lived on the same continent for the last twelve years—in her place. Senior year in high school? I figured it was a shame to let their distant past blight her life.

Lorelei must have been six feet tall, slender and elegant, with perfect bones and flawless skin. That face had gazed out from hundreds of magazine covers over the years. This was the woman who had snagged the role of spokesmodel for Face It cosmetics at the age of forty-five and in many ways had changed the way America regarded women as they hit midlife. She had the confidence that would come naturally to someone with a perfume named after her. I had noticed the soft exotic scent of *Lorelei* as soon as I'd arrived. Lorelei's personal tragedies had not marred her classic features. The tiny lines that were visible when you sat next to her never made it into the advertising shots, but even if they had, they didn't diminish her beauty.

She tucked a strand of her silver blond hair behind a perfect ear. "Hmm. You're still single?"

"Happily so."

"What happened to what's-his-name? That young man you were engaged to in Manhattan? Didn't he give you a lovely ring? I seem to remember Esme raving on the subject the last time I saw her. She was very excited about it."

My mother had indeed been over the moon about both what's-his-name and the ring. And when I told her I'd tossed the square-cut diamond solitaire into the swirling dark waters of the Hudson, she'd been devastated. After four marriages and countless near misses, she was used to the idea that the man you loved could be a cheating hound. But it had been a new experience for me, and I had no plans to get used to it.

"Didn't work out. Sometimes a person needs variety." I grinned to leave the impression that I'd been the variety seeker. I was glad I'd taken care in choosing my outfit. My crisp white shirt had a flattering row of ruffles, and my venerable black pencil skirt was perfect with it. I'd splurged on a pair of open-toed red patent platform heels and a pedicure. When you're barely five feet tall, shoes matter.

With the large pair of gold hoop earrings on long-term loan from my mother, my classic wide woven leather belt, and a vintage lapis lazuli bracelet I'd scored at a garage sale, I could pass the Lorelei test, barely.

"I suppose." She produced a soft smile. "Although Harry has never sought variety in thirty-five years."

"Never have, never will, Lorelei darlin'." Harry still hadn't shaken off his soft southern drawl after more than thirty years in the Hudson Valley.

I knew he was telling the truth. I'd never seen a man quite so besotted by his wife. A couple of my mother's husbands had been head over heels, but none of them lasted past five years.

"In fact," Harry said as he got to his feet, "I think it's

time to celebrate that with a champagne cocktail. That's the current house specialty, Charlotte honey."

Of course it would be the house specialty for Lorelei Beauchamp. The color was right for one thing. Same pale shimmer as her famous hair.

As Harry was talking, Lorelei turned and stared out the expanse of fourteen-foot-high windows; her mind had drifted elsewhere. I didn't know what part of Harry's comments had triggered a troubling thought.

Harry glanced her way, then mine. "I have a special technique. Want to step into the kitchen with me and see how I do it?"

"With pleasure." Actually I was very happy to step away from Lorelei. Maybe she needed to be by herself. Harry had always functioned as Lorelei's white knight, manager, and protector. Now apparently he'd added mind reader to his résumé.

I followed him along the stark minimalist hallway to the mostly concrete and stainless steel kitchen. This house had been featured twice in major architectural magazines. The kitchen had scored a full page in both, although I couldn't imagine anyone cooking anything in it. Harry stopped at an immense cooler designed especially for white wine and, I supposed, champagne.

This seemed like a good time to tell Harry that I don't drink much and never when I'm working. I need my wits about me.

Harry grinned and nodded toward the cooler. "New toy. It keeps the bubbly at a perfect forty-two degrees."

Harry opened the door and produced a bottle of Veuve Clicquot. No cheap and cheerful sparkling wines for the Beauchamps' champagne cocktails. He grinned as he twisted off the foil and eased the cork out with the gentlest of pops. "We're having mimosas today. Does that work for you, Charlotte?"

He took down three crystal flutes from the bar cupboard and set them on the glossy counter.

"Not for me, Harry. I hope you don't mind. I'll stick with the orange juice."

"Charlotte honey, that's no problem with me. I squeezed the juice fresh just before you got here. I'll go easy. I imagine you'll need your wits when you tackle those closets." He stepped over to a refrigerator that was bigger than my entire kitchen and reached in.

More like when I tackle Lorelei, I thought. Most closets are a piece of cake for me. These seven would come with stacks of Louis Vuitton suitcases and tons of emotional baggage.

"How is she doing?" I asked, nodding back toward the seemingly endless living room where Lorelei sat staring out the wall of windows and seeing nothing.

Harry paused, still bent over. "Ah well." He picked up the pitcher of fresh orange juice. "Not too good."

"She seems so sad."

"She can't believe it. Anabel being gone. Like that." He straightened up and snapped his fingers. "One day she's our perfect girl, the next . . ." His eyes filled.

Sally had shown me the newspaper coverage of the tragedy when I returned from my trip, and I'd been shocked by the image of Anabel's covered body being carried from the muddy construction site where she'd drowned. It still distressed me when I thought of it. I hoped that wasn't the picture that stayed in Harry's head. I felt a catch in my throat as I watched Harry struggle to control his emotions.

"We were lucky to have her. So lucky. At least we have those beautiful memories."

I understood what he meant. Anabel was five years younger than me, but I always remembered her open smile and sturdy good nature. Harry's girl for sure.

"She was wonderful. Everyone loved her."

"Thank you, Charlotte honey." He turned his attention to the flutes and poured in the orange juice. "Juice first. The alcohol mixes down."

"And she was lucky to have you. You gave her a very joyous life."

At least Harry had.

"I hope so."

"Trust me."

Harry had been a wonderful parent, warm, uncritical, yet no pushover, the master of the gentle correction and the quiet life lesson. Anabel must have felt loved and cherished every day of her life. As for Lorelei, she hadn't been unkind, merely remote and always all about Lorelei. But then again, you can't have everything.

Harry smiled as he arranged the three flutes on a stylish tray from the Museum of Modern Art. "I'm awfully glad you agreed to come. You can see that she needs some kind of distraction. She's not getting back to normal. Not at all. I have to confess, Lorelei sounded intrigued when I told her about your new occupation. That's when I got the bright idea to call you. I thought that playing in those closets would be fun for her and would give her a chance to spend time with someone who was almost family. And I felt confident that you would understand if she's not herself."

"I'll do my best. I hope it works." I knew the closets might be improved when we finished, but there was no way of fixing Anabel's death. No surprise that Lorelei wasn't herself.

Harry picked up the MOMA tray and nodded for me to lead the way back to the living room. "And if you find Lorelei sometimes makes comments that are a little less than kind about your own mama, I hope you won't let that get you down. It's not personal. You know she has her funny little ways. But she thinks the world of you and she always has."

—+—

I shouldn't have been surprised a half hour later when Lorelei threw back the ebony-trimmed etched-glass doors to her own dressing room, the first of many closets that lay ahead of me. Like everything in the house, the doors were custom-made. She'd stood there for a while inhaling softly before the dramatic opening flourish. I admired her perfect posture as I believed I was intended to.

"What do you think? It's a bit like a Jackson Pollock, isn't it? All jumbled up."

It might have been, too, except that everything in it was a soft shade of white, cream, gray, or the official family color: champagne.

How to respond? "It does have a certain artistic purity."

She laughed, showing her perfect teeth to advantage. "You are a cute little thing, Charlotte. I hope Esme realizes what she has in you."

Let it go, I told myself.

"Is this closet a problem? It looks as though it was custom designed for you. Am I wrong?"

"No, you're not wrong, and you know it, Missy Smarty Pants. It *was* designed for me. They all were, naturally. It only makes sense."

Great. We were getting nowhere. "Why don't you give me an idea about what you'd like to achieve in this project?"

Lorelei nodded, approving. "Nicely done. And now the ball's in my court. Well, of course, it is and it should be. Let me see, what would I like to achieve? That's a very good question, Charlotte Adams. And I don't know the answer to it. Do you have to know right this minute?"

I chuckled politely. "I don't. But we're unlikely to achieve whatever that turns out to be if we don't figure out what it is."

Lorelei sank into a soft gray velour chaise that sat in the middle of the dressing room, like a fainting couch perfectly positioned for those days when there was a wardrobe malfunction. With those gorgeous looks and all that money, it was hard to imagine Lorelei ever having any kind of problem at all. But of course, Lorelei had a huge problem and one that money couldn't fix. Nothing would bring Anabel back. It would take more than a closet makeover to bring the meaning back to her mother's life.

"Sometimes I can't seem to find something."

I blinked and Lorelei laughed her silvery laugh. "I don't mean that I have nothing to wear. Of course, that's ridiculous. But I often can't find the one perfect article I'm looking for. I don't know where it is, and I don't even know where to begin looking. Finding what I want, that is something I'd like to achieve."

"Sounds well worth striving for."

"Hmm." She yawned languidly. "I suppose it is. What else am I going to do with my time?"

She got to her feet with one fluid movement, and we passed through her bedroom on our way to closet two. I gave a backward glance at the room with the largest bed I'd ever seen, no doubt also custom constructed for Lorelei. The headboard must have been six feet high and upholstered in white leather. A shimmering white silk spread covered the bed. I supposed the eight pillows would be enough even for Lorelei, with one or two for Harry.

As we turned to go, she stopped abruptly. "I don't think I can cope with any more today."

I raised an eyebrow without thinking. If she couldn't cope with looking at the second of her seven closets, I wasn't sure how she'd react to the more challenging part of sorting them out, not that I believed for a second she was serious about the project.

"I can tell that you think I'm being silly."

"It's your project, Lorelei. Naturally, you make the decisions. I have to say that it doesn't get any easier. And looking at the closets is usually the first step."

"I get so tired lately. You have no idea."

I found myself regretting my raised eyebrow and stodgy comments. Lorelei was so beautiful, so elegant, and so inclined to play to the imaginary camera every minute, it was easy to forget she'd suffered such a terrible tragedy so recently. I'd always found her hard to deal with, but that didn't mean I could overlook what she'd lost. I reached out and touched her hand.

"When would you like me to come back?"

She smoothed her already smooth hair and smiled wanly. "Can we be flexible? I never know how I'm going to feel."

"I'm booked up lately, but I was able to pop in when Harry called because I leave my Sundays free as a rule. He's very persuasive."

"Isn't he? Well, I don't know what to do, Charlotte."

"No pressure. Call me when you feel like going ahead and I'll come as soon as I'm free." I was surprised at myself as I am a stickler for making and keeping appointments. But then Lorelei always expected special treatment and got it. She has that in common with my mother.

"Monday then. Monday would be good for me."

"You mean tomorrow?"

"Isn't tomorrow Monday?"

"It is, but . . . okay, let me check." I fished out my agenda, the old-fashioned paper kind. Sure enough. I had a two-hour opening in the middle of the afternoon. I'd planned to use that to work on a time management seminar I was designing, but I could accommodate that easily enough later. The irony wasn't lost on me.

I looked up to find Lorelei watching me with interest, all signs of fatigue gone.

"Three o'clock? I can be here then."

"I know I'm not always easy to deal with. Harry's been suggesting that I try harder."

I kept my mouth firmly closed.

"Thank you, Charlotte." Lorelei clasped my hand.

"You're welcome. I hope I can help. Why don't we agree that tomorrow we'll take a look at the other closets? And then I'll have a better idea where to take it from there."

"Lovely."

She was getting paler by the minute. A modern Lady of Shalott. She'd tossed back that mimosa. Had it combined with some sedative she was taking?

"Perhaps you should lie down, Lorelei. You seem unwell."

The silvery laugh echoed through the room. "Unwell? I suppose I am."

"I'll let myself out."

As I reached the bedroom door, Lorelei swayed and sat on the edge of the shimmering silk-covered bed. "Charlotte?"

Reluctantly I turned back. "Yes?"

"Do you think we will ever find out who murdered my beautiful Anabel?"

2

I tracked down Harry in the rock garden by the back of the house. He'd changed into khaki Bermudas, a faded blue cotton shirt, and a pair of thick rubber gardening gloves. He was leaning forward on a garden kneeler, yanking out weeds, surrounded by the hum of bees. He had a determined look on his deeply tanned face, as if he was trying to avoid sympathy for the trespassing greenery. That look was overtaken by a smile as he saw me approaching. He stopped and got to his feet.

I took a deep breath first. "I don't know quite how to say this, Harry, but I had no idea that someone had killed Anabel."

The smile vanished. His brow furrowed. "Oh, Charlotte honey. What has Lorelei been sayin'?"

"She wondered if we would ever find out who murdered Anabel. I had no idea that anyone had. I thought . . . well, a horrible, tragic accident."

I actually felt my stomach lurch. I've had way too much murder in my life these last two years.

"Charlotte honey, it was an accident. There's no question about that. Everyone agrees. The police, the witnesses. Everyone except Lorelei. Some days she seems to accept it, but then, when I least expect it, she'll start up about Anabel being murdered."

"Oh. So . . . ?"

"A tragic misstep. There's no reason to think otherwise, except perhaps if you are a heartbroken mother."

I glanced at him. In my opinion, Harry was far more heartbroken than Lorelei. What impact would this talk of murder have on his healing? "I'm glad to hear she wasn't murdered."

His shoulders slumped. "I do not want to think that my beautiful baby girl was killed by anyone. I always wanted the best for her, and now I need to know her spirit will rest gently."

I felt tears sting my eyes. I found myself patting his arm to comfort him. "I can certainly understand that. I would want the same thing."

"Lorelei is having problems. She can't process it. Things have always gone so well for her and now this senseless tragedy."

I nodded.

"Try not to let her distress you, Charlotte honey."

"Lorelei won't distress me. And I can understand why you both feel the way you do."

"That's real good. Let me know if she asks you to do anything too . . . unusual."

"Thanks." I smiled at him.

"I'm so sorry, Charlotte honey. I should have realized when I suggested the closet project that she might have wanted you especially because of all your involvement in, well, um, you know what I mean."

"That makes sense. She doesn't seem to have much interest in the closet refit."

"As usual, I walked in with my eyes wide open and still not seein' what she actually wanted."

Damn. I was doing my best to steer clear of murders for the rest of my life. At least this one wasn't real.

"I can't look into murders, and I don't want to mislead Lorelei about that."

"Don't you worry about misleadin' her. I'll try to make sure she doesn't mislead *you*."

Was it possible that Lorelei could truly mislead me? I consider myself to be practical and not in the least naïve. Of course, I have been known to be wrong on both counts.

"Don't worry about it. She took me by surprise."

"She takes a lot of people by surprise. You'll find yourself bamboozled again when she doesn't pay any attention to whatever you have both agreed to. Maybe you should humor her. I think in time she'll come to accept what's happened as I have. She'll never have any closure otherwise. I was hoping that you would distract her with your organizing project. You're young, you're a real pretty gal, and she's known you since you were this big. If you can steer her mind away from this crazy idea, it'll be good."

"I'll tell her that I'm happy to do the closets or to come and visit, but I can't investigate."

Harry squeezed my hand.

"Great. I'll see you tomorrow then. And Harry, I am so sorry for what you've been going through."

"Why thank you, Charlotte honey."

I hated to take Harry from the solace of his garden, but I did have to say, "One more thing. Lorelei didn't seem to be feeling all that well and I wondered if you should check on her. Maybe it's sedatives and mimosas? She didn't seem herself at all. I wasn't sure, but it worried me."

Harry hurried back toward the hard-edged glass and rock architectural marvel, and I headed for my Miata and home.

—••—

I would have gone straight home, too, if I hadn't stopped
at Hannaford's to restock my supply of Ben & Jerry's New
York Super Fudge Chunk. I dashed over to my favorite section and squealed to a halt at the end of the nearest aisle. I
spotted a familiar redhead. In front of the ice cream cooler
was one man I wasn't sure I wanted to see. Detective Connor Tierney of the Woodbridge Police managed to look
like a million in his jeans and T-shirt. He was taking his
time over the ice cream and jingling his keys.

That's the strength and a weakness of living in a small
city. You are bound to run into people you know in the
main grocery store, restaurants, movies, and any place you
might want to frequent. Two and a half years after I moved
back from Manhattan to my hometown, and I couldn't go
anywhere without tripping over people I knew.

Not this time, I decided. He was turned away from me,
so I didn't have to meet his ice blue eyes.

I backed up quietly and whipped around on my platform heels. I had other sources of ice cream. And after
one lackluster date three weeks earlier, with no call the
next day, I sure didn't want Connor Tierney to get the impression I was following him. I snatched a giant box of
Cheerios as I flew down the cereal aisle. No point in going
home completely empty-handed. Truffle and Sweet Marie,
my miniature dachshunds, like them, and they make great
training aids in my ongoing battle to keep them from barking their pointed little heads off. We need training. I spotted some jumbo bags of Mars bars at the end of the row and
picked those up, too. I'd need some soothing when training
was over. Of course, this all meant I had to go through the
checkout lane.

Tierney emerged from the end of the coffee aisle as I
reached the cashier. Just when I thought I was in the clear.

He grinned. "You're in a hurry."

"Forgot my list," I said breathlessly.

"Cheerios and Mars bars. I can see where you'd need a list for that. What would be on the list? Buy? Not buy?"

"Ha-ha. There were other things, but I can't remember what they were. Of course, the dogs may have eaten the list. You know what they're like."

I tossed my money at the cashier and added, "Gotta run. Very busy day. Good to see you."

"Wait, there's something I—"

But I'd already waved good-bye.

I zipped out the door of Hannaford's, head down and speed walking to the Miata. I floored it for the few blocks to Tang's Convenience where I had the privilege of paying a higher price for my New York Super Fudge Chunk while being glared at by my good friend Margaret Tang's mother. I could have stopped at another convenience store, but when it comes to B & J's, Tang's is the only other game in town. I ignored the cost and purchased a half dozen tubs. You never know when there will be an emergency.

As I headed for home, I kicked myself for not asking Tierney about Anabel Beauchamp's death. I would have felt more comfortable resisting Lorelei's requests if I had some common sense answers from a working police detective.

Of course, it was too late for that.

I didn't want to make a move. It wasn't only his ice blue eyes or the red hair or the silk shirts. I never felt that I was completely in control. My behavior in Hannaford's being Exhibit A. When you make your living as an organizer, it doesn't pay to become unglued in public.

＊

After I left Tang's Convenience, I drove by the spot on Friesen Street where Anabel's body had been found. I pulled up and stopped. The construction site for the new condo project was set off from prying eyes by a high chain-link fence. As if that wasn't enough, pressed-wood panels kept the project from view. Still, the fence had one of those convenient mesh window slots that keep the curious happy. I fell into that category, although I had to stand on my tiptoes to see in, and I didn't find much of a view. There hadn't been a lot of progress on this building. There was still a gaping hole in the middle, with a narrow pathway around it. The hole was easily fifteen feet deep and cluttered with boards and metal debris, and our recent late spring rains had left what looked like a foot of water. It was framed with wooden walls that I assumed were the formwork for the foundation. Like the narrow, slippery path around the excavated area, the wood was a muddy mess. My guess was that the project had stalled after Anabel Beauchamp's accident and had yet to get going again. I'd heard that the foundation had been full of stagnant water when Anabel had slipped from the narrow walkway and fallen into it. I felt a chill at the thought. I shivered and not because the afternoon was unseasonably cool. What a place to die. So close to people and yet absolutely invisible. I tried not to think about poor Anabel slipping beneath the dark water when no help came. She was in the wrong place at the wrong time.

I did wonder what she had been doing there. No one seemed to have any idea why Anabel had been in such a spot alone. And more to the point, how had she managed to get in? I walked along the boarded-up front of the site and couldn't see a way in, not that I had any desire to check it out in person. An access door was firmly padlocked. Perhaps the wood and chain-link fence and the padlocks had been a response to Anabel's drowning. I certainly didn't want to question Harry about the circumstances of his daughter's death, and that would go double for Lorelei, but I figured I could find out elsewhere. Not from Connor Tierney, though. I knew the idea of me asking questions about a death would not go down well with him.

I glanced around at Friesen Street. It was a peculiar part of Woodbridge, a mix of older homes that had been converted into apartments or businesses and low-rise office buildings, many with *FOR RENT* signs in the windows. Unlike some of the funkier uptown and downtown neighborhoods, it hadn't yet been discovered by the artsy crowd, but this condo development was designed to change all that. In two years, if the development went ahead, Friesen Street would probably look quite different.

I wondered what that would mean for the apartment building across the street, a six-story relic from the sixties boom, now slightly shabby, if still respectable. Some sweet soul nearby seemed to be baking bread. I liked the idea that many residents had small but flourishing gardens on their balconies.

The rest of the street was normal. A mix of businesses: a dingy dry cleaner, a sandwich shop. The storefront office for the building project had the dustiest window I'd ever seen in a commercial enterprise. Behind the layer of grime was a glossy concept drawing of how the tiered condo would transform this street. Anabel had worked her heart out for Hope for Youth at Risk. That window was spotless, and the howling yellow sign brightened the row of businesses, all closed for Sunday. I didn't spot any of the street kids or troubled youth who were the clients, although there was plenty of graffiti on the boards around the site. Still, there were signs of life and community. A few seniors were ambling by, and a jaunty man in his sixties wearing a straw fedora and riding a motorized scooter went buzzing past me. He tipped his fedora and grinned. I grinned back. An old Civic sputtered before it turned the corner where an elderly gentleman was making a slow approach to the mailbox at the corner. Friesen Street was still home to perfectly normal-looking people.

—◆—

Lucky me, I had a baby gift in the tiny trunk of my car, waiting for the right moment to drop it off to my once again friend, Pepper Monahan. The right moment was defined as the one when her husband, Officer Nick (the Stick) Monahan, was nowhere to be seen. Next stop, Old Pine Street and the Arts and Crafts home that Pepper shared with Nick and the baby. I grabbed the gaily wrapped gift and turboed up the walkway.

Pepper answered the door in saggy jeans and a stained sweatshirt and carrying her son in her arms. They both seemed to be wearing a good deal of orange goop. Pepper even had some in her hair, which was due for a cut. The baby kept trying to make a swan dive toward the floor to reach the purple sock monkey he had tossed there.

I said, "Is this a good time?"

She rolled her eyes. "Are you kidding? I am desperate to socialize with someone who knows words and who won't spit strained carrots at me."

"I'll do my best to deliver."

"Cute." She bent to pick up the sock monkey. The baby hugged it with his orange-stained hands. "He can't live without this or his yellow ducky. Thank heavens they're both washable. Come on in. Nick's working overtime again, so Little Nick and I are hanging around throwing food at each other. Well, one of us is throwing food, the other one is wiping it up. Whoops! Almost lost him."

I followed Pepper into her living room. The formerly trendy space had been transformed by acres of baby gear. I found an empty section of the sofa and sat down. I waggled the wrapped baby gift.

I refused to call the child Little Nick. "Look how big he is. It seems like yesterday when he was born."

"I can't get over that he'll be eight months old soon. He has four teeth already. I have the bite marks to prove it. So much for breastfeeding. Anyway, we're getting ready to show them off at his christening party."

I hoped she meant the teeth. "But the christening was months ago."

"We waited for the big party because Nick's mom hasn't been all that well, so she couldn't come all the way up from South Carolina. Now she's doing better and we are going to have a big bash. I meant to send invitations, but I'm behind schedule. I can't even keep up with the house. It's a disaster here. I sure miss my cleaning lady. I let her go because it's not so easy on the one salary and I should be able to keep it up myself."

"You're too hard on yourself, Pepper. Get Nick to help."

"As if. I believe that he'd lay down his life for me or Little Nick, but that doesn't mean he would change a diaper or run a vacuum cleaner. That's a different part of his value system." She positioned the baby so that he could hold on to the large ottoman, and he seemed to have fun alternating between clinging to the ottoman and bouncing while holding on to the purple sock monkey.

"Come on, Pepper. You had a hellish pregnancy and a difficult birth and a baby who was sick for weeks. Who cares if your house has a few things scattered around? Let it go."

"That's funny coming from you, Miss Obsessive-Compulsive Organizer Freak. Of course, I mean that in the kindest way."

"I accept the title, but believe me, my obsessions are only about things that matter."

The familiar grin showed. "I'm bitching because Nick's

never home lately. Little Nick is crazy about his daddy, and he's missing the small amount of attention he gets."

"My friend Lilith Carisse is always looking for an hour or two here and there, especially if she doesn't get her shifts. She's working a batch of part-time jobs to put herself through college. If you let yourself see past the teal blue hair and the new nose ring, she's a dream employee. She could do some of the heavy work for you or even vacuum the house or weed the garden—"

"Weed the garden? My mind never even gets that far. Sorry, Charlotte, I'm so tired of eating canned spaghetti when Nick's not around and it brings out the worst in me."

Canned spaghetti? I had actually noticed the half-eaten plate of orange food congealing on the table. It went well with the strained carrots she was wearing.

Pepper continued. "Anyway, the party's in St. Jude's Hall two weeks from Saturday. To be followed by a big Irish party with religious overtones and lots of drinking."

"Wonderful. I look forward to that."

"I'm planning to invite Sally and Ben and Margaret and Frank."

"Don't forget Jack. He can help, too. He loves babies more than anybody I know."

"I already asked him because he's been by a couple of times to visit Little Nick."

"He has?" I felt the little frisson of jealousy that comes over me when Jack, my own personal Jack, my best friend in the world and my landlord to boot, hangs out with other people and their babies. I have to work on that.

"You know what Jack's like with babies. I wish Nick was as excited about being a father. Sometimes he seems to be a bigger kid than the baby. Have you been talking to him?"

"Nick?" I shook my head. "Nope. Haven't seen him for months."

I'd been dodging Nick for years. I didn't find Nick in the least bit appealing, but Pepper sometimes got ideas in her head that there was something between us. It had led to a years' long rift, and we'd only put that behind us in recent months. I wanted to protect the new harmonious friendship. A distraction seemed called for.

"Crazy question. Do you remember the accident that killed Anabel Beauchamp about six months ago?"

"Of course I do. I went to the funeral. Weren't you there?"

I shook my head. "It happened when I was on vacation in Europe."

"Right, of course. I forgot about that." Pepper reached over to steady the baby. "She did a lot of work with a group that tried to divert kids from crime and poverty and life on the street."

"Yes, the Hope for Youth at Risk organization makes a difference. Lilith Carisse was one of their clients. They helped her get a place to live and her first part-time job. Look at her now. She'll have that college degree before you know it."

Pepper said, "Anabel didn't have to do that. The Beauchamps are loaded, and she would have been able to have a glamorous job somewhere. Anywhere. Paris. London. Rome."

"Actually, Anabel never needed to work at all, but she was a very down-to-earth person, not at all materialistic. I always thought of her as a person with no edge at all."

Pepper's cop training showed. "But of course, *I* have edge. So I'll have to inquire why you're asking."

"No reason. I'm doing a closet organization job for her mother."

"There's always a reason when you ask something, Charlotte. And I'm guessing it's not closets. You might as well come right out with it."

"Fine. Lorelei Beauchamp seems convinced that someone murdered Anabel. So I'm wondering what you've heard."

Pepper shook her head. "I haven't heard a whisper that it was anything but an accident. Nick was one of the first people on site. I've seen my partner Frank quite often, and he didn't mention it."

"Of course, he might be distracted since he married Margaret."

"He wouldn't be too distracted to be a first-rate detective," Pepper snapped.

"Right."

Pepper must have felt the need for a little rant. "What is it with parents that they want to believe their kids were murdered instead of dying accidentally? I think I'd prefer the accident. Murder is so horrible, and to think that someone would kill your child, it's incredible." She gave Little Nick a tight squeeze. He pulled her hair.

"Agreed. Lorelei came right out and said it. I'm sure it's the grief talking."

"Yeah well, don't let her talk you into driving everyone in the department nuts again."

"Absolutely no warning needed, Pepper. I have no intention of doing anything but straightening out the closets at the Beauchamp home. Not interested in foul play or dirty deeds."

"Or snooping around in investigations that don't concern you and stirring up trouble."

I straightened up. "Is there an investigation? I thought—"

"There isn't one. It was an accidental death. And the local force has plenty to do without you meddling and wasting people's time. I hope you've lost that habit."

I can always tell when Pepper's lying, the legacy of growing up together and telling our share of whoppers. If she believed Anabel's death was an accident, that was good enough for me.

"I've been enjoying my quiet, normal life lately."

Pepper gave me an appraising glance.

"Let's open the baby's gift." I'd picked up a selection of books at Cuddleship, my favorite uptown kids' shop.

Pepper squealed when the books came out "*The Very Hungry Caterpillar*! I loved that when I was a kid."

"Me, too!"

Her face softened. "And *Goodnight Moon*. My mom used to read that to me."

"Mine, too." Well, at least she'd arranged for someone to read it to me. "I got them in the board book format so they may survive longer."

Little Nick reached out for the caterpillar with both pudgy hands.

"He loves it," Pepper said with a wide smile.

He clamped his new teeth on the corner and chewed away happily.

"He sure does." I laughed. "While you two are enjoying story time, how about I get us some coffee?"

"That would be lovely. I forget what it's like to get waited on a bit."

Nick, Nick, Nick, I thought, *better pull up your socks.*

I could hear Pepper reading the text to Little Nick as I made a pot of her favorite Kona blend. When I headed back in with two steaming mugs, the door opened. Nick stuck his big handsome empty head in the front door. He swaggered into the room. Being a father hadn't hurt Nick's figure. He still looked good in his uniform, and as always, he was well aware of that. "Hi, babe, thought I'd come by and say hi to my girl."

Pepper scowled. She knew Nick would have spotted my Miata in the driveway.

"Well, hey, Charley. What brings you here?"

"I wanted to hang out with Pepper and the baby for a bit."

"You're looking good."

Honestly, Nick had the brains of a shoelace.

"I can't get over how terrific Pepper looks. A lot of women would be jealous."

"I guess." Nick scratched his head.

"And I wanted some advice from Pepper, too. There was an accident a few months back. Anabel Beauchamp."

Nick's face clouded. What was behind that cloud, I wondered. He muttered, "I remember her. Good-looking chick. That was too bad."

"Right. Her mother thinks—"

Nick rolled his eyes. "Her mom? The model? Now she's hot!"

He seemed immune to the glares that both Pepper and I were shooting at him. You would have thought he'd have been rolling on the floor in agony. I decided it must be great to be as oblivious as Nick was. You'd never worry about anyone, unless of course, you thought they were *hot*.

As if I hadn't heard, I said, "*Mrs.* Beauchamp thinks that someone murdered Anabel, and I wanted to get Pepper's opinion. I'm glad to hear that there's nothing—"

Nick scratched his blond head. "Huh. Murdered?"

I added patiently, "And I guess there's nothing—"

Nick nodded. "You know, I was a first responder when she died."

"He was pretty shaken." Pepper stroked his hand. "He had nightmares for weeks."

"Ah come on, babe. I didn't have nightmares."

Of course, Monahan men wouldn't have nightmares.

Pepper clamped her mouth shut. As annoying as Nick was, she probably hadn't intended to diminish him in front of me.

I steered away from the nightmares. "I'm sorry to hear

that you were the first to arrive. That would be rough for anyone."

Nick's mind seemed elsewhere, remembering the accident perhaps. He kept nodding like a bobble head.

I found myself wishing I was far away. "Gotta run. Great seeing the three of you."

Nick snapped back to the present. "I thought there was something funny about the way she died, but it turned out there wasn't. Just an accident. That's all."

Now why didn't I believe him?

3

Sunday night was party night in our little two-unit enclave. The attendees were, as usual, Jack, Truffle, and Sweet Marie. It was Jack's turn to get the party food. Sure, he doesn't cook and keeps the overstock from his bicycle shop in the kitchen of his first-floor unit, but he has a talent for ordering out. I was the last to arrive, and it looked as though they'd started the party without me. The Ben & Jerry's had been in the car for a while, but at least it hadn't turned into a puddle.

I puffed up the stairs to my apartment in the converted Victorian home that Jack had grown up in. I was met by the dogs. They barked on principle and hurled themselves at the Hannaford's bag and the ice cream. "Be quiet and try to remember who feeds you."

Speaking of food, I sniffed the air.

I'd been hoping for pizza.

Or a shawarma platter.

Even sushi.

But I was happy to settle for Chinese. The Kowloon has excellent food. Jack always buys enough for an army, so lunch tomorrow would be taken care of with leftovers. Extra points to the man.

Jack and I were working on rebuilding our companionable relationship, which had taken a pounding last fall. Jack had also taken a bullet. We were each slathered in guilt over the events leading up to that. I supposed that time would take care of those emotions and we could get back to the easy carefree way we'd always been. In the meantime, we were both far more polite than we'd ever been. I was looking forward to our post-politeness period, when we could go back to trading insults and stealing each other's food. We weren't there yet.

The dogs were very excited to see the jumbo box of Cheerios. Low in calories and small, they worked well for portly little pooches that required a lot of food-based positive reinforcement to be good citizens and not bark. "Quiet" was the word of the week. Too bad I was the only one who understood what it meant.

Jack stuck his head out of the kitchen. His hair was its usual spiky disarray, and his latest Hawaiian shirt looked as though he might have slept in it. Lucky for him, he's one of those tall rangy people whose clothes always look good on them, regardless of wrinkles or whatever. "I've been working on the training with Truffle and Sweet Marie. I know you're worried about the retake of their Therapy Dogs evaluation."

"Worried doesn't begin to cover it, Jack. I noticed they barked at me when I came in. I believe they're actually getting worse."

"Hysterical then. I didn't want to come right out and say it."

"I am not hysterical. It's a serious goal and having them bark all the time is hard on the nerves."

"They're dogs. They bark. Get over it. I bought a double General Tso's chicken. You want lots?"

"Lots is good."

"Moo goo gai pan?"

"Absolutely."

"So do you want white rice or fried rice?"

"Both. And any other happy carbohydrate you have hanging around. I hope there's plenty of MSG, too."

I squeezed past him to tuck the Ben & Jerry's in the freezer. Good thing it starts out hard as a rock. At least the two of us could still fit in my tiny galley kitchen. People have been telling me now that I'm past thirty (a mere matter of months) I won't be able to eat the way I always have. So I have to make every junk meal matter.

I ducked into the bedroom and quickly changed into my frog pajamas. I took the minute to hang up my skirt neatly and toss the no-longer crisp white blouse into the hamper. The red platforms went on the shoe rack. Now I could relax.

I picked up the chopsticks and drinks on the way back to the living room before Jack arrived at the coffee table with our plates heaped high. I fed Truffle and Sweet Marie their kibble, while he was getting things settled, safely. Jack and I knew that all it would take was a random blink for them to pilfer our food. That's why the containers stayed in the kitchen and Jack served.

"Truffle and Sweet Marie will do well the next time. People are rooting for them. Are there enough garlic spare ribs for you?"

Apparently everyone in Woodbridge knew that the dogs had blown their first evaluations. Of course, they always did everything that Jack asked them and did it right the first time and every time.

"I appreciate it, Jack. It's not that they haven't learned all the commands. They have. They either bark at the other dogs or the person doing the evaluation or both. I believe I have explained this a hundred times."

"They didn't bark at me."

"That's because you're family."

"And anyway, they have to behave for me, because I'm the person who's going to take them to visit people and cheer them up. We can't be barking in a hospital or a seniors' residence. Do you hear that, you turkeys?"

But Truffle and Sweet Marie were now in the tiny galley kitchen staring up at the containers from the Kowloon. They looked like they might be hatching a plot. But at least they weren't barking.

"You seem down, Charlotte."

"I guess I am. I'm thinking about Anabel Beauchamp, and how one day she's happy and beautiful and helping people and making the world a better place and the next day she's dead." I snapped my fingers. "Gone. Like that."

"I knew her, too. That was very bad."

"Remember I told you I was doing a closet job for Lorelei? Seven closets jammed with high-end goods?"

"You didn't say who for. But I guess I should have figured it out. Who else would have seven closets? Sort of our local glamour queen. Would you call her a celebrity?"

"I don't know. I've known her as long as I can remember. She and my mother had a strange, love/hate relationship. At first I thought she was deluded by grief. Now I'm not so sure. Maybe, she's just—"

"Huh. Are you going to eat the rest of that General Tso's chicken?" This came as no surprise. Jack took a lot of calories to keep that rangy frame of his filled.

"Yes I am, and exactly what do you mean 'huh'?"

"It's an expression."

"It's an expression that means 'I think that's a crock.' "

"I—"

"Don't bother to deny it."

"I am denying it. It's a speech filler, like, 'um' or 'like.' "

"Is not."

"Is."

"Listen, Jack. We're getting our groove back, but you can't play word games with me."

"Okay, fine. Huh! It means in this case, don't go finding more trouble, Charlotte. You almost got killed last time. And the time before and . . ."

"And you took a bullet to save me. I am very grateful and sorry I dragged you into it, Jack. You take the chicken."

"It's not about the chicken, Charlotte. It's about you living a normal life without murders in it."

"I'm trying. These are my clients, and they, well, she brought it up."

"And you should let it go."

"Trust me, there's nothing I'd like better. And I think I can. Anabel's father said there was nothing odd in the way she died. He thinks this is the form that Lorelei's grief is taking. What I have to do is get enough information to reassure her."

"Must be awful for the parents."

"The pits. Anyway, I had already decided that there was nothing to it. A grief-stricken mother seeking answers, although there's nothing high-strung about Lorelei. So I asked Pepper what she thought."

"You saw Pepper? And the little dude?"

"Yes, today and—"

"Did you ever see a baby so cute?"

Here's where I was in an awkward moment. I don't mind babies. But I am not captivated by them. For one thing, they all look alike. Give me a toddler any day. Naturally, I would have cut out my tongue before I admitted this.

I tried a neutral comment. "He's cute all right."

"Unbelievable," Jack said.

I upgraded my end of the conversation to say something sincere. "Pepper wanted that baby so much. She seems happy."

"Who wouldn't be?" Jack said.

Well, I for one wouldn't be. Particularly if Nick the Stick came as part of the package. I felt a chill. Better to let it go. The thing was, of all my baby-crazy friends, Jack turned out to have the worst case. I'd learned to change the subject, early and often.

"I figured Pepper would be in the know, and sure enough, she had even been to the funeral."

"So was I," Jack said. "St. Jude's was overflowing. Everyone liked Anabel."

"And Pepper said to her knowledge there was nothing untoward about her death. Tragic, but an accident."

"That's good."

"It was. I need to know how to deal with Lorelei. Harry seems to humor her. Maybe I need to, too, but if she's going to badger me to do something about this death, then—"

Jack's level blue eyes met mine. "Then you tell her you're not going to. Period. No arguments."

"My plan exactly, perhaps stated with a bit more tact, considering this is a grieving mother."

"Excellent," Jack said. "Are you finished eating?"

"No! I told you to take the leftover chicken, but I still want the rest of my meal."

"I'm just asking."

"And I'm just saying no. With an exclamation mark. Maybe two."

Jack shrugged, resigned to not getting the rest of my food.

We both knew that he doesn't give up that easily.

I said, "So it was all good until Nick came home, in the middle of a shift."

"I thought Pepper realized that you don't have designs on her sleazy husband."

"She does, but that's not the issue."

"Let me guess. It has to do with Anabel."

"Got it in one, Jacko. Nick was on the scene immediately after, and he'd thought there was something not quite right about the whole thing. But then he realized it was an accident. Of course, he's having nightmares."

"But Charlotte—"

"So before I go back to see Lorelei and her exploding closets, I should get a third opinion. A tiebreaker. Someone neutral. And knowledgeable."

"You mean a cop?"

"Makes sense, no?"

"Like the guy with the silky shirts? And the creepy eyes?"

"They're not creepy. They're just icy blue."

"Like from a horror movie. Bad idea to talk to him, Charlotte."

"I thought you might come with me."

Jack's jaw dropped.

I said, "I gave you the General Tso's chicken. You can have all the leftovers. Everything. All I want is one fortune cookie."

My fortune cookie said, *Everything is not as it seems.*

Jack's said, *Beware a tall man.*

———⋆———

Mondays are busy. I always try to hit the week running, so I was up early. As it seemed to be closet season all over Woodbridge, I had three potential closet clients waiting for a slot and one lined up for a consultation in the morning, as well as a lot of people I'd referred to my website for information. If I ended up doing the job for Lorelei, her seven closets would extend the waiting time.

My To Do list said:

+ *Call Connor Tierney*
+ *Dog training—find anti-bark techniques*
+ *Client consult: 10 a.m.*

+ *Library: Ramona re: Anabel*
+ *Keep lunch for Tierney?*
+ *Lorelei: 3 p.m.*

I put on the coffee, walked the dogs, apologized as they barked at an elderly couple, and returned to enjoy a cup of medium Guatemalan. Before I took the first sip at seven fifteen, I left a message for Tierney asking if he could join me and Jack for lunch to discuss something. If lunch was not possible, we could probably make it for breakfast.

I took a quick shower and got ready. I put on the outfit I'd laid out the night before, right down to the underwear and spangly earrings to perk up the look. I fixed my hair and did a better than usual job on my makeup. I changed my shoes twice, finally settling on a pair of electric blue leather spikes with four-inch heels. I felt like Superwoman in them.

The dogs watched me suspiciously. They can always spot the most minuscule change in pattern. Must have been the extra makeup.

Tierney called when we were in the middle of a training session. It involved startling them with a loud noise and them not barking. I did my part well, but that was still one of our tricky ones. So I was embarrassingly breathless when I answered the phone.

"Breakfast would be better," he said. "Betty's Diner? Half an hour."

"Sure thing. But make that forty-five minutes so I can locate Jack." I did not emphasize the fact that Jack and I live in the same house and he would still be snoring away. I'd have to throw a bucket of water on him or something. He sleeps like the dead.

"Come on," I said to the dogs. "We're going downstairs."

Jack doesn't lock the door to his first-floor apartment.

Hell, sometimes he doesn't even shut it. This was one of those times.

"Go get Jack," I said. "He has treats in his bed."

It wasn't good news for my anti-bark program, but the resulting yelps were quite amusing. I hoped I didn't crack the layer of foundation I'd slathered on my face by laughing too much.

Jack sat up in bed, by which I mean his mattress on the floor, and said, "Wow. Are we going to a party?"

"What do you mean?"

"You seem, well, I don't know. Maybe I shouldn't say anything."

"I'll say this. Betty's Diner, forty minutes."

"But it's a twenty-minute drive."

"Right, so don't waste time picking fights."

I stomped back upstairs and scrubbed my face. I removed the three applications of midnight blue mascara and went back to my usual look. I replaced the blue spike heels with a pair of tan sling backs and the spangly earrings with my trusty gold hoops. Smart, businesslike, but not quite so ready to party.

—◆—

As we arrived at Betty's just after eight that morning, I mused that I never saw police officers in that particular diner. As usual, our server was Patsy Magliaro, always on duty when I show up. Patsy's one of Woodbridge's longtime hippie residents as evidenced by her tie-dyed skirt and hemp peasant top. Sometimes I think there's a bit of marijuana mist surrounding her.

"Three for breakfast," I said when she sashayed over, Birkenstocks slapping on the floor.

Across the room, I spotted Tierney already waiting in a booth. Jack gave him a dirty look, maybe because Jack's idea of getting dressed up is a clean pair of baggy shorts and a fresh vintage Hawaiian shirt. Jack had found today's shirt at the Goodwill and it featured dancing pineapples. Tierney was as usual dressed to kill.

I said, "Just don't."

Tierney was looking particularly silky when we approached the booth. He was also jingling his keys. That meant something I supposed, but who knew what.

Tierney had coffee going already.

Patsy hovered. "Breakfast folks?"

"Coffee for me." Tierney probably didn't want to get crumbs on that immaculate shirt.

I slid into the battered red leather booth ahead of Jack and across the table from Tierney. Even so, every now and then I got a gentle whiff of his aftershave. I am particularly susceptible to that.

"Wheat toast with raspberry jam and cream cheese," I said.

"Are you people crazy?" Jack said with the enthusiasm of a person who has no kitchen skills, and who finds himself in the place that serves the best breakfast in town, poised to order said breakfast on someone else's dime. Mine in this case. "I'll have the Americano special, extra eggs, extra hash browns, extra bacon, and extra toast. Extra jam, too. Very large coffee."

"Cheese with those eggs?" Patsy said.

"Sure."

"I'll make it extra then. Orange juice?"

"Absolutely."

"Large, I'm guessing."

Patsy filled up my coffee cup, sauntered off toward the kitchen, her tie-dyed skirt swaying, her gray braid keeping time with it.

"I don't know why we came all the way out here if you guys don't even want breakfast," Jack said. "The food is great."

I had a theory that Tierney probably didn't want to be seen eating breakfast with me. I don't know how he felt about my buddy, but Jack's hungry presence certainly made me look less like I might be pursuing Tierney.

Jack's food arrived in what seemed like seconds. We'd hardly got past the awkward part. While Jack stuffed his lanky frame, I filled Tierney in on the background of Anabel and her parents and then got to the point. "I know you haven't lived in Woodbridge all that long, but I wondered if you could tell me, honestly, if there was any question at all about the way she died."

I felt the ice blue eyes on me. Tierney can be a disturbing man.

Jack swallowed and said, "I told her that she shouldn't get involved in anything to do with murders. What if—?"

"Jack," I snapped. "I'm merely getting information so that I can reassure Lorelei, that's all. I need facts."

"Lorelei? That's the mother? Cover girl? Model?"

"Right."

"I remember her."

"Oh. I guess I should have realized that."

"I do live here now. And I'd met Anabel, too. She wasn't much like her mother. Very down-to-earth, casual dresser, kind of boyish even. I don't think she wore makeup."

I was glad I'd scrubbed my face. "I didn't realize you'd met her."

Still jingling those keys. "Woodbridge is a pretty small place, hard to avoid people."

Was he talking about yesterday? Was he talking about me avoiding him or him avoiding me?

Back to topic. "How did you meet her?"

"She was working with some kids at Hope for Youth at Risk, and we thought they were a little too close to some badass types we were keeping an eye on. There are some serious criminal activities in that area, and we're having trouble keeping a lid on."

This took me by surprise. "Did she cooperate with you about that?"

Tierney laughed. "Not even a little bit. Basically told me to get lost. Her job was helping these kids, not the police."

"Do you think there's some kind of connection? I mean with these badass types you were keeping an eye on?"

"No I don't. We didn't find any connections, so I don't think there's anything there. Bad as they are, these people have no history of attacking unconnected civilians. Anabel was a special young woman, and she died accidentally. It was a horrible tragedy, but it shouldn't be too surprising. I saw the site myself. It was a muddy mess the day she died. It had been raining for a week or more, and the earth from the excavation had turned completely to mud. There must have been five feet of water in that hole. The walkway around the inside of the site was a slick disaster waiting to happen. And anyway, it was all investigated thoroughly by competent personnel." He paused before adding, "I hope you realize that not every police officer is like Nick Monahan."

I nodded. "I do."

Jack said, "Five feet of water and a slippery walkway. Sounds like the company was irresponsible."

Tierney shook his red head. "I heard there's a lawsuit pending, but Anabel was definitely trespassing. She wasn't wearing any safety gear, and she had the wrong kind of shoes for sure. I think it would be hard to make the case that she died because of negligence, but I'm no lawyer. The main thing is that her family has a lot of influence in these parts, so there were no chances taken in the investigation, no sloppy work."

"I suppose you talked to every possible witness and all that?"

"We did, in fact. Even though we didn't think it was

murder, we still needed to know what had happened. Our guys interviewed people on the street, neighbors, and anyone who might have been able to see the site."

I said, "But—"

"They even did a door-to-door. I'm telling you: This is not some rinky-dink force and Anabel Beauchamp's death was taken seriously. Her father thanked us for everything we did."

"And her mother?"

Tierney shrugged. "Can't blame her. But it doesn't change the facts any."

Harry was always gracious. Lorelei's words wouldn't count as she was not the most grounded woman in the world even when not ripped up by such a tragedy.

"Okay then, so I'm going to ignore what Nick said about his own initial impression."

Oddly enough, Tierney didn't ask me what Nick had said. "Sometimes you have to consider the source."

"That's more or less what Jack told me. Pepper didn't seem to think anything was out of the ordinary."

"You should listen to her. She's a first-rate detective."

I smiled and lifted my coffee mug. But the unwelcome thought kept skittering through my head. If someone *had* killed Anabel, then they definitely got away with it.

4

I arrived at the home of my other new client ten minutes early. I like to build in a time buffer in case of traffic. I sat in the car and used the buffer to check my voice mail.

At ten sharp I knocked at the door of the faded bungalow. The paint was peeling slightly, and the awnings showed rust at the edges. Still, the lawn was neatly kept, and the place had a welcoming air about it. A pair of hanging baskets held impatiens in a riot of color. I felt a cheerful vibe about this home.

The door swung open and a round smiling face greeted me. I swear the woman actually bubbled. "I am so glad you are here! I can't wait. Come in! Bluto is very excited to meet you, too."

Beside her a golden retriever wagged his tail furiously, waiting—without much patience—to be stroked.

I stepped through the door into a home: a real home, not just a house. Unlike Lorelei and Harry's glamorous glass and metal sculpture, this was a place where people lived and loved and relaxed. I always approve of that. A stack of sports gear was contained by a plastic bin in the front hall. Four pairs of running shoes—in giant sizes—sat on a mat near the front door.

Wow, I thought, *who lives here and what species are they?*

"I made some—" She stopped herself. "Oh boy. I almost forgot to introduce myself. I'm Wendy Dykstra." She ran a hand through her curly salt-and-pepper hair.

I grinned. "In that case, I must be Charlotte."

"Everybody in Woodbridge knows you after . . ." She turned pale and averted her eyes.

"Don't worry," I said soothingly, "I'm well aware that in the last year and a half I've been all over the WINY news showing up on every television in town looking crazed and dangerous."

"You don't look *dangerous*," she interjected. "And not crazed, either."

"I've seen the tapes. I've adjusted to it. Anyway, this is the real me. Sort of normal."

"I got your name from Rose Skipowski. She was a pal of my mom's, and she speaks so highly of you. She said you solved the second biggest problem of her life."

"Rose is a good friend. Makes great cookies, too."

"Oh boy, that reminds me. I whipped up some ice tea for you and lemon squares, too. Please come in and have a seat."

I would have liked to take a peek at Wendy's kitchen. Sometimes you get an idea of how the household is run by checking that, but I am well aware of the etiquette of waiting until asked. People need to keep their dignity when allowing someone like me to see into their darkest organizational problems. It also pays to see their living rooms. Wendy's was a celebration of her family. A wedding picture of a much younger Wendy and a huge grinning groom sat on the mantel. It shared space with larger framed photos of three boys who took after their father: big lads with oversize grins. All of the photos seemed to involve sporting events or graduations.

The coffee table held magazines: *Woman's Day*, *National Geographic*, and *Sports Illustrated.*

Wendy was back in a flash with a glistening pitcher of ice tea and lemon squares that looked like they'd melt in my mouth.

"I am so nervous," she said, putting the plate of lemon squares on the Formica coffee table. "This is a big deal for me."

"Please don't be worried."

"I know I'm going to feel pretty goofy when such an organized person sees the state of my closets."

"If it's any consolation, I could no more make lemon squares like these than I could fly."

"They're as easy as pie."

"I can't make pie, either, although I could eat one all by myself."

Wendy passed me a napkin with the image of a golden retriever. I had a feeling there would be more retriever icons around the place. I wasted no time in testing the lemon squares. Perfect. The ice tea was perfect, too. I made a bet with myself that Wendy was a woman with firm priorities and that she herself came well down the list of those priorities.

I said, "These are fabulous, so tangy."

"One other thing that's kind of embarrassing," Wendy said.

Of course, I'd popped my second lemon square and my mouth was full. I lifted my eyebrows to indicate that she should go on.

"I, um, don't have a lot of money for this project."

I nodded.

"Money is tight because we have three boys in college."

This time I managed to say, "Expensive time of life."

"They all work part-time during the term, and Seth is able to live at home, but Aaron and Jason are at Cornell. Jason has a scholarship, but we're scrimping. I'm not complaining. I think it's the best investment we could ever make, and our boys deserve everything we can do for them."

I nodded again. Nodding is a good way to keep the conversation going.

Wendy continued. "What I'm trying to say is that my hubby and the boys chipped in to give me a hundred dollars and told me to get as much closet advice as I could for that. Is that nuts?"

"Not at all."

"I realize now that I should have told you this before. You probably charge that much to look at a place."

"Well, I sure won't be charging you for the time and opportunity to eat these fabulous squares. But let me have a look at what we're dealing with, and I'll give you the best value I can. You may have to do some of the groundwork yourself, but we'll make that one hundred dollars go as far as we can."

"Thank you! I'll throw in the recipe for the squares, if that helps."

"Sure does." Maybe I could talk Sally into making them.

I smiled and raised an eyebrow at Wendy. "Let's have a look. If I stay here any longer, I might even eat the plate those squares came on."

"All right," she said, "but I'll be holding my breath."

The bungalow had three bedrooms, and it must have been bursting when those boys were all under the roof.

Wendy said as I followed her down the hallway, "Luckily my boys spend a lot of time in the rec room downstairs. You must be wondering if anyone can even inhale in this space."

I admired the framed photos of the boys that decorated the hallway walls. "Wendy, your home is obviously full of love."

"That's kind of you to say."

It was a sincere comment. My own upbringing had been in a series of fairly glamorous surroundings with whomever my mother's latest husband had been at the time. My happiest years had been growing up in Woodbridge when hubby number three, an IBM executive, had been in the area. I'd always envied the kids whose moms made cookies and squares. I'd had lots of smoked salmon and caviar as a child, but I'd hidden most of it behind the designer cushions.

Wendy had a sheepish grin as she opened the bedroom door. The furniture was probably the same set they'd bought when they married more than twenty years ago. Seemed as solid and enduring as it was dark and gloomy. The closet doors stood open, revealing everything that Wendy was worried I would see. Clothing hung on a sagging closet pole that was so jammed it would be hard to extract anything. I spotted a mix of women's and men's duds as well as what looked like uniforms.

"Is it beyond hope?" she whispered.

I said, "No way. This may be the best hundred dollars you've ever spent."

"Really?"

"It's a promise."

I spoke with absolute confidence. I could see at a glance at least ten minor modifications that would make Wendy's closet easier on the eye and improve her life at the same time. I liked this woman. She seemed to have no connection whatsoever with murder, madness, schemes, or any of the other plagues I'd faced in recent months. I decided on the spot that if I gave her the lowest possible hourly rate, that was no one's business but my own. That was the great part about working for myself.

She sat on the bed and said, "Oh boy, that would be wonderful."

"Is your husband handy with tools? Or are the boys? Or maybe you are?"

"Not me, my talents are in the kitchen, but all the boys are except for Jason. Why?"

"We'll probably need the odd bit of hammering and a shelf or three. Do you want to put them on alert?"

"Sure will. They won't mind a bit."

"So now I don't want to waste any of our time. Tomorrow I'll be here with some bins and we'll sort out your clothing into keep, toss, donate, and sell. Do you want to prepare yourself mentally for the big purge?"

"Whatever it takes."

"Good, then get used to thinking about these questions, because we'll be asking them over and over again." I ran through my standard pre-purge queries for her.

Do I love it?
Do I wear it?
Does it fit?
Is it still in fashion?
Does it go with anything else I own?
Does it make me feel good?

I added, "The only right answer to each of those questions is yes. Be wary of anything that makes you feel bad."

Wendy interrupted. "Feel bad? You mean like fat? Old? Dumpy?"

I said, "You definitely want to turf anything that brings out those reactions."

She grimaced. "Might be quite a high percentage."

"We'll see how that plays out. Part two of the question series goes like this:

Can somebody else make use of it? Can I sell it?
Can I donate it to a worthy cause?
If I didn't have it already, would I want to buy it?
Is it too small? Too large? Needing repair?
Why am I keeping this?

"I can do that," she said, nodding a bit uncertainly.

"It's all a bit more challenging than you might think.
So here's a little tip sheet to remind you of the questions.
I'll be back tomorrow with a contract for one hundred dollars' worth of work. I'll try to keep your costs down by
bringing my assistant and letting her oversee the purge. I
hope she's available. If not, we should rejig our schedules
to mesh with hers. She's also a college student, she has no
family, and she's putting herself through. And by the way,
she's always hungry."

"Music to my ears. I love to cook, and I can't imagine
what it will be like when the other two boys move out on
their own."

"I'm sure Lilith will be happy to help out with your need
to feed. You might actually know her. She lives with your
mom's friend, Rose Skipowski. They have an arrangement
so that Rose isn't alone and Lilith has a roof over her head.
If you'll excuse me a second, I'll give her a call."

I flipped open my cell phone. Lilith is on speed dial.
She can't always answer when she's knee-deep at one of
her three part-time jobs. I left a detailed message and mentioned Wendy by name.

Wendy blurted out, "Lilith! Of course I know that girl.
Well, I met her a couple of times. She's made such a difference for Rose. It shows you with some kids you have to
look past the piercings and the tattoos and the hair to see
the person underneath."

I knew that would work out. Lilith's hair was stunning
teal blue this month, and I'd detected a new facial piercing

last time. I was glad that Wendy was planning to look past all that. Of course, it helped that she knew the difference Lilith had made in Rose's life.

That made me think. Lilith had been living on the streets when she first came to Woodbridge. I'd never found out what terrible things had happened to her during those dark times, but I figured she'd either know about Anabel Beauchamp's work with troubled kids or she'd know someone who would.

"Charlotte?" Wendy was staring at me anxiously.

"Sorry. I thought of something."

"Is it a problem with my closet? Or—"

"Nothing to do with it. And your closet will be finished before you know it. See you tomorrow. I am free for a few minutes early in the day, so I'll drop in and get you started once I make arrangements with Lilith.

Wendy hesitated, usually a sign that someone's not quite ready to take the plunge.

"You have no idea how wonderful you will feel when it's over. By the way, this consultation's on the house. The meter doesn't start ticking until tomorrow."

"I'll start getting ready. Rose is a great cook, but even so, that Lilith's a skinny little thing. I'll make sure she gets lunch, on the house."

I left feeling very good indeed and with time to get to the library and check out something that had been troubling me.

— ❧ —

Luck was with me and my friend Ramona was working reference. I spotted her silver brush cut and denim skirt across the room. A ray of sunshine caught her dangling silver earrings. Ramona is not always such a ray of sunshine herself, but she is invariably intelligent, businesslike, and up for finding whatever you seek.

"You're keeping out of the news lately," she said as she approached.

The reference regulars shot her dirty looks for daring to speak while they read their *New York Times* or *Atlantic Monthly*. Of course, Ramona can trade dirty looks with the best of them, so they quickly transferred their pursed lips and narrowed eyes to me. I'm not nearly as sensitive as I was before I got hauled off to the police station in my frog pajamas and bunny slippers while the WINY cameras were rolling.

What doesn't kill you makes you stronger.

"So," Ramona said. "To what do I owe the honor?"

"Just saying hello. I planned on checking the library's supply of organizing books and magazines for a client who's on a tight budget. I couldn't come by without dropping in to see you."

"I'm always a bonus. Make sure you use the online catalog, too. We have tons of stuff and it's not always in, but your client can request items online and we'll let her—or him—know when they come in."

"Perfect. And it's her. For some reason, all my clients have been female. By the way, you've lived in Woodbridge all your life, haven't you?"

"Except for the two years getting my master's in library science."

"Great—I wondered what you know about—"

Ramona threw back her head and guffawed. "I knew you hadn't just dropped in, Charlotte."

Naturally that drew another round of disapproving stares from the category of folks that Ramona calls the Information Prima Donnas, IPDs for short.

"No need to break a rib laughing. But, you're right. It so happens there is a matter that I'm curious about."

"Out with it. I don't have all day."

"Fine. Anabel Beauchamp's death."

"Whoa. No sugarcoating there."

"No. I'm doing some work for the family, and there's been a suggestion that—well, that someone killed her. It's crazy, I know."

"Not so crazy to want to know that. I would in your position. Of course, I'd probably start by asking the police."

"Been there. Done that."

"And?"

"And it was a straightforward accident, with the slightest hint it might not have been."

Ramona nodded; the silver earrings actually jingled up close. "They would prefer an accident, of course."

"What do you mean?"

"They're a city department, like us. Their funding depends on getting results. We all measure our results using stats. That's what keeps us afloat. Every time you walk through the door and ask me a question, Charlotte Adams, I add you to the tally."

"So you think the police wouldn't acknowledge that Anabel's death might not have been an accident to keep their stats up?"

"Of course not. But I do think they wouldn't go looking for extra murders because they're curious. They have plenty to do with the deaths that are obviously foul play, not that Woodbridge has all that many. Plus, a big chunk of their activity seems to be chasing after you."

"Very funny."

"Maybe you could become a departmental line item."

"You've given me something to think about, Ramona. So tell me, did you ever babysit for Anabel or have any other connections I should know about?"

"I knew her through her work, but not well. I do have a lot of clippings and information about her. I can gather them up for you. She was very well thought of, and she made the papers with her work before her death. She wasn't afraid to stand up for what she believed in. And the funeral was a big deal. I don't remember seeing you there."

"She died while I was in Europe, visiting my mother, who managed to give me the slip quite a few times. We didn't find out that Anabel had died until too late." I was starting to feel very guilty about missing this funeral.

"People spilled out of the church. I never saw so many tears. All kinds of people, rich and poor, old and young. Lots of media, too, but that might have been because of her mother."

"Right. She's the one who thinks that Anabel's death was murder."

"Oh right, Lorelei. She's nothing like her daughter, that's for darn sure."

"And that's supposed to convey some information?"

"And come to think of it, you dropped the ball, Charlotte."

"In what way?"

"In the way that you asked about Anabel but never questioned if I had any dealings with Lorelei."

"Did you?"

A library page skittered out an office door and up to Ramona. "They want you in the office. Now."

Sometimes I wondered if there was someone on the management side who tried to break up every conversation that I had with Ramona. But of course, that was silly.

5

I made a note to myself to ask Ramona about Lorelei when she called to say the clippings were ready. Knowing Ramona, that would pay off. In the meantime, I had plenty to keep me busy. I hoped she'd call before I headed back to the Beauchamps' house at three that afternoon.

In the meantime, I hit the nearest Dollar Do! to see what might help in Wendy's closet upgrade. I checked the storage and the kitchen section, identifying lots of useful little tools. I didn't buy anything, because Wendy would be making those decisions and there was no point in starting until we knew what she'd be keeping in her closet.

Next I hit the building supply store to check out inexpensive closet organizers. It looked like even the most cost-effective systems were going to put her over the hundred-dollar mark, but a double-hanging closet pole could come in very cheap and double her hanging space for shirts and jackets.

I had more luck at the new linen store. I'd noted some deals on the flyer they'd sent around. What was more, I had a coupon. Sure enough, the cost of the slim-line closet system, pole, matching hangers, and a system to hang belts, scarves, pants, and shoes would come in well under Wendy's budget. This would be our first stop when it came time to make decisions about how to settle the closet. I also liked the deal on the hanging cloth shelves—less than twenty dollars. We were unlikely to get a dresser with the amount we had, but these could go a long way to corralling T-shirts, sweaters, and anything that needed to be folded. I noted everything down in Wendy's file and left smiling.

I didn't plan to charge Wendy Dykstra for my browsing time. It's all part of business reconnaissance and built into the charges for most clients. She was my first client for a hundred-dollar closet makeover, but she might not be the last. My clients tend to be quite affluent because getting the services of an organizer is perceived to be a luxury. Not that it should be: Everyone who does a thorough organizing job—on their own or with professional help—finds that it saves them time, money, and misery. Even so, it's well down the list of most people's perceived necessities and as scary as a root canal for lots of folks. With this in mind, I decided it would be worth developing a kit to help people do the bulk of the work themselves, with me teaching them to analyze their needs and get started. I could provide reading material, photos, illustrations, checklists, worksheets, and resources, and, if necessary, a couple of phone calls or a visit to incite them to keep moving.

This idea was all quite a bit of unexpected fun, and I took notes at a furious rate in my little paper organizer. I didn't want to lose any of the ideas dancing in my brain. There's something nice about coming up with an extra line of business. I stopped off at my apartment to let Truffle and Sweet Marie out for an extra walk.

When we came back, I checked the food supply. There's empty and then there's my fridge, which gives new meaning to empty. My Betty's toast and jam was long gone, and I didn't want to eat the B & J's New York Super Fudge Chunk, the Cheerios, or the Mars bars for lunch. I wondered if I would ever turn into a Wendy, happily feeding a family and humming as I did so. Somehow I suspected it wasn't in my genes.

People who have it in their genes seem to accumulate families or open restaurants. I headed for my favorite café. Ciao! Ciao! has the best takeout in town, and this seemed like the right day for it. About once a week, I drop by Jack's bicycle shop and bring him lunch. He does a lot for me. I had a very reasonable rent on the entire second floor of the Victorian house Jack had inherited from his parents. I had someone to walk the dogs without even being asked whenever I was in a bind and frequently a Hawaiian-shirted shoulder to cry on. The occasional lunch seemed a small price to repay. And that morning he'd done me the favor of getting up early to meet Tierney. Mind you, he'd glared at Tierney throughout breakfast. For a guy who was just short of a PhD in philosophy, every now and then Jack's a bit light on subtlety.

I arrived at CYCotics carrying three prosciutto and provolone on ciabatta bread sandwiches, and a pair of jumbo coffees. I figured Jack's breakfast would have worn off by now. I opened the door to CYCotics and was stunned to see a customer. Who knew? He always maintained he had clientele and that CYCotics did a good business. He even claimed to have two part-time employees who did repairs and tune-ups. I had never seen any sign of that. Jack and the customer engaged in a long and esoteric discussion of Italian bike pedals. As usual, Jack was physically into the discussion, waving his long arms, as the pineapples on the Hawaiian shirt swayed along. I sipped my coffee and thanked the universe that I had my job and not his.

"Told you," he said when the customer had departed,

but not before making a serious deposit on a pair of astronomically priced pedals. "I have customers. So what do I owe you for the lunch?"

"On the house. I am grateful that you came with me this morning."

"Always glad to help you. You don't have to buy me lunch, although you did have to buy me breakfast."

"Accept it, Jack."

"All right," he said, giving up without a fight. "But why did you need me to be there? That was the most banal conversation."

I wasn't sure I'd agree as Jack and I have had some conversations that would make the banality Olympics. When we got going, either one of us could bore for the U.S. of A. "I didn't want him to think I was making a play for him."

Jack's hand stopped inches from his mouth, the sandwich so close and yet so far away. "Why would he think that?"

"I don't know. He's got a sense of himself. We had a date a couple of—"

The sandwich hovered. "A what?"

"A date. You've heard of dates, Jack."

"Yeah, but you had a date with him? I didn't hear anything about that."

"Maybe I forgot to mention it. Maybe you were tied up with the shop. Maybe I was busy. Maybe I thought I mentioned it and I didn't. Maybe it was when what's-her-name was in the picture."

"Huh."

"Not again with the 'huhs.' You can't read anything into that, Jack. Anyway, even if you did read something into it, there's nothing to read, because he never called me back for another date."

"Not so fast with all this information. You said a date. Where did you go? What did you do? What—?"

"Boundaries, Jack. Remember boundaries?"

"Well, I'm supposed to be your friend. I've been in your life since grade school, and now you're sneaking around with this silky—"

"He's not a silky anything and I wasn't sneaking. Didn't you have a relationship with that woman last fall?"

"Now it's a *relationship* with this dude? Out of the blue, like that? Upgraded status?"

"It is not necessary to snap your fingers. *You* were the one who had the relationship with you-know-who."

"That was not a relationship. It was a series of misunderstandings, miscommunications, and deliberate misleadings."

"A long series."

"But all that stuff is over. And we have to move past it. You know that, Charlotte."

"Well, I can't move past the thing with Tierney. One date does not a relationship make."

"If you say so."

"You heard me. Particularly as he never called me for a second one."

"I told you there was something wrong with that guy. Is that second sandwich for me, too?"

––⊬––

I had enough time to drive down Friesen Street again. I parked and walked along the block nearest the construction site. It looked much livelier with people on the street. The dry cleaner and the sandwich shop were both busy, and the office door of Hope for Youth at Risk was open. I stepped in and smiled. A tall, intense-looking young man in a battered leather jacket brushed by me. He had cheekbones you could cut glass with. And if he hadn't been in this particular location, I might have taken him for a star in some movie shoot. A woman's voice called out, "See you later, Dimitri." But he didn't turn around.

Inside there was no sign of recent tragedy: The walls were covered with encouraging posters, and there was a grouping of chairs and a coffee table with magazines. The message was, *We're here for you.* A boy and girl who couldn't have been more than fifteen and who must have been living on the street judging by the whiff their clothes gave off treated me to a look of suspicion, vacated the chairs, and vanished through the door. A miasma of cigarette smoke and sweat lingered behind them.

I stared after them before turning to check out the staff. A curvy woman with huge dark eyes and luminous ebony skin chuckled softly from behind a desk. As I approached, I noticed that there was an overlay of air freshener in the office. A good idea, I thought.

I had no choice but to grin. "I guess I'm scarier than I thought."

She stood up and nodded agreement. "You got it. In that outfit, you look like you're representing some kind of authority. That's never good news for some of our clients."

That explained her plain long-sleeved scoop-neck white tee and the jeans with a studded belt. She may not have been dressed for business, but even so she radiated equal parts in-charge and empathy. A nice combo.

"They're safe from me," I said. "Not that I'd ever catch up with them to tell them that."

"I'm Gwen Jones." She extended a hand. Gold bangles jingled on her wrist. They matched the substantial gold studs in her ears.

"Nice bangles," I said. "I've been meaning to get some."

"They're cheap and cheerful," she said. "Genuine goldium. You don't wear the real thing around here."

I knew they weren't real, and agreed you might think twice about wearing gold bangles in this neighborhood.

"What can I do for you?"

"I'm Charlotte Adams, and this will sound stupid. I wanted to see the site where Anabel Beauchamp died and I remembered that she'd worked here."

The smile dipped. "Oh yes, Anabel. But why?"

"I knew her practically all her life. The way she died was so tragic, I find it keeps bothering me."

"Me, too, and I guess it always will. Such a horrible waste of a wonderful, caring person." A tiny frown flickered across her lovely face. "I don't remember seeing you at the funeral or the family reception. Are you a reporter?"

"A reporter? No! I missed the funeral because I was in Europe. I didn't even find out she'd died until much later. Our mothers have known each other all their lives, but my mother was also traveling at the time. I guess that's why I'm here. Needing a bit of closure."

"Closure doesn't always come easy."

"I took a look at the site and it seems like . . ."

She raised an eyebrow.

I said, "Such an awful place to die. For anyone, but especially Anabel." I glanced at Gwen Jones. I thought she blinked away a tear. That surprised me. I supposed you would toughen up working in this environment.

"For anyone indeed," Gwen said. "It was incredibly shocking that she died that way. I still can't get used to the idea."

"Thank you for saying that. Her mother is convinced that she was murdered, and I guess that's why I've been thinking about it. It appears that she was the only one to think that."

Gwen said, "Most people accept that Anabel was in the wrong place at the wrong time and she was the victim of a freak accident. Anabel's mother is a strange person, maybe not living entirely in the real world." She slumped back in the chair. "You know, some days I still don't believe it. She brought such energy to this place, and she was an amazing fund-raiser. That's an endless and often thankless job. I have to say her connections came in handy and she didn't mind mining them."

"Quite a loss for you, too," I said.

"For the organization. And for our clients."

I wondered for a second if that included Gwen herself.

"So you don't think she was murdered?"

Gwen shook her head.

"I guess her mother is the only one who does."

That drew a blink. "Maybe not the only one, but one of a very few. Some people around here have trouble accepting it, too."

"Like who?"

Her expression shifted to caution. "People have to grieve and move on. Anabel's death was an accident. Nothing more. If you don't believe me, please check with the police."

"Oh, I'm sure it was, but I wanted to rule out—"

"Rule out?" Her full contralto voice rose. "Do you have any idea how hard it is to help these kids get their lives together? Do you think we need foolish talk of murder to mess up our city funding and alarm our donors and supporters? I'd like to rule out *that*."

I know when I've been dismissed, and this was one of those cases. To make the point that much clearer, Gwen stood up and turned her back to me, slapping around some files on the table by her desk.

Anabel hadn't been murdered. Merely an accident. Just ask the police. This was what I wanted to hear, so why didn't I feel happier when I left?

—◆◆—

My cell phone rang as soon as I climbed back into the Miata. I was asking myself who else might be thinking that Anabel might have been murdered, although I knew Gwen wasn't likely to give me that information.

Lilith Carisse was on her break from her job at a nearby nursing home and returning my call.

"Sure," she said when I explained Wendy's situation. "I'll be glad to help. I know Mrs. Dykstra and I think she's great. I don't mind giving her a break on the price. I know they're tight for money keeping three boys in college."

I loved that. There was Lilith putting herself through school on three jobs with no help from anyone in her family and she could still offer some assistance to Wendy.

"That's nice. But I'll pay your regular rate. There are other ways to trim costs. By the way, I wouldn't be surprised if there were a few meals in it for you."

"Awesome."

"And I may have a much bigger job coming up and I'll probably need a team of packers. I'd like you as team leader if that works for you."

"Thanks. What kind of job?"

"Can you get your head around seven custom-designed closets stuffed with designer clothing, accessories, and goods, much of it probably with the tags still on?"

"Whoa. That is hard for me to imagine. What kind of a person has that lifestyle?"

"A cover girl. Well, a former cover girl with a wealthy, indulgent husband and a contract as the face of a major cosmetics company."

"Oh. Sounds like Lorelei. I bet she's the only person in this area who fits that description. Is it confidential information?"

"Not if you're going to be the team leader for the packing."

"I have to head back to work in a minute, but that sounds very cool."

"It will be a different kind of project for all of us. I'm not sure Lorelei's completely committed to it. But I'll keep you in the loop."

"Sure. Gotta go."

"Right. Before I forget, did you happen to know her daughter, Anabel Beauchamp?"

Lilith paused. "Sure. I knew Anabel. But those patient bells are ringing and I'm back on duty. I'll talk to you tonight."

Was it my imagination or did Lilith's voice have an edge in it when she said Anabel's name? That didn't make sense, because everyone, absolutely everyone, had loved Anabel. Hadn't they?

—◆◆—

The Beauchamp home was a pleasant drive out of town, across my favorite bridge and into the much more affluent town of Rheingold. I love Woodbridge for all its quirky history, artistic and entrepreneurial population, not to mention the splendid Victorian-era houses, but in Rheingold you can practically smell money in the air. It was the right place for the Beauchamps to have their "summer home," no question.

Rumor had it they had an ocean-view condo in Palm Beach, Harry's family home in Georgia, and a pied-à-terre in Paris. Regular folks, but with all the seasons covered.

I realized as I checked my watch that I was going to be five minutes late for the first time in my working life. There's always a real reason for being late, I reminded myself. I always told clients that. And it's not bad traffic or a flat tire or a broken heel. It's something in your head. I knew darn well in this case Lorelei was in my head. As I drove along I felt a chill that had nothing to do with the mild weather or the warm Miata. A glance at my speedometer indicated I was way under the speed limit, which is not my style.

A ray of hope glowed softly in my brain: Maybe Lorelei would change her mind about the project. While I would be sorry that Lilith wouldn't get that job as team coordinator, I would have been quite pleased. Besides, I always had plenty of work for Lilith, often more than she could handle.

Even the crunch of the car tires along the long driveway had an ominous sound. I was ten minutes late by this time. When I got out of the car, Harry was waiting near the door.

"I am sorry that I'm late." I did not offer an excuse, as I could hardly say I'd been creeped out by the idea of coming back.

"Don't you worry about that, Charlotte honey. We're glad you're here." Harry exuded southern warmth. He sure didn't seem to be aware that I was creeped out.

Well, Harry might have been glad I was there, but Lorelei was nowhere to be seen.

"Lorelei's getting freshened up. I'll keep you company."

Such a warm, reassuring man. I wondered how he could stand this sterile environment and the ice queen who was Lorelei. Of course, I know from my mother's life, my own, and those of my friends that there is no accounting for taste in lovers and husbands.

"Sometimes it takes Lorelei a fair amount of time to feel ready to meet the world," he said.

I refrained from comment. I'd been late and had no business criticizing others. And it was hard not to smile at Harry.

Harry headed toward the kitchen. "You have a seat here. I'm fixin' today's special cocktail. It's a champagne julep."

"Thanks so much, but it's a bit too early for me. I need my head about me."

He called back over his shoulder. "What's that charmin' expression? Somewhere in the world it's the cocktail hour?"

"It probably is. Can you make mine a virgin champagne julep?"

"Well, that's a good idea."

Harry returned with three champagne flutes. They all looked pretty much the same. Mine turned out to be a gentle ice tea with sugar syrup and mint. I had to admit it was delightful.

Harry sat on the opposite sofa and raised his glass in a salute.

I raised mine in turn.

"She'll be down in good time, don't you worry."

"I'm sure she will. But I'm glad to have a chance to talk to you, Harry."

"Really? Why?"

I liked the way he said it. Sounded like "wah." Musical.

"I get the impression that Lorelei isn't hugely enthusiastic about the whole closet reorganization project."

He shrugged. He was an engaging man; he could manage a shrug without looking rude. It seemed to say, *Well, what can we do? We are all in this together.*

I pressed on. "Am I right?"

"Sometimes Lorelei needs a little nudge in a particular direction."

"Am I a little nudge?"

"You are a lot more than that, Charlotte honey. You could be a very pleasant and even productive diversion for a lovely lady who is in desperate need of bein' diverted from her own thoughts."

"I'm not so sure I'll be able to provide that diversion."

"I don't know anyone who loves clothes more than my girl, and I think when you all get right into the project, you'll both enjoy yourselves thoroughly."

"She didn't seem very engaged yesterday. We only saw one closet out of the seven."

"Seven? I think there might be more than that."

"More than seven?"

"Well, I'm not certain. I don't ever think much about closets. I can go check for you. Count 'em up."

"It doesn't matter how many. It only matters if Lorelei wants to get involved with the project. It won't work otherwise."

"Oh, I'm sure it will work."

"Well, if her first closet is anything to go by, she'll most likely have to sort things out and get rid of some items."

Harry's eyebrows shot up. "Lorelei likes to hold on to things."

"I suppose there are ways around that. You could add some more closets or convert a bedroom to storage space with racks or get some off-site storage for surplus clothing and gear, but she'd still have to decide what items would go where."

"I hadn't thought of that. There must be more to this whole closet business than meets the eye."

You bet your champagne cocktail, I thought, *and that's why I can make a living at it.*

"It's an expensive business, and if she's not keen, it will be a waste of your money and my time."

By now, I was wondering how many ways I would have to make my point with Harry.

Harry said, "I don't give a fig about the cost, Charlotte honey, if it makes a difference. I'm at my wit's end trying to find distractions for her, so she can let her mind rest a bit."

I cleared my throat. "I can only imagine how awful this whole situation is for both of you. Losing a child must be—"

Harry's brown eyes filled. "The day Anabel died, the light went out of my life. I couldn't ever have dreamed how empty I would feel. Nothing can prepare you for that complete devastation. Imagine how your own daddy would react."

"Actually, I never knew my father. My mother divorced him a month before I was born."

Harry stared at me for a very long minute. "And you never met him? Your own daddy?"

"That's right. I had a series of stepfathers who were all very pleasant and kind enough. Generous, too. So the situation with Lorelei—"

"Is he still alive?"

"My father? I don't know."

"Your mama doesn't know?"

"She never told me and she won't talk about it. All I know is he was French from somewhere in Quebec. She'd moved on."

Harry shook his head. "Seems to me a child should know her own daddy, but Mama knows best. I guess she has her reasons."

"I imagine she does. They may even be good ones. But I prefer to believe that somewhere near Quebec City there's a man who looks a lot like me and has spectacular storage units and a color-coded closet."

I sensed relief in Harry's laughter and took advantage of it to say, "But on a serious note, Lorelei probably needs to deal with her grief. She needs to get professional help. The closets could come afterward. If ever."

"Honey, we've had lots of professional help. Psychologists, psychiatrists, grief counselors, even a medium. Like you say, she needs to deal with her grief. In fact we all do. Each in our own way. But the point is that all the professionals in this whole world won't bring Anabel back."

That was true enough. "I'm sorry," I said. "I am trying to help and maybe I am making things worse."

"Don't you let yourself think like that. Now you make yourself comfortable and I'll go check if Lorelei is able to get out of bed yet. I won't be but a minute." He patted my hand and left the room.

Five minutes later he descended the long architectural staircase and shook his handsome head sadly. Lorelei would not be making our meeting today.

6

The trip home was a lot faster. This time I was a bit over the speed limit. As I crossed the bridge to Woodbridge, I didn't even notice the fast-flowing Hudson below. I was too busy thinking about the charged atmosphere in the Beauchamp home. Maybe that's why I didn't hear the siren until the dark car was on my bumper.

I pulled over with my heart thumping. How fast had I been going? It couldn't have been that bad. I'm not much for speeding. I felt almost panicked as I rooted in my handbag for my car registration and license. Naturally, I always have them easily accessible.

I jumped when I saw the man loom in the window.

Connor Tierney leaned over and fixed those ice blue eyes on me.

"Pants on fire?" he asked.

"Very funny. I wasn't going that fast."

"How fast were you going?"

I hung on to the shreds of my dignity. "I don't actually know the precise speed, but I am certainly not in the habit of . . ." I tried not to be distracted by the slight hint of his sexy aftershave. Why is that a weakness for me?

"Rule one: Don't argue with the nice policeman."

"Oh. Is there a nice policeman around here somewhere?" I glanced out my rear window.

He crossed his arms in front of him and leaned into my open window. "I wanted to talk to you."

"Write the ticket. If I was speeding, I'll pay the price. I didn't even know detectives carried radar guns with them."

"We don't. Like I said, I want to talk to you."

"About what?"

"Well, about this situation with the Beauchamps for one thing."

"I'm not sure there's going to be a situation. Lorelei can't even get out of bed today. She's not in emotional shape to take on a big complicated project."

"Big complicated project. Closets?"

"Don't denigrate my work. That is surely outside the scope of your job description, Detective."

"Speaking of, I hope you are not going to nose around about Anabel Beauchamp and get everyone all revved up."

"By everyone, do you mean the Woodbridge police?"

"I mean some of the Woodbridge police and the library staff and who knows who else."

I was outraged. "The library staff? They're supposed to keep inquiries confidential. Wait a minute. I do not believe that Ramona would—"

"Rat you out to the fuzz?"

"Hilarious."

"One of the patrons called the station to make a complaint that you were disturbing the peace in the library and stirring up controversy over Anabel Beauchamp's death."

"Wow. Crime rates in our city must be at an all-time

low if detectives collect information about people asking questions in the library. Do you keep track of everyone's overdue books, too?"

"Let's say I happened to be passing by when the call came in."

"Lucky me."

"I need you to promise me you won't get yourself involved in another investigation."

"Seriously, there's no way I intend to get involved in an investigation. I am merely worried about Anabel's mother, who may or may not be my client after today. She thinks someone killed her daughter. I don't know why, and I don't know anything about the circumstances. I have known Mrs. Beauchamp for years, and I knew Anabel slightly and liked her very much. I got the impression when I was talking to Nick that he saw something that didn't look right. Now, I'm fully aware that Nick Monahan is an idiot, and I can always tell when Pepper's lying. So as she believes it was a tragic accident, I am prepared to accept that."

"What about me? Didn't you think I was telling the truth?" I heard the jingle of his keys.

"Not sure. I don't know much about you."

"But we had such a great evening out a few weeks back."

"Right. I have vague memories of that."

"I thought we'd have more of those."

"Did you?" My voice was chilly enough to frost up the windows.

"Yeah. But then I had to take leave and fly back to my hometown to handle some urgent family business. My brother was injured on duty. He has a young family and he needed help. I should have called you, but everyone in my family dropped whatever they were doing and pulled together for his wife and kids."

"Oh." I felt about as tall as Truffle and Sweet Marie.

"I'm sorry I didn't get in touch sooner. I didn't want to mention it today in front of your shadow."

"His name is Jack. And I apologize. I should have figured there was a good reason why you never called back."

It sure was my day to say sorry a lot.

"I did try a few times, but that guy always answers."

"Jack."

"Is he always around?"

"He's my oldest and best friend."

Tierney watched me carefully for a while. "So I wanted to ask you out again this morning, but then you showed up with him. Is he your pet pit bull?"

I couldn't hold back a bubble of laughter. The notion of baby-crazy Jack as a pit bull was nothing short of hilarious.

"Don't curl your lip like that. Jack thinks you are going to arrest me or hassle me or something."

"I think he's jealous. Did you take a look at his face?"

"Not the case. You can always ask for me if he answers the phone, you know. Does he say I'm not there? He never even mentioned you called."

"I hang up. If you're there with him, it's not the time for me to explain why I didn't ask you out again."

"What's your excuse now?"

He grinned. "My excuse must be in my other pants pocket. So would you like to go out to dinner tonight?"

"Oh. I can't."

"Why not?" I guess if you're a detective you get used to asking the questions and expecting answers.

"It's girls' night with Sally and Margaret. It's a sacred tradition. I wouldn't dare miss it."

Tierney had met both of them, and in fact he'd been invited to the dinner after Margaret eloped with Frank, one of his colleagues. I didn't mention that Jack often turned up for girls' nights as the silly boy continues to be unclear on certain concepts, such as who's a girl and who isn't. When challenged, he claims reverse sexism and hauls out the heavy artillery from his many logic courses to win his point. Usually one of us real girls falls asleep from the sheer tedium.

"Tomorrow then?"

I looked up at those ice blue eyes and smiled. "Tomorrow will be great. My schedule's absolutely clear."

—++—

I swung by Rose Skipowski's place, hoping to catch Lilith between shifts, chowing down at Rose's seventies-style dining table. Their deal for a roof over Lilith's head in return for helping Rose was working well for both. I was lucky and caught her as she was leaving. Rose opened the door. She was resplendent in a lilac jogging suit and neon runners and lit up at the sight of me. Despite my protests, she immediately began to pack cookies for what she called my "trip home." There seemed to be quite a few cookies, considering the trip was walkable on a good day. Still, I was thankful.

Lilith was rushing to get ready to work the dinner shift at a nearby seniors' residence. "I have fifteen minutes to get there. Six ladies need me to accompany them to the dining room for the five-thirty dinner. One at a time!"

"Lilith," I said a few minutes later as I walked with her toward Rose's car, "I was curious. You are one of the few people who don't sing Anabel's praises. Is there something I should be aware of?"

Lilith turned away. I waited. Finally she said, "Maybe it's me."

I continued to wait, trying not to be distracted by the scent of the freshly baked cookies.

Lilith blurted, "She had everything. The gorgeous home, the famous beautiful mother, the adoring father, whatever college she wanted, no worries about money. She was naturally beautiful."

This was all true, of course, but even if you left out narcissistic from the beautiful mother description, although it belonged there, you'd still have to think it was a tragedy that Anabel had died the way she did.

"That sounds horrible, I know." Lilith kicked a stone. "But she didn't have to work at Hope for Youth at Risk. She didn't have to work at all. She had the world. Why did she have to have—?"

"Have to have what?"

"Who," she said. "Why did she have to have who?"

"Okay." I smiled encouragingly.

Lilith snorted. "You look like you need an antacid."

"Fine, tell me who the 'who' is and I'll go take one. Did Anabel get involved with someone you cared about?"

"Yes. No."

"Ah. The old yes-no thing."

She laughed despite herself. "Not someone I cared about, although I think he's okay. But one of my friends."

"Just so you know, I'm not giving up."

She sighed and I had to remind myself that Lilith was still in her teens and not long off the streets herself, in part because of Hope for Youth at Risk. Once again, I waited.

"Jewel, my friend, was always good to me. She hasn't had it easy." Lilith could have written the book on not having it easy, but I refrained from comment. I nodded, though.

Lilith continued. "Jewel had a thing for this guy named Dimitri. He does a lot of work with Hope for Youth at Risk. She had no one, nothing. She's beautiful and lovely and sad. Trying to get her life together. Dimitri liked her, too. I know it and—"

I interrupted, "Dimitri? Is he kind of attractive? Young?"

Lilith snorted. "Kind of attractive? Um, yeah. Like every woman's fantasy kind of attractive."

"I think I saw him at their office."

"Leather jacket? Tormented soul expression?"

"That's the one."

"Anyway, then Anabel arrived at the agency. Even with her jeans and plaid work shirts, she still had those rich-girl looks. And pow! Dimitri got knocked off his feet."

"Well," I blurted, "I know what that's like."

"You mean your ex-fiancé?"

"Yeah."

"You don't know. What did you have left at the end?"

"No fiancé, for starters!"

"But everything else. Your car. Your job. Your savings. Your friends? Your life?"

I stared at her. "You mean that because of Anabel, Jewel lost everything? Didn't she—?"

"She left. How could she stay connected to Hope for Youth at Risk if he was there drooling over Anabel? It was horrible for her. And because of this, I didn't think that Anabel was all that saintly, you know? She could have let him down gently. Or meanly. She could have left herself, found another agency to play with. Why did she have to take everything away from Jewel?"

I considered what I knew about Anabel. "Do you think Anabel knew how Jewel felt? Or Dimitri for that matter?"

Lilith stared at me solemnly as she opened the door to Rose's car. "I think she did. But if she hadn't noticed, that would make it worse, wouldn't it?"

———

The dogs were waiting with their legs crossed when I got home, so it took a while before I picked up my voice mail.

I slipped them each one of Rose's cookies and put the rest aside for Jack and me.

There were a couple of hang-ups from an unknown number that I figured might have been Tierney. Maybe I'd have to start calling him Connor if we were going on a second date.

There was one call from Wendy Dykstra, a pleasant and cheerful request that I call her back. The second was from Lorelei Beauchamp. Ramona had left a few brisk words to say that my clippings were ready. I had three potential clients wanting information about my services. I was slightly surprised by the message from Pepper.

"Call me on my cell phone," she insisted. "Not at home."

I couldn't figure out what that might be about.

I returned the calls in order, Wendy first.

"Does it matter where I get rid of my old clothes?"

"Not at all. I always ask my clients to think about a charity for the ones that don't fit but are in good condition. We'll figure out what we can do with the rest. Don't try to match each item to the perfect new home. Find one or two deserving places and let them go."

"Oh boy, that's great. I do a bit of volunteering at Galilee House and I was hoping I could donate them there. And I can take some of my old T-shirts to the animal shelter. They're always looking for soft fabrics for bedding. I'll do a bit of that ahead of time. Maybe it will make our job easier."

I knew that our job would be easier anyway because Wendy was positive and enthusiastic and spent the bulk of her time thinking of other people. She'd given me a good idea.

I hesitated before I called Lorelei. Perhaps I could wait until after I'd returned the other calls. Get at it, I told myself. You can't afford to waste energy because of procrastination.

Harry answered, sounding gallant as always. "Lovely to hear from you, Charlotte honey. Lorelei was up and around and in much better spirits this afternoon."

Not if the tone in her message was anything to go by, I thought.

"Charlotte?" she said when she came on the phone. "I must apologize for this afternoon. I don't know what came over me. I assure you that I will be ready for you for the rest of this project. I'd like you to come again tomorrow if you would. I'll be waiting and willing."

She was trying; I had to give her that.

She added, "I know it's an imposition."

I flipped open my agenda and said, "Sorry, Lorelei, I have only one o'clock tomorrow. Will that do?" It would come out of my business-planning time, but what the hell.

She said, "One o'clock's too early for me. Tomorrow night, then? Harry would love to make you dinner."

I noticed Harry hadn't been consulted.

I said, "I have a previous engagement." Tierney's date was coming in handy already.

"You can't change it?"

"Sorry. It took several weeks to arrange." I felt a smile bloom.

"That's a shame."

"I have more flexibility on Wednesday. You can show me around, and if you aren't feeling well, perhaps Harry will. Or if you prefer, we can decide to do the main closet in your dressing room."

"Harry thinks it will keep me busy. He's right. You may as well come tomorrow afternoon."

Ignoring her total lack of enthusiasm, I said, "Lovely. And Lorelei?"

"Yes."

"I have a little homework for you."

"Homework!"

"That's right. But you'll be equal to the task."

"What is it?"

"I need you to come up with a charity to donate your surplus clothing to. That is anything we decide not to keep or sell or throw out."

"A charity?"

"That's right. Lots of them use clothing donations to fund their services to people."

She hesitated. "All right. I'll think about it."

"Excellent. See you tomorrow."

"A lot of those clothes have never been worn, you know."

"That's fine, too. You don't have to donate them if you don't want to. Give some thought to which charity you will use for whatever you do discard."

"All right. I don't know what to suggest. Harry takes care of all that sort of business."

"Why not discuss it with Harry in that case? I'm sure you'll find some group that you like the sound of, someone who is doing good work with disadvantaged people in Rheingold or even Woodbridge. Even a national charity. You've lent your name and face to support more than one organization."

As we said good-bye I was reminded of why Wendy's project would be so much more fun. I knew that Lorelei needed this project, needed to reach out to me, and even more needed to give her wounded heart a rest. It had nothing to do with closets at all.

I finished up by making consultation appointments with two of the three potential clients for the following week. I figured Wendy's job would be done very quickly, even if

Lorelei's might drag out. I decided to dash into the library that evening. I hoped I wouldn't run into the rats who had reported me.

For some reason, Pepper wasn't answering her cell phone.

7

Girls' night was at Sally's place. By the time I drove up, Margaret's glossy black Volvo S80 and Jack's dung-colored Mini Minor were parked side by side behind Sally's huge SUV. It takes a lot of vehicle to haul Sally's family from place to place. Not that she's on the run that much: Four young children keep her fairly tied down. Sally's husband, Benjamin, was a busy physician. He'd wisely scheduled a meeting for that night. No sign of his Lexus.

Margaret and I were exhausted by the time Dallas, Madison, Savannah, and little Shenandoah had settled in. Of course, we'd been left downstairs to straighten up. Sally and Jack got the kids to bed. Apparently there's something about me that keeps them revved up for hours.

Margaret wasn't into kids, although her parents made up for that. May I add they were not shy about mentioning it? She must have had a rough day in court, as she was snoring softly on Sally's white leather sofa by the time Sally and Jack tiptoed down the stairs. That sofa had been the height of cool when Sally and Benjamin purchased it.

It didn't look as sleek now with the felt-tip marker designs that decorated one arm.

I said, "I'll make the s'mores. You wake up Margaret."

"I'll make the s'mores," Jack and Sally said in unison.

"No way. What are you two, chicken? What do you think she'll do to you anyway?"

"Remember last time?" Sally said.

"Oh right. Yeah. Well, let's let her snore then. Newlyweds need their sleep."

"She better get it now," Sally said. "She won't have a hope once 'baby makes three.' "

Margaret opened her eyes and yawned. "Someone change the subject."

"Did any of you know Anabel Beauchamp? I know you did, Jack. I'm talking to Sally and Margaret."

"Anabel Beauchamp?"

"Lorelei and my mother go way back. I have a job to do for her, and I've been thinking about Anabel."

Sally scrunched up her face. "Well, she was the opposite of Lorelei, that's for sure."

Margaret yawned again and said, "She was a couple of years younger than us. I heard that she had a very good brain and her parents wanted to send her to an exclusive boarding school, but she insisted on St. Jude's. I thought she'd go on to Harvard law or medicine or something. She had the smarts and the family money."

Jack said, "I knew her from some of the animal rescue activities. She mobilized some of the kids she was working with to help at events. What does that mean, 'the opposite of Lorelei'?"

"Well, working on a volunteer event would be one example, I'm guessing," Sally said. "I can't see Lorelei ever doing anything like that, can you?"

I said, "She does lend her name and face to some high-profile fund-raisers, but doesn't seem involved with community activities. I suppose I shouldn't say that when she's been through a horrible tragedy."

I didn't mention that Lorelei had no idea where to donate her clothes, although I was bothered by that. Most people have some charity or organization that they donate a bit of time to, even if they can't afford to donate cash. Lorelei's annual income was probably worth more than most of the annual budgets of our local nonprofits. Perhaps her inability to think of one grew from the concentration problems that often accompany trauma.

Sally was on a roll. "And the other thing was that Anabel didn't give a hoot what she looked like. She never wore makeup, and she always dressed like a construction worker. What? What are you giving me the evil eye for, Jack?"

"That seems unkind, Sally. It's easy for you. You always look pretty."

"Without trying," I added, "which is actually a form of cheating."

That was true enough. Sally wasn't quite in Lorelei's league, but she was a knockout. Her naturally tumbling blond curls and bright coloring worked in her favor. A touch of lip gloss was all it took to dress her up. Plus she was tall and her figure snapped back almost audibly after she gave birth. If I didn't love her, I would find her quite annoying.

Jack wasn't done, though. "She was a person who made a difference in the lives of vulnerable people. And animals. Who cares what she looked like or how she dressed?"

Sally flushed. Of course, a flush looks good on Sal. "No. That's not what I'm saying. We were talking about how she is the opposite of Lorelei. You were the one who asked that particular question. I'm answering it. She didn't care about her appearance. She was clean and neat and full of energy. But she wore work clothes, plain and practical. Lorelei probably doesn't appear for breakfast unless she's in full makeup and wearing designer loungewear."

I said, "You know what? That's true."

Margaret lifted an eyebrow. "Big deal. Not like we're paying for it. She's a successful model and a business-woman. She can do anything she wants with her money."

For some reason, Jack seemed to be sulking. "Why did you even bring this up, Charlotte?"

"I'm sorry I did. I am trying to figure out what's going on with her, that's all. Lorelei's not an easy person to connect to. And she is convinced that someone killed her daughter. The police don't believe this and I have to admit, I have trouble buying into the idea, too. "

"You never know. Maybe someone hated Anabel. People aren't always what they look like." Was Sally deliberately trying to get under Jack's skin?

Jack said, "Yeah. Sometimes pretty people can turn into real bitches."

Margaret said, "Ouch!"

Sally lobbed a cushion at Jack's head. "I speak the truth. Whether you can take it or not, dude. I've seen them both in action and Charlotte's right. I'd say they had nothing in common at all."

"When did you see them in action?" Margaret asked.

"Benjamin and I were invited to a cocktail party at their home. Harry had made a substantial donation to the Woodbridge General Hospital Foundation and had a party to celebrate it."

Margaret said, "A money man then. What's he like?"

"Lovely," Sally said.

"A big courtly bear," I added. "Kind and gentle."

"Generous to a fault," Sally added.

Margaret said, "Sally, may I remind you that a minute ago you said that people are not always what they look like."

I shook my head. "Forget the cross-examination, Margaret. I'll go with my instincts on this one. Harry's a wonderful man."

Jack said, "Your instincts aren't always the best, you know."

Margaret and Sally both shot him a look. Those looks flew right over his messy head.

I said, "Well, Harry is not a problem. He's trying to find a way to help Lorelei cope with her horrible loss. He's suffering himself. And he's still looking out for her."

Jack piped up, "Time for a DVD?"

"Wait a minute," Margaret said. "What's in the closets, Charlotte?"

"I don't know. I'm betting spectacular designer stuff, high-end. Amazing stuff. It will be like looking through *Vogue* and *Glamour*."

"Didn't you once tell me that every closet has a secret?" Sally said.

I grinned. "I did. And I found yours, if I remember correctly: a framed head shot of the teeth that walked like a man, Todd Tyrell. How was it signed? Oh yes: *To my ardent fan! XOXO, Todd*."

Margaret snorted. "Ooh. Hiding that from Benjamin, I bet."

Sally flushed. "Benjamin's a busy man. No need to hide anything from him. He'd never notice. And if he did, he wouldn't react. He's a man of great confidence, not always merited. But what's the secret in your closet, Margaret?"

"Nothing you'll ever find out about."

Knowing Margaret, I suspected that was true. If she had secrets, she'd know how to keep them.

Sally turned to me. "And you, Charlotte? Do you have your own secrets in your color-coded cupboard? Are they in alphabetical order?"

"I must be the only person who doesn't have a hidden secret." Time to change the subject. "Except Jack, of course."

We all chortled at the idea of Jack keeping or even having a secret. Even his close-call relationship with a woman I loathed had been fairly obvious some months back. Jack said, "Don't underestimate me."

I was glad when the conversation switched to a lively debate on which DVD to watch. I like to keep my own closet off-limits.

—◆◆—

Margaret and I tidied up after the movie as Sally and Jack had put the kids to bed. They kept saying, "Fair's fair." Jack headed out, claiming he had to get up early the next morning.

"How's it going?" I asked Margaret as we finally tucked the last glasses into the rack and closed the door of the dishwasher.

"Life is good. You'll notice I'm yawning a lot. Interpret that in a romantic way."

"I thought you might have had a rough day in court."

"Nothing to do with court."

"Well, I'm glad you are still hanging out with the misfits, seeing as you're practically still on your honeymoon."

"We all need space. Frank went out with some guys from the station tonight."

"That works well."

"Speaking of guys, Frank says that Connor Tierney brings up your name in every single conversation."

"What's that about? He stopped me for speeding today. They must be desperate to fill their ticket quotas."

"Detectives don't have ticket quotas. It's a ploy."

"I've had some bad luck, or bad choices if you prefer. I don't know how ready I am to see anybody. But you're the first to know that we're having dinner together tomorrow night."

"How's Jack taking it?"

"What does Jack have to do with it? What? Why are you looking at me like that? Do I have to clear every date with my friends? And this from the woman who surprised us by eloping with a man she'd kept secret."

"For someone so smart and together, Charlotte, you are pretty thick sometimes."

I was still puzzling over what she might have meant when I drove into my driveway. Jack's Mini was already parked, and the lights were out in his apartment. I hustled the dogs outside for a good-night trip. We paraded up and down in the little strip in front of my house.

"Hurry up. It's getting nippy and it's dark. That translates into make it snappy."

Behind me, a car door opened. I started and whirled, and to tell the truth, squeaked. One too many guns in my recent past.

The dogs pulled out their Rottweiler barks. But those are much more effective if they're out of sight. It was obvious by looking at Truffle and Sweet Marie that they were just over twelve pounds each. They could savage your ankles, though.

"Charlotte?"

"Pepper?"

"Can you call off those hounds?"

"I'm sure they won't ever bite you again, Pepper. You were trying to arrest me that other time. Remember?"

"I'm not likely to forget. Tell them to be quiet. I don't want them to wake up Little Nick."

"Little Nick? He's here? You're out driving around near midnight with the baby in the—?"

"Calm your dogs. We're going inside."

Once we were settled in my living room, Truffle and Sweet Marie sniffed the baby. Pepper glared at them. I parked them at the end of the sofa and placed myself between them and Pepper. "I did return your call, but then I had to go out."

"I didn't want to do it by phone."

"Do what?"

"Have this talk."

"Oh. You mean you do know something about Anabel Beauchamp's death?"

"Are you still harping on that?"

"Harping? Okay, never mind, no more harping. What is it about?" I tried to keep a pleasant tone. Pepper had once been my best friend, and we were making amends after years of insults and the occasional frog marching of me to the police station. Again, that would have been Pepper's doing. Although it's possible I may have contributed in some small way.

"It's Nick."

Of course. It would have to be. I prepared to put on my most sympathetic voice. I figured she'd need it if God's gift to women had been out catting around again. On the other hand, I didn't want to give her bad advice, such as *This will pass, give him space* or other foolishness. No matter how you cut it, Nick Monahan wasn't what you'd call prime husband material.

"Do you think it's serious?"

She frowned at me. "What?"

I said, "Whatever brings you out here for moonless midnight madness with your baby. I didn't think you wanted to discuss sandwiches for Nick's lunch."

"Have you heard anything?"

"About *what*?"

She snapped, "Nick, of course. The person we're talking about."

I shook my head. "No. Nothing. His name hasn't come

up. And the only time I've run into him for months was at your own home."

"Hmm."

It had to be another woman. Nick has a hard time keeping his mouth shut and his fly zippered. And he is damned good-looking. He makes Connor Tierney, Todd Tyrell, and even Margaret's tall, dark, and granite husband, Frank D'Angelo, look like also-rans.

I said, "Would this be a good time for New York Super Fudge Chunk?"

She nodded. "Got lots?"

"Believe it."

I gave Pepper her own tub of ice cream. As underhanded as it seems, I was prepared to slip the Anabel Beauchamp issue back into the conversation once we were past the latest Nick crisis.

Little Nick at least was cooperative. He lay sleeping happily, punctuating his breathing with the occasional squeak that even I had to admit was adorable.

Truffle and Sweet Marie were poised by my side throughout the ice cream eating. They like to make off with the empty containers. I wasn't sure the vet would approve, but then again, there were no vets in sight.

"So," I said, as we polished off our ice cream a few minutes later. "What seems to be the problem?" I stopped myself from ending it with *this time*.

"Sorry for snapping. I don't know what's going on. First I thought it was another woman. Nick hasn't dealt well with all the changes of pregnancy and motherhood. He likes a woman to be trim and neat and wearing sexy underwear. Lactation freaks him out. Naturally, that's what I suspected when he first started to act differently."

"Well, Nick's a big boy now. He'd better get used to real life." I refrained from saying it was high time he grew up.

"But it's not that."

"So . . . ?"

"I'm not sure what's going on."

"Why are you worried?"

"Huh. Well that's it. If he's interested in a woman, and I always know when he is, he takes extra care with his appearance. Works out more than usual. Takes a razor to work so he can shave after shift. Showers there and not at home. Finds fault with everything I do. There's a whole vibe. You don't want to know."

"But he's not doing that now?"

"No. He hasn't been to the gym. He doesn't bother shaving on his off days. His clothes are sort of . . . rumpled. He hangs around home looking gloomy, or he pretends to be working extra shifts, even though I know he's not."

"Don't take this the wrong way, Pepper, but maybe he's adjusting to the whole idea of being a father."

"I'd buy that idea if he was spending any time with Little Nick. I don't mean feeding him or changing him because neither of those things are in the job description of the male Monahans. But if he'd even pay attention, make goofy daddy faces, give him shoulder rides, the way other fathers do. Hell, Jack even plays games with Little Nick, and he's as single as you can get."

"If he hasn't seen it in his family, I guess the models aren't there and—"

"Knock off the amateur-shrink routine, Charlotte. I'm not here to get a pep talk straight out of some useless woman's magazine. It's not about that anyway."

"Help me out here, Pepper. I don't know what you want from me."

"I want you to listen. I want to talk about this out loud, and I'm not even sure what will come out of my mouth."

"Deal. Talk. I'll listen."

"Then, when I'm finished, I want to hear what you think about what I've said."

I nodded. There wasn't much else I could do.

"He's slumping around, not sleeping properly, and jumping at shadows. You know, the way *you* do."

"Thanks," I muttered under my breath.

"It's not like him. He's not afraid of anything, even when he should be. He has the judgment of a rubber ducky, you know that."

I held my comments back. Pepper has always seemed to be in denial about Nick. For all I knew, she'd be back to normal the next day and mad at me for having listened to her.

"He won't answer the phone, and he's incredibly secretive."

"Like you were tonight?"

"I didn't want him to pick up one of my messages and figure out that I was coming to see you. He'd show up and I wouldn't be able to have this difficult conversation."

Pepper bit her lip, a little-girl gesture that was completely out of character with the hard-edged detective she'd turned into.

I said, "I'm not married. I never had a dad or even a stepdad who stuck around and did dadlike things with me. I don't know what normal daily family life is supposed to be like. I won't be much help to you here, unless I fall back on my useless women's magazine advice."

She grinned wanly. "I am worried sick and I can't cope with this on my own. That's why I called you."

"I'm happy to be here for you, Pepper. Although I'm not doing much good."

"This is very hard for me to say." She met my eyes and glanced away.

Little Nick stirred and whimpered. He squirmed and scrunched up his perfect baby face. He opened his perfect rosebud mouth and let out one hell of a holler, without even a warm-up.

Truffle and Sweet Marie quivered before racing into the bedroom and hiding under the bed. I would have joined them, but I didn't want to sever this new bond between Pepper and me.

She picked up Little Nick. "He's hungry and I have to take care of that. It's midnight, his last feeding. And I must be nuts," she said.

"What?"

"What am I doing here with you talking about my husband?" She stood up and turned toward the door.

I said, "You thought I could help."

"Seriously, how could you help? You're an organizer, not a therapist. And you're bossy and opinionated on top of that."

"I'll admit to all of those things. I'm so happy to be your friend again. And I'll do whatever you want me to . . ." I obviously couldn't say "help" again as that hadn't worked out so well the last time I'd said it. "I'd like to hear what you have to say. Maybe you'll feel better for saying it, too."

She stared down at me, jiggling the squalling baby. "Sorry I bothered you. I have to go."

Truffle and Sweet Marie emerged as soon as Pepper left. I sat there, stroking their fur, stunned. What had happened? I couldn't let it go by. I thundered down the stairs and out to Pepper's new bright red Ford Edge. She was leaning her head against the wheel, weeping. Little Nick was screaming his head off.

A light went on in Jack's apartment, and he appeared barefoot and wearing pajama bottoms. "Did I dream I heard a baby crying?"

"Look who's here, Little Nick. It's Uncle Jack," I shouted to the wailing baby. "Uncle Jack's going to fix your problem. Open the door, Pepper, and give Jack the baby and the bottle."

Jack said, "What?"

"Be quiet. Don't argue. You'll love it. You know what you're like."

"Sure," he said. "I'll take him upstairs. Let me know when you want him back."

I reached in and picked up Little Nick and transferred his enraged being to Jack's arms. "Hey, little buddy, pipe down," Jack said.

The howl died on Little Nick's lips. He stared. He reached out his tiny hand for Jack's glasses. I took the baby bottle from Pepper's hand and passed it to Jack. "You're on your own," I said. "The dogs will be no help."

As Jack headed toward the house, I climbed into the car and put my arms around Pepper. "You're not getting rid of me that quickly this time."

"There's nothing you can do."

"Try me. I'll understand."

"You couldn't even begin to understand, Charlotte. You're not involved in law enforcement." She managed a weak smile. "Except on the other side."

I knew this meant something big. Pepper is the third generation of her family of police officers. And Nick's father, grandfather, and great-grandfather had all been cops in Woodbridge. That's not even mentioning the uncles.

"Why did you come to see me then?"

She turned away, stared out the window. "Exactly because you're not a cop. I thought it was a good idea, but now I realize how stupid it was."

"Yeah well, that's misfits for you. Dumb as a bag of hammers."

She gave a weak smile, leaned back against the headrest, and closed her eyes. "I'm so desperate, Charlotte. I think Nick is involved in something seriously bad."

"We've ruled out women, so what does that leave?"

"Think about it."

"Oh! A crime?"

"It must be."

"What kind?"

"I have no clue, but he's put his foot in something, and I'm so afraid he's going to get himself hurt or even killed."

8

"For the last time, I don't want you to do anything. I needed to say it out loud." Pepper followed this by blowing her nose emphatically.

All right, I may have overreacted to her comment about Nick getting himself killed.

For the fifth time, I said, "But—"

"But nothing. Your job is to listen. That's what friends do."

"We can't let Nick get killed. I have to do something about that."

"That's right. When our lives are in danger, we call our closet organizer to fix it all up."

"Wouldn't be the first time the closet organizer solved the crime." Maybe I snapped that.

"He's not *your* husband."

"True, but he's . . ."

"I feel that he's involved in something. And don't ask me for details again, because I don't have any. It's intuition. And yes, cops use that."

"So you think criminal?"

"I don't *know*." She blew her nose again to make the point.

She meant yes. I decided the best thing might be to sit there and quietly listen, just as she'd suggested. Perhaps that would bring out a bit more information.

After a minute, Pepper glared at me. "If you're trying to wait me out, I know all about that. I've interrogated enough people. It won't work."

"I'm trying to listen. What do you want me to do?"

"I don't know that, either." She managed a weak grin. "Let me rage and carry on in a paranoid manner, I guess."

"Okay. Rage away."

She leaned back on the headrest of the driver's seat and closed her eyes. "I can't. I'm too tired. I haven't been sleeping, and that may be all there is behind this. Nick is not the easiest person . . ."

I bit my tongue to keep myself from finishing her sentence with "at the best of times."

"He's not good at communicating. And he doesn't have a knack with looking after Little Nick. He's not natural daddy material like Jack."

I turned to look at the lights in my apartment where apparently he was being natural and entertaining Little Nick. It kept me from saying, *Damn straight Nick's not good at communicating*. Still, I had to contribute something. "So what made you think that something's wrong with Nick?"

"He jumps at his own shadow."

I raised an eyebrow. Whatever you could say about Nick, he'd never been a coward.

"Sometimes I'll tiptoe into the room trying not to wake the baby and he'll freak."

"Whoa."

She nodded. "Yeah. Not like him."

"Well, after I was attacked last year, I screamed at every loud noise. And some not so loud ones. I had flashbacks, too. And nightmares."

"I thought of that. But except for those two incidents that involved you, he hasn't had any bad encounters. He hasn't been shot at or shot at anyone else. He hasn't even had a chase. And after that dangerous situation that you were involved in, he didn't lose any sleep, although you were both nearly killed."

"And Jack, too. Don't get mad, but I understand that this happens to lots of guys: Do you think it's fatherhood?"

"I asked myself that, too. I think he's not all that interested in Little Nick yet. I don't think he's afraid of him or afraid to be a father. I'm sure he'll be better when the baby starts to do things. And if you are planning to suggest that he's afraid of me because I look like hell, you can forget that."

I gasped. "I would never suggest that. You are too hard on yourself. You look fine."

"And he's keeping strange hours and going out in the middle of the night sometimes. But he doesn't get himself fixed up as if it were a woman he wanted to impress." She chewed her lip.

"Perhaps it's all in his mind, a bit of delayed posttraumatic stress disorder. Do you want me to talk to him?"

"That is the last thing in the world I want. What could you do for his PTSD, not that he has that?"

"Okay. Well, if you do want me to help in any way, let me know. If you want me to come over and let you catch up on your sleep sometime, I can do that. I can plan for it. I know you don't have your mom to help out. New mothers need—"

"Thanks. I appreciate that. Little Nick's not so new anymore. That reminds me. I'd better go get him before Jack decides to keep him."

"Pepper, I keep saying, let me know what I can do to help."

She opened the driver's door and hopped out of the vehicle. "You have helped, Charlotte. A lot. More than you know. I'll be able to sleep tonight."

Which was a lot more than I could say for myself.

—••—

Tuesday was fully booked. By nine thirty I had headed out to Wendy's place, carrying a file full of ideas, sale brochures, and digital photos from the dollar stores and my other favorite haunts. I had my digital camera with me to take a "before" photo. People are always amazed to see where they started from at the end of a project. After the strange conversation with Pepper the night before, it felt very good to be meeting Wendy, kind, uncomplicated, agreeable. I put the contract in my briefcase, told the dogs to behave, and headed over to North Hemlock to pick up Lilith at Rose's place.

I had turned onto Long March Road when I jerked at the sound of a siren behind me. A patrol car was on my tail, roof lights flashing. I pulled over, heart thumping. What had I done now? Was I so caught up in my own schedule that I hadn't signaled? Had I cut someone off? I knew it wasn't Tierney this time. He wouldn't be caught dead in a patrol car.

I opened the windows, fished out my license and insurance papers, and did my best not to look guilty. Until Nick Monahan's face loomed in the open window on the passenger side. He opened the door and got in.

I said, "Oh, what the hell? Are you trying to give me a panic attack?"

"Hi, Charley."

"This calls for more than 'hi,' Nick. This requires an apology for practically freaking me out. Sirens and flashing lights? What's that about?"

"I wanted to talk to you."

"Trust me, there are easier ways."

"I know, but I saw you and I got the idea. You don't mind if I pretend to be giving you a ticket?"

"What?"

"You don't mind if—?"

"I heard you, but why would you want to pretend to give me a ticket if all you want to do is talk to me?"

"Because I don't want anyone to know."

"Anyone? You mean Pepper?"

"No, I mean anyone. So let's see your license."

I handed it over, but at least I got to roll my eyes. He took my info and pretended to write a few things.

I said, "I think you need my registration, too."

"I know that, Charley."

"I'm sure you do, but in case anyone is watching, we might as well look realistic."

"Good thinking."

"And I believe you need to take my documents and go to your squad car and check them on the computer. I don't think you're supposed to sit in my passenger seat and have a heart-to-heart. Although I'm not the cop here."

"We're just talking . . . but maybe you're right. I'll be back in a minute."

A few minutes later, he returned and handed me back my documents through the open window. "You're clear," he said.

"Imagine that. Okay, what are we talking about?"

"Pepper."

"What about her?"

"She came to see you last night. What did you talk about?"

"How do you know that she came to see me last night?"

"Because I . . . you know what, Charley? I think you better come with me to the squad car. To look realistic."

"Um, I'm not sure that is realistic, Nick. Do you put many of the people you ticket into the squad car?"

"Good point. Okay, I'll get in yours."

"No. Stay where you are and keep talking. How do you know that Pepper came to see me? Did you follow her?"

"No way."

"You're a lousy liar, especially considering all the practice you get. Following your own wife around? Shame on you, Nick Monahan."

"I didn't follow her. I happened to turn onto your street and I saw you sitting in the car together. I need to know what she said."

"She didn't say much of anything, Nick."

"Come on, Charley. This is Nick. You can't fool me."

I don't know where he would get an idea like that. My dogs are harder to fool than Nick is. "Believe me. It was all girl talk."

He snorted. "Pepper's not much for girl talk."

"As a rule, I'd agree, but she's been changed by motherhood. It was girl talk, Nick. Accept that."

He stared at me for a while, trying to read my thoughts, I guess. "Like what?" he said finally.

"Oh, you know, hair and stuff."

"You mean she's going to do something with her hair? That would be good. She's let herself go."

"You listen here, Nick Monahan. Your wife is up half the night with your son. And then she's there alone with him during the day. Babies take a lot of time and energy. How's she supposed to spend time on herself?"

"Okay, okay, don't get your thong in a twist. I thought her hair used to look better."

"Haven't you ever heard of hormones?"

He blinked. Of course, Nick was a walking hormone, but that didn't mean he'd be up to speed on the effects of a birth on skin, hair, and mood. "What's that got to do with it?"

"New mothers, lots of hormone changes. Get used to it. Be a man." I wasn't sure if hormones would be much of a factor after nearly eight months, but what did I know. Anything to distract him.

"It's not easy to get used to, Charley. But forget the hair. Did she say anything about me?"

I sat back and pretended to think. "Like what for instance?"

"Nothing special. Didn't she mention me at all?"

"She usually talks about you, but I honestly don't recall."

Of course, I'd said honestly, which is always a clue that I'm fibbing. A white lie in this case, because I had good reasons. Whatever Nick was mixed up in, it wouldn't do any good to have him think that his wife might be blabbing it all over town. If it was dangerous for him, it could be dangerous for her, too.

"That's kind of weird, you know, Charley."

"It was late. She was tired. The baby woke her up. I think he's teething. You sleep through that usually. She did mention that. So I guess she did talk about you. You know what, Nick? You'd better try to take better care of your wife and child."

He stood up and looked down at me with sad puppy eyes. "That's what I'm doin', Charley."

Through my rearview mirror, I watched him walk back to his police car, no sign of his usual swagger. No question, Pepper had something to worry about, all right.

———

It was only after Nick peeled away in the cruiser that I realized I had missed an opportunity. I was still distracted by that when I picked up Lilith. Of course, her enthusiasm could always bring me back to the moment. And if that didn't do the trick, then her teal blue hair sure would.

I knew she'd already picked up the bins from my off-site storage and delivered them to Wendy's place using Rose's car. I had to give some serious thought to investing in a more practical vehicle. Of course, I love my Miata. It's paid for and we've been through a lot together. So rent-by-the-day vans and Lilith's services would have to do for the time being.

"This will be awesome," she said, hopping into the Miata. "And in case there's not enough food at Wendy's place, Rose sent along some of her Toll House cookies."

"No danger of there not being enough food," I said, sniffing the air. "But I don't think the cookies will last long anyway."

"Rose thought Wendy might need a break from baking if she's working on her closet."

The drive to Wendy's was long enough that I got caught up on what was happening to Lilith at college and her three jobs, and how Rose was doing.

"I'm sorry about my outburst over Anabel. I know you knew her and liked her. I was bothered by that thing with Dimitri, but I realize it wasn't fair to her memory."

"Don't worry about it," I said. "Up until that point, Anabel had seemed way too good to be true."

That reminded me I had intended to follow up on Lilith's friend Jewel and Dimitri.

"Thanks. By the way, Rose wants you to come by and bring the pups," Lilith said. "Schopie misses having smaller dogs to boss him around."

Schopenhauer, like half the dogs I knew in Woodbridge, had been rescued by Jack, who has a rare talent for that. Schopie had a history with Truffle and Sweet Marie, and I had narrowly escaped being his owner myself, even if he was roughly the size of my kitchen.

"And Charlotte?"

"Yup?"

"Thanks for the vote of confidence on the big closet job, if we get it."

"You're more than equal to it. But it won't be as much fun as this one is even if it will be a lot more money."

"Money's not everything, Charlotte. I know that more than most people."

"You're a great friend, Lilith. By the way, I've been meaning to ask, did you keep in touch with Jewel? It sounded like she might have needed a shoulder to cry on."

She shrugged. "I tried, but I think she wanted to put the whole thing behind her. She headed out to California, I think. Too bad, because now Dimitri's . . ."

I could tell Lilith hadn't meant to suggest that with Anabel gone, Dimitri might have turned back to Jewel. And she didn't want me to think about the implication.

—◆◆—

Wendy answered the door with a mile-wide smile. "You won't believe it! I did all my homework. I practiced the questions. I am ready to purge. Ooh, Toll House cookies? Let me guess. Rose sent them. Nobody makes them like her."

She reached out and gave Lilith a big motherly hug. Lilith managed to look surprised and pleased in equal measure. I got a smaller, shyer hug. I was pleased, too. Motherly hugs are not part of my unique heritage.

"Great. I have the contract and some ideas to explore."

"Coffee's ready and I'll put out the cookies!" Wendy said.

"Please do. I've been inhaling the aroma all the way over and they've made me a bit crazy."

At the table, I pulled out the contract, and Wendy signed it without even looking. Lilith's eyes widened. Luckily, I'd never take advantage of her trusting nature.

I said, "First thing we're going to do is take every single item out of the closet."

Wendy nodded. "Lilith hinted at that when she dropped the bins off."

"Great. Now Lilith will give you a hand to sort your clothing. You'll have to work fast so there's not a pile on your bed when it's time to go to sleep. You'll have a bin for the stuff that you want to toss: stained, unfixable, worn out, or faded. WAG'D, the dog rescue group, can use nice used cotton material for bedding for doggies in shelters. If something needs to be mended or cleaned, we'll find a spot to put it aside.

Lilith picked up there. "Then we'll get a bin going for donations. I can drop it off at the youth shelter tonight. They'll be glad to get whatever we bring, and they'll give you a tax receipt, too."

"Wow. You're sure not wasting time."

We grinned in unison, and I said, "You got it. The more time you give yourself, the less likely you'll succeed in clearing things up and meeting your goal."

"I see you two run a tight ship."

"We'll see if there's anything that we can sell. We have a bin for that, too."

Wendy laughed out loud. "That's funny. Can't see anyone wanting to buy any of my worn-out rags."

Lilith said, "You might be surprised."

I said, "You should be left with things that you love, that you wear, and that suit you and your life. Once we know what they are, we can talk about how to store them."

"Good thing I gobbled those cookies."

"Right," I said, "you're going to burn them off."

The door squeaked as it opened behind us, and a young man ducked to get in. I couldn't imagine what it would be like to be taller than the door frame, but, if the giant athletic shoes were anything to go by, that was the norm in the Dykstra home, Wendy excluded, of course.

"Toll House cookies, Seth?" his mother asked.

But Seth was staring at Lilith, his mouth open.

"Seth? Don't be rude, honey. We have guests. This is Charlotte Adams and her assistant, Lilith Carisse. Lilith lives with my friend, Rose Skipowski."

Without saying a word, Seth disappeared from the room, his face and neck bright red, his size-fifteen feet tripping over each other.

"Well, I don't know what got into him today," Wendy said. "He's usually so polite."

Lilith gazed at the cookie in her hand without comment, but I noticed a patch of red glowing on each of her cheeks. I never thought I'd see Lilith blush. The tips of her ears were red, too. Didn't go all that well with the teal blue hair, but Lilith has never been one to be conventional about colors.

We listened to a stumbling up the stairs and at least two muffled "ows." An upstairs door slammed.

Five minutes later, Lilith, Wendy, and I gathered in Wendy's bedroom and stood staring at the closet.

"Although my husband and I sleep here, this isn't the original master bedroom," she said. "Seth has that because he keeps his desk and his musical instruments there. So we're kind of wedged into the second bedroom with the queen-size bed and all. I'm not sure there's room for all three of us at the same time to sort through it." She chuckled. "But from the bed we have a great view of the closet, and now, thanks to your tips, Charlotte, I know what I want it to be like."

"What?" Lilith beat me to the punch.

"I want to be able to see everything at a glance and I want to be able to find things right away and I want to feel good when I look at it. So it has to look neat and orderly."

"That's one of our specialties, ma'am," Lilith said.

Once I took the "before" shot, it didn't take long to empty the closet. Soon the bed was piled high, and Wendy was breathless and laughing. There was a slightly hysterical edge to her laughter.

I said, "Remember the key questions?"

She rhymed them off and added, "Does it make me feel fat? Old? Dumpy?"

I waited long enough to see how it would go. Wendy went to reach into the middle of the pile. I said, "It's best not to cherry-pick. It adds to the time. Take the first item and make a decision. Then the second and so on. It's good to have a buddy to bounce your reactions off. Your buddy, Lilith, will help you keep on track."

The first item was a stained T-shirt from a PTA fundraiser in 1999. Lilith held it up.

Wendy hesitated.

Lilith rolled her eyes. "I hope you're kidding. Animal rescue!"

Wendy gave a squeal as it went into the bin for WAG'D. The second item was a pair of sprung leggings. They joined the T-shirt. I leaned back and watched Wendy and Lilith whip through a dozen items. Only one was a keeper: a crisp white shirt, never worn.

"Does it fit?" That's always my first question.

"It does."

"And you like it?"

She nodded.

"That's good, because almost everyone's wardrobe needs at least one."

"It's new because I don't have anything to wear it with," Wendy said.

"When we're done, we'll see what else turns up that might look smashing with it. Charlotte will give you some advice there," Lilith told her. "You'll be surprised."

The shirt went into the *Keep* pile.

"This is kind of fun," Wendy said.

I agreed. I figured it was way more fun than I was going to have dealing with Lorelei's perfect wardrobe in her perfect and perfectly depressing house and the even more perfectly disturbing belief that her daughter had been murdered.

9

I toodled home after Wendy's, still feeling good because that project was going well and in part because I'd had all those cookies. I knew Wendy and Lilith would accomplish a lot in the short time they had. I walked the dogs, chastised them for barking at a small child, and sent them back to the sofa to resume their nap while I changed to go to Lorelei's for one.

On the way there, I found myself once again driving slowly. I was ahead of schedule and, whatever else, I didn't want to be early for the Beauchamps. I drifted past Stewart's, hoping to see Nick scoring a coffee. No luck. I cruised around to Tang's. But there was no sign of Nick attempting to con Margaret's mother out of free chips, another regular pastime.

I had one more spot to try: Hank's, the greasy spoon that Nick had been hanging out in since he was a teenager. Sure enough, there was the Woodbridge Police Services black-and-white parked outside.

I peered in and spotted him, alone at a table, staring

morosely at a hamburger and a pile of fries. This would be my chance to push back a bit and find out what he knew about Anabel's death. I tapped on the dingy front window. I thought Nick's beautiful head would hit the ceiling and dislodge the flaking paint. I saw panic fill his eyes. He did his best to cover it up, but he was still pale under his rugged-guy tan when I approached his table. "Ow, Charley, what are you doing?"

I tried not to inhale the smell of ancient grease that has always been the signature scent of Hank's. Even if Wendy hadn't stuffed us full of snacks, nothing would induce me to eat anything I could hear sizzling on the grungy grill.

I said, "Turnabout is fair play."

"Ha-ha." Nick tried a sort of smile.

I could tell that whatever else was going, Nick didn't want me to know that he'd had a scare. Wouldn't want that to slip out during casual girl talk with Pepper.

"I'll try to help you with whatever you are worried about, Nick. But I also need a favor."

"Worried? I'm not worried about anything, Charley."

"Tell it to someone who believes you."

"There's nothing you could do to help me, and you shouldn't be involved in this. I'll work it out without involving anyone I care about."

"Okay. If you change your mind and need to talk about whatever 'this' is, you know where to find me. In the meantime, I need to know why you thought there might have been something funny about Anabel Beauchamp's death."

"I don't know what you are talking about." Of course, the fact Nick turned white put the lie to his words.

"Well, to refresh your memory, you mentioned there might have been something 'funny' about that death. I assume you meant disturbing or unusual and not humorous."

He shivered. "Come on, Charley. That was terrible. There wasn't anything funny about it."

"But there must have been something that felt wrong."

"Hey, they bumped me down from detective because they said I get stuff wrong. Maybe this was one of those things. Anyway, it was an accident."

"Why don't you tell me about it, Nick? Explain what seemed odd. Maybe you didn't get it wrong. I could—"

Nick banged the table, causing the dishes to clatter. "Do you have a death wish?"

My jaw dropped. I managed to shake my head no anyway.

"Me neither. And that means you have to stay away from me."

"You mean that I might be in danger by chatting with you?"

"Well, duh."

"But you just—"

"You keep pushing me, Charley. I have to warn you."

"Warn me about what exactly?"

"Girl talk wouldn't be enough to save you, Charley. You gotta believe me. This is serious."

"But—"

"Leave it alone, Charley. It's none of your business. And don't be around me. It's bad enough I have to worry about Pepper and Little Nick." He turned his handsome head and went back to staring at his hamburger and the pile of fries rapidly cooling on the plate next to his coffee.

As I headed back to the Miata, I turned back to Nick again. The waitress scowled at me through the window.

—※—

On the road out to the Beauchamps', I thought about Nick and his reaction. Pepper was right. He was definitely jumpy. And he was very worried about Pepper, too. What kind of problem could he have that would have him afraid for her? And what about her reaction? She knew his weaknesses. He wasn't very bright. He was lazy and shallow and vain. He was useless around the house and unlikely to rise in the police. He couldn't resist women or trucks. But she'd known his flaws before she married him. Whatever she was worried about was much more serious. To the best of my knowledge, Nick didn't gamble. Didn't have the concentration, I'd once joked. He didn't do drugs. Wouldn't want to mess up his body or end up with bad hair. If it was a woman, Pepper would have gone after her and made her wish she'd never been born.

Maybe I was wrong about those things. *Did* Nick have a gambling problem? Was he being threatened by someone he owed money to? Could he have been stupid enough to get into drugs at this age? He wouldn't have been the first person I'd known who'd done that. Or, despite Pepper's protests, was it a woman? Someone with a blackmailing streak or a murderous husband?

Of course, he'd said it was none of my business. But whatever was wrong in Nick's life was very serious, and if he'd put Pepper and the baby in the middle of it, this truly was my business. Especially since after all these years, she'd come to me for help. I wondered if I should talk to Tierney about it. Too bad I didn't have even a scrap of useful information to share with him or with Pepper as a result of this talk. I didn't think I'd get far on my gut feelings.

———

This time Lorelei was not only out of bed but also dressed and in full makeup. I was glad I'd taken the time to change from my closet-busting clothes into a pin-striped cotton jacket and trim gray pants and my teal blue heels. I hoped the jacket would give me a bit of authority with Lorelei, something so far sadly lacking.

"Harry's been hovering," she said with a blasé laugh. "His hand's been over the Veuve Clicquot since noon."

From far away, Harry said, "That's not at all true, Charlotte honey. But it does remind me that today's cocktail is a green dragon. Midori and bubbly."

How could these people get through the day if they were tossing back cocktails from noon on?

"I think Lorelei's ready."

"I am," she said.

I glanced at her and wondered if she'd taken some kind of mood-altering substance to get herself going on this day. If so, could a double slug of booze be anything but trouble in conjunction with it? On the other hand, Harry was crazy about Lorelei. He wouldn't risk doing anything that would harm her.

"Charlotte honey?"

"No, thanks." I was getting prissier by the minute. Was that what it meant to be over thirty? The next thing you knew, I'd be eating regular meals and exercising. Game over.

"All right then, but y'all let me know if you change your mind in a little bit."

"Sure thing."

Lorelei smiled slowly at me, the way you smile at the camera when your heart's not in it.

"Are you looking forward to our project?" I asked as Harry arrived with the drinks.

She lifted one shoulder in an elegant gesture of unconcern. "As much as I am looking forward to anything."

"Well, I hope it might be a bit of fun. Did you give any thought to the charity for donations?"

She glanced at her husband. "What was it again, Harry?"

"We do support Hope for Youth at Risk, because Anabel was so committed to it. But I don't know if they have a clothing resale shop. Do they, Charlotte?"

"I don't believe so. But there are lots of wonderful charities that do."

Lorelei interrupted. "If there *is* anything to donate. I'm not sure. All my things are in beautiful condition, so maybe not."

Harry gave her a startled glance. After all, she had seven closets crammed with high-end stuff. How could she begrudge a few cast-offs to the charity her own daughter had devoted her life to? Or any other charity for that matter. I reminded myself that Lorelei had been through a lot and perhaps that was why she was hanging on to what she could.

I whipped out the paperwork with a flourish. "I brought the contract with me. This might be a good time to have a look at it. You'll see the terms set out there. Because this is an unusual job with so many closets, I'll be charging by the hour, with a minimum number, in order to reserve enough time for you. My rates are on the last page. Take a look and see if it suits you. You should know what you're getting into and feel no pressure, Lorelei."

I've learned the hard way not to do anything past the initial consult without a contract. The consult is free if a contract comes out of it. Otherwise, it's a one-hour job at my top fee. At this rate, I figured I would be spending untold hours at the Beauchamps' and losing other clients as a result.

Lorelei shooed the contract away with a languid wave of her wrist. "Harry handles paperwork for me."

I found myself checking Harry's expression yet again. I wondered if he got tired of being the person who did everything. Or did it help him to keep busy? After all, he'd lost his daughter, too. Lorelei wasn't the only one with a heart full of grief. From what I'd observed, Harry had been the parent who was always there for Anabel.

But Harry kept any emotion off his face as he checked out the terms of my standard contract.

Conversation stopped and I sat, waiting in a room that seemed to be full of ghosts.

A minute later, Harry raised his head and said, "This is fair and comprehensive, Charlotte. I'll sign it right now. I see you've already signed both copies yourself."

I smiled at Harry. "Can you sign both copies, too, please?"

Lorelei was busy staring out the window at nothing. If her demeanor was any indication, it was going to be a long day. My cell phone vibrated in my pocket. I don't answer it when I am with clients, but I have to admit that I sure felt the urge. Instead, I turned to Harry and grasped for a conversational loophole. "I assume you have a closet, too?"

"Thank you for asking, Charlotte honey. I sure do."

"Let me know if you want me to have a look at it. I'd be glad to."

"You're welcome to check it out, but you won't find much of interest. Just the basics, hanging up, waiting for something to happen to get them out."

"Why don't we do that? And give Lorelei a moment with her thoughts."

I don't know if she even noticed us leave the room and walk up the long sculptural glass and metal staircase to the second floor. My cell phone vibrated again and again. Harry had his own room. The next one down from Lorelei's, but not connected by a door inside either room. Harry's room had an old southern elegance about it. Heavy, dark mahogany bedroom furniture that looked as though it might have been in the Beauchamp family for generations. A four-poster bed, a campaign desk. A gentleman's highboy wardrobe. All polished to a fine patina and neat as a pin. On the campaign desk was a fairly recent picture of Harry and Anabel laughing and eating cotton candy at what looked like the Woodbridge Fair. Anabel had a large pink blob on her nose, and Harry seemed to find that funny. Anabel was forever captured in that happy moment.

Harry turned out to be absolutely correct about his storage. His closet was spare and orderly. He had the minimum of elegant menswear wear, hung neatly. The space between each hanger was the width of two fingers. A dozen crisp white shirts, five suits, a handful of sport jackets and pants. A place for everything and everything in its place. Even down to the polished shoes on the shoe trees. I approved. You don't see much of that anymore.

Of course, seeing Harry's closet was all a ploy, and the ploy was entirely mine. I had to admit it wasn't unduly subtle, either. I wanted to talk to Harry out of Lorelei's hearing.

"Harry, I'd never make a living if everyone was like you. This is like a work of art. But you probably figured out, I'm not here about your closet."

"As you can tell by looking at me, I wasn't born yesterday, Charlotte honey."

"The thing is, I'm a bit worried about Lorelei. She doesn't seem to be . . . entirely in the moment."

"In the moment? No, Charlotte honey, Lorelei is never in the moment, as you call it."

"Never?"

"Not in the thirty-two years we've been together, thirty of 'em married, too. Did you know that?"

"I did and it's a pretty darn good run in this age."

"And in the business that Lorelei's in, it's very unusual."

"But I have known Lorelei for a long time, too, and this seems . . ." I hesitated. "More extreme than usual. She clearly doesn't care at all about it. I don't think she's the least bit interested. If you want me to visit and talk to her, I'll be happy to do that as a family friend. I'd prefer it to this pretext. We don't need a business arrangement. Do you think there's any point in doing the closet project? We can tear up that contract if you want. I have plenty of people waiting for my time, so you wouldn't need to worry about that side of things. I could drop in some evenings to chat."

"I know you've got a good head for business, Charlotte honey. And I know you're kind and care about Lorelei. That's why I want to stick to our agreement. It's fair to you, and I'm hoping it will be good for her, too. Get her mind off things, you know what I mean. She loves clothes. She loves pocketbooks. She loves footwear. Those things make her smile. So maybe that will provide a break from sitting and brooding. I can't ask for anything more of you. If the closets get rearranged, that will be a bonus. You have probably already figured out that Lorelei is more likely to value something you pay for. That's the other reason it's a good idea."

My cell phone vibrated again in my pocket. I continued to ignore it and was regretting not turning it off.

It was hard to know what to think about Harry's idea. On the one hand, I felt aware of the pain Lorelei and Harry must have been feeling. On the other, I'm an organizer, not a physician or a psychologist. I had a feeling that Lorelei needed one or both of those professions desperately. It would be a long time before she could turn her mind to her closets or anything else. If there was a third hand, it would be that I don't want to take advantage of vulnerable clients. And I sure didn't choose to spend my time keeping people's minds occupied so they don't seek the help they need.

Okay. End of soapbox.

Harry said, "Excuse me, Charlotte honey, I think we should hurry back and see if she's all right."

The phone vibrated yet again.

Who the hell was in such a hurry to speak to me?

I said, "Do you want to go ahead? I'd like to use the powder room."

Harry hurried ahead of me, after apologizing and pointing to a door to the left off the corridor. Inside the lovely pale marble room, I checked the pesky cell phone.

Pepper.

Three voice messages.

And three texts.

That was even more than the number of vibrations had seemed to indicate. I checked all. The essence of both texts and phone messages was, *Have you seen Nick? He's on duty, but he's not responding to calls.*

Typical Nick. So why the panic?

I sat on the lush upholstered bench and rubbed my temple. Oh well, not much choice but to respond with a text that summarized the news that I had indeed seen Nick at Hank's and he had seemed morose but otherwise fine. I flushed the fine imported European toilet and ran the water quickly. I stepped out into the upstairs corridor and glanced both ways. I seemed to be alone, and something had been bothering me since I'd been in Harry's room. I stepped into Lorelei's palatial bedroom to verify. Sure enough. Unlike Harry, Lorelei did not have a single photo of her late daughter, Anabel. Now what was that about? Was Lorelei unable to bear seeing an image of her daughter? Had she packed away the photos?

I shivered in the warm June air, straightened my back, and headed downstairs.

Lorelei was still stretched out languidly on the pearl gray leather chaise staring at the view. She didn't turn around as I arrived and cleared my throat. Harry must have stepped back into the kitchen. Not for more drinks, I hoped.

"Such a beautiful house," I said. "I am looking forward to the tour of the closets."

Harry hustled out of the kitchen holding a fresh champagne cocktail for Lorelei. I figured I'd be kissing the closets good-bye again that afternoon.

"I'm sorry, Charlotte. I don't think that Lorelei will be up to anything today."

I barely managed not to say, "because she's had a snootful."

He said, "It goes without saying that we will pay you for your time this afternoon, including travel."

I said, "I hope that Lorelei will feel well enough to try tomorrow."

Harry said wistfully, "We take it day by day."

"I'm sure. Do you mind if I take a look at these closets?" I almost said "alleged closets." I added, "It will make it easier for me to get an idea of what we want to accomplish."

If indeed we wanted to accomplish anything.

Lorelei turned her head and adjusted her facial expression, an infinitesimal frown, but enough to convey that did not suit her in the least.

"Of course, it can always wait." Although, I myself could hardly wait to get away from this strange house with its tragic undercurrents and the beautiful damaged woman at the cold heart of it.

Harry walked me to the door. In the amazing domed entrance, he opened a mirrored door and pointed to the contents of the front entrance closet. It was an unremarkable collection of jackets and coats, capes, shawls and wraps, with boots and walking shoes neatly arrayed. Lorelei's side was jammed. Harry's was perfect.

"Harry, I need to say this: There's no point in my coming if Lorelei is going to have a couple of cocktails and put the brakes on every time. And there's less point in me coming when she can't get out of bed."

"Charlotte honey, I told you we'd pay you anyway."

"It's not about money, Harry. I'm not helping her in the least. And I'd like to. So how about you let me know when I can catch her awake and not yet anesthetized and we can see if I can do something useful. Otherwise, it's not going to work out."

It was hard for me to meet Harry's eyes. And for the first time since I'd visited them, I noticed how much he'd aged in the past year or so. He moved more slowly, favoring his left leg. His handsome face was losing the crisp edges, and even his usual good spirits seemed forced. I supposed in the troubling atmosphere of their home, this was the last thing I'd notice. Lorelei seemed almost to be made of glass like the house, in danger of shattering at a wrong word or look. She needed to heal, not that she would ever get over Anabel's death.

"All right," he said. "I'll try. How about eleven o'clock tomorrow? If she won't take you, I will. After that, we'll have to play it by ear."

"I'll be here. We'll hope for the best. By the way, I was wondering, did you and Lorelei stay in touch with Anabel's friend from Hope for Youth at Risk?"

"You mean Gwen? Now, I feel real guilty about that. They were congenial colleagues rather than friends. We should have stayed in touch with Gwen. She was so good to Anabel. Anabel always respected her. I'll see if Lorelei is up to having her over for brunch next week. And if not"— he glanced toward the other end of the house—"then I can take her to lunch. I'm sure they have some project we can help out with in some small way."

"No, I meant Dimitri."

Harry's expression landed somewhere between surprise and shock, a look that's hard to fake. "Dimitri? You mean that haunted-looking boy in the leather jacket? I don't think he was a special friend."

"No? I must be mistaken. I thought there might have been something between them. I had heard he had a bad case on Anabel."

"Well, if he did, she didn't tell us."

"Would you have minded?"

"I wanted my little girl to be happy. If she cared about him, I would have bent over backward. And Lorelei would have been tickled pink."

"She would have?"

"Sure. She's a romantic. She wanted her little girl to be beautiful and popular, too. She wanted the big white wedding for Anabel. The whole three-ring circus. Anabel didn't care much about boyfriends or clothes or makeup or fairy-tale weddings. She could never hope to meet her mother's expectations, so she declined to try."

I wasn't ready to let this topic go. "I understand that Dimitri was on the streets for a while and he's managed to build a life for himself. That's admirable, don't you think?"

Harry said, "I do. Everyone deserves a second chance, and sometimes even a third."

He gave me a fatherly hug, insofar as I understand such things, and I escaped the gorgeous glass prison and made tracks for the Miata.

I wondered if, in truth, the Beauchamps would have been happy to learn that Anabel had a relationship with Dimitri.

10

I called Pepper before I turned the key in the ignition.

"Why did you talk to him?" she shrieked. "What the hell are you doing behind my back?"

Sometimes Pepper can push me too far. "Pull yourself together. You came to me, remember? You cried on my shoulder, and then your husband pulled me over this morning and scared the wits out of me."

"What?"

"Do you know why?"

"Make it good."

"It is good. Because he followed you to my house last night. He was worried. He wanted to know what you said to me."

"And what did you tell him?"

"Girl talk."

"Did he buy it?"

"Eventually. He's worried and upset about something."

"Did he give any idea what?"

"None."

"What time was this?"

"Before ten. I was on my way to see my first client."

"And that's the last time you saw him?"

"No. On my way to the second client, I happened to be driving by Hank's and I spotted him in the window."

I didn't mention that I had checked out all Nick's usual haunts.

"Why didn't you call me?"

"I suppose because I didn't have anything new to say. He seemed agitated and worried. He was barely coherent."

"All right. That was what, an hour and a half ago?"

"Less. And it didn't look like he was going anywhere fast. Maybe you should drive by Hank's and get some fries. Bring antacids. I guess it's one of the familiar old places that he would head for when he's upset and worried. I suppose there are more—"

Pepper cut in, "You're right. It *is* one of the special places. We used to go there when we were dating over my father's objections." To my surprise, she chuckled. "And Charlotte?"

I held my breath. Pepper so often takes my head off at the shoulders.

"Thanks. I know you're my friend."

I dug into my supply of courage and managed to say, "Any time you need me. If he's scared about something real and serious, maybe we should try to figure—"

But she'd already clicked off. I suspected that she was also thinking about drugs, gambling, murderously jealous husbands, and other dangers due to Nick's never-ending bad judgment. I was about to start the drive home when I realized that I still had to collect Lilith at Wendy's. I guess I was more rattled than I was letting on. The wonderfully normal family atmosphere at the Dykstras' drew me and my Miata like a tractor beam.

—••—

Wendy's hair was damp and her T-shirt rumpled. She looked hot and sweaty and I hoped happy. I knew the sorting stage can lead to the most bizarre emotions. Happiness isn't always the main byproduct.

She smiled tiredly. "Boy, do we need you."

"Good thing you're here," Lilith called down the stairs. "We're about to go to war over a bridesmaid dress if you can believe that."

"Cookies?" Wendy said. She was obviously seeking allies in the war, like the man standing behind her. He was shorter than his boys, but still quite tall, with a buzz cut that made him look tough and a shy grin that made him look like a teddy bear. He had to be Wendy's husband, Brad. His shy grin appeared again. "Let me out of here while it's still safe."

Lilith arrived downstairs two at a time and said breathlessly, "You are going to freak when you see what we've done."

"Great. Done is good."

"We are smoking hot! With the exception of the bridesmaid dress from yellow hell."

"Matron of honor," Wendy said. "And that thing cost two hundred bucks. It stays."

"It can stay, but I'm leaving." Wendy's husband headed quickly for the door. "Where's Seth?"

"Run away, see if I care," his wife said. "And Seth hasn't come out of his room all afternoon. I think we scare him."

I said, "Bridesmaid dresses are always good for a lot of high emotion on both sides of the keep-it/get-rid-of-it fence."

"Matron of honor," Wendy said again. "A whole 'nother thang."

"I can't wait to see the source of the discord." My money was on that dress being gone before the day was out. I tried to appear neutral, though.

We gulped a couple of cookies and glasses of milk. Wendy and Lilith both felt they needed their strength. When we headed back upstairs, Lilith said, "Close your eyes when you get there."

What the hey? This was so much easier than the Beauchamps'. I shut my eyes and didn't open them until Lilith and Wendy squealed.

I couldn't believe those eyes when I did look. The bed that had been piled high with clothing when I left was nearly empty.

"We're coming down the homestretch," Lilith added. "A few contentious items and the shoes, of course."

The shoes had been stacked in a corner for separate consideration.

She kept talking. "I offer you Exhibit A. May I add that A stands for 'awful.' "

Wendy sputtered. "Awful? I told you I spent—"

"Whatever it was, you were robbed. For one thing, the color wouldn't suit you at all."

Yikes. I wasn't so sure I wanted Lilith with her piercings and teal blue hair and distinctly Goth vibe to be giving fashion advice to plump middle-aged motherly types.

"As Charlotte would say, trust me," Lilith said.

"I can't throw away all that money. It wasn't even that long ago. My best friend's third wedding."

"You wouldn't be getting rid of the friend," Lilith said. "Just the dress. Your husband will thank you."

Wendy threw back her head and howled with laughter. "He's glad to escape, if you ask me. You two terrify him. He'd back me up, but I'm not sure he has the guts."

"What does he do?" Lilith said.

"He's a paramedic. I think he wishes he was on duty today!"

"Well, he'd need those skills if you went anywhere public in this."

Luckily they were having fun. All it took was one look at the yellow horror with the ruffles to know that I'd be siding with Lilith on this issue, if I ever got a word in. But it was time to assert a bit of authority.

"You are way ahead of schedule. Why not grab the shoes and purse and everything that goes with it, Wendy, and try it on? See if you still love it in the cold light of day."

She raised her dusty chin. "I will love it. Two hundred bucks and worn once. Dry cleaned, too."

Five minutes later, she showed up. Lilith flopped on the bed and said, "I can't bear to look."

I bit my lip.

"What?" Wendy pretended to pout.

"Try the mirror," Lilith said.

Wendy slowly turned and stared at herself in the mirror.

Lilith didn't hold back. "It's like the reverse of the dream come true. You are like a giant grapefruit on steroids. A dancing—"

I don't know who collapsed laughing first, but soon the three of us were in a heap.

"Oh well," Wendy said when she caught her breath. "Now that I see myself, I can't believe that so-called friend talked me into buying this monstrosity. And I wore it in public!"

"Brides," Lilith intoned as if she had firsthand knowledge. "They like to be the center of attention. No bridesmaid is ever supposed to look good. That's their subtext. Don't let yourself be fooled again."

"Matron of honor!"

"Goes double," Lilith muttered.

Wendy sighed. "No wonder Brad wouldn't comment. I could try to sell it, but who in their right mind would buy it?"

I said, "Don't worry about that. If you're lucky you'll get

twenty percent of the original value, but every forty dollars counts. The shoes and evening bag are keepers. Nice and neutral classics. You'll get to use them for years."

Shortly after, Wendy was back in her closet-cleaning gear and the monstrosity was lying in its protective zippered bag on the *Sell* pile.

"How does that feel?" I said.

"I'm surprised, but it feels good to send it packing. I didn't like it, of course, but all that money and the sentimental value. But of course, you've explained the politics of all that."

"When something's hard to get rid of, maybe it's an investment or sentimental object or it's you wanting to be a different size or a different age or in a different life, but the minute you decide to turf it, you can feel the weight lift off your shoulders."

"Yeah and I want the forty bucks, too. We're not through here yet."

The remaining items at issue—pants that were too tight, a gift sweater that was the wrong color, and a yoga top that clung like freezer wrap—all hit the *Sell* pile in a flash.

"And we're done with Phase 1," I said. "We can see the bed. I'll leave you two to sort the shoes, and I'll see you tomorrow to plan how we'll store your remaining clothing. Have a look at the pictures I left behind. Decide if you like things open and visible or closed off and neat. We're nearly finished."

Wendy gave me a big hug.

I said, "Lilith will cart away the toss and donate stuff. And if you want, I'll take the *Sell* pile to the consignment shop tomorrow. That will save you from having a midnight change of heart."

"I'll come tomorrow, too," Lilith said.

I glanced at her sharply. The hundred dollars wouldn't

last much longer, even with me charging for portions of an hour and subtracting any minutes that I was eating, drinking, chatting, or laughing.

"No charge," Lilith added quickly. "I'll do it as a friend. Anyway, I haven't seen too much of Charlotte in action and I'd like to watch how she measures and helps you decide about storage."

Wendy gave her a mom-size hug. "I'd love it if you came over. We're great buddies."

Right, I thought. And Seth didn't have a thing to do with it.

Speaking of buddies, my cell phone vibrated angrily for the third time during that short conversation. I decided to take it.

Pepper.

What the hell was wrong now?

—◆◆—

Whatever was troubling Pepper, she didn't respond. I sat in the Miata and thought about what to do next. Ever since Wendy had mentioned that her husband was a paramedic, I'd been wondering about what the emergency personnel might have observed on the scene when Anabel's body was found. I knew the police believed it was an accident, but, face facts, the best detective in Woodbridge was definitely Pepper and she was on leave with her baby at the time and pretty much obsessed with that baby. Her partner, Frank D'Angelo, was seconded to yet another task force, as well as being a distracted newlywed. They weren't exactly plugged into the pulse.

Tierney seemed sharp enough, but he was new to Woodbridge. And he wouldn't tell me even if he did think there was anything suspicious about Anabel's death. We didn't seem to have a trusting relationship. It couldn't hurt to have a chat with the paramedics, but I knew that Tierney would never tell me their names. Nick would know who the emergency workers had been. He'd been there early on. With Nick that couldn't be a good thing. No doubt he'd blundered all over the walkway, trampling evidence. It wouldn't have been the first time. Wendy's husband, Brad, might have known their names. I should have asked him when I'd had the chance. Maybe the next time I was there. I left another message for Pepper and headed home to catch up on my calls and clients, check e-mail and phone messages. Halfway there I made a U-turn and headed for Old Pine Street. I pulled up in front of Pepper and Nick's place. I peered into the garage window. Only Nick would have a window so he could admire his vehicles while mowing the lawn. Of course, the garage had the kind of security that the governor's mansion gets. Nick's Mustang and truck were still parked inside. I hoped I didn't set off any alarms by peeking in. Pepper's new Ford Edge was gone. No one answered the front door. Where were Pepper and Little Nick? Pepper was so overprotective. She'd never leave the baby with any mere mortal babysitter. Was she scouring town in her agitated state of mind looking for Nick?

I decided that my office duties could wait. It had been that kind of day. The advantage of keeping on top of my schedule as a general rule is flexibility when I need it. My friends usually roll their eyes if I mention that. Of course, with all the complications provided by the Beauchamps, Pepper, and Nick, I'd be seriously behind in no time. There are limits to flexibility.

Pepper was not at the Woodbridge Police Station, although I suppose it was a ridiculous idea to think she might have gone looking for Nick there. As all the squad cars look alike, I couldn't tell if Nick was there, either, though it must have been near the end of his shift. I straightened my blouse and checked my makeup in the rearview. I walked into the station with my head held high.

I asked the desk sergeant if I could speak with Officer Nick Monahan.

"Sure can."

"Thank you," I said with my warmest smile, secure in the knowledge that there was no lipstick on my teeth.

"Course you'll have to find him first."

"Everybody's a comedian," said a voice behind me. I turned to find Connor Tierney grinning.

"As long as they don't give up their day jobs first, I guess that's all right."

"Nicely put," he said. "Why do you want to talk to Nick?"

"Just saying hello."

"Try and remember that I'm the bad policeman with the good instincts and you're the lady who gets arrested. How many times is it now?"

"Never for asking if I could talk to someone, though. I see that the law-and-order approach is gaining ground in our town."

"Nick doesn't seem to be reachable."

"Crap," I said.

"Do you know anything about that?"

"No. Yes. Maybe I do. But not much. I wanted to discuss something with him, but I'll try again when he's not on patrol."

"How do you know he's out on patrol?"

I found myself biting my lip yet again. "I don't. But I did see him a couple of times this morning. I'm sure he's out patrolling diligently. Maybe he had a flat tire or something."

"Could be, and maybe that flat tire happened at the same time as he stopped responding to his radio."

The desk sergeant was grinning along with Tierney.

"I guess it's funny," I said. "I was a bit worried, but if you guys are practicing your stand-up comic routines, I'll head home to mind my own business."

Tierney caught up with me. "Don't take this the wrong way, but it's not like you to mind your own business."

"People change. I'm going home. I have a lot of work to do tonight."

"Work to do?"

"Yes. I—"

I couldn't believe it. Of course. Dinner! I had it written on my list, but the problem with Nick and Pepper and my lack of sleep and my worry about Lorelei had all driven it out of my mind. I was losing it. And that is so not like me.

"Until dinner, of course," I said. "And allowing time to get ready before."

"I thought maybe you might have forgotten."

"Ha. Are you kidding?"

"Do I look like I'm kidding?"

"You look like you're annoyed."

"I'll see you tonight. I need you to promise me that there will be no meddling."

I was still having a bit of trouble making eye contact. I let my eyes stray behind him to a poster of police, fire-fighters, and paramedics. It was attractive and soothing. Made you feel safe looking at it. It didn't seem like the right time to ask Tierney if he knew the names of the paramedics who were first on the scene when Anabel Beauchamp died.

—••—

Pepper still wasn't answering. I sure hoped she didn't end up home with a cranky baby and an infantile husband on suspension. She was already on the edge. I thought if we misfits had to help out, there'd be a fight to see which of us got the baby, as a couple of hours consoling Pepper and Nick would seem a lot longer.

I glanced over my shoulder on the off chance that Tierney was behind me. On this crazy day when the police seemed to have nothing at all on their To Do lists, anything was possible. The coast was clear, so I veered off and retraced the route I had taken that morning when looking for Nick. He was a creature of habit. I tried the doughnut shops, the drive-thru coffee shops, the movie theaters, although that seemed unlikely. I even returned to Hank's. No Nick. No Pepper.

I glanced at my watch and reminded myself that an organized person has learned to deal with shifting priorities. I was and I had. So. New first priority: Find Nick. Where else would he hang out?

I even drove by my place, but neither Pepper nor Nick were parked in the driveway. I zipped along and down Long March Road to Jack's shop.

Jack was in the shop looking bemused. With his free hand he was spinning the wheels of two Italian bikes that were suspended from the ceiling.

"Guess what?" he said.

"Let me think. You're holding a baby?"

"Yeah. Of course, you're cheating since you can see him."

"Since I'm on a winning streak, I'll hazard another guess. Pepper left him with you?"

"She did. And the little dude and I have a great time playing with these excellent toys, whenever we get tired of the sock monkey and the ducky."

"Huh."

"Isn't that neat?"

"Sure is, Jack."

Little Nick squeezed his soft plush yellow duck and it squeaked.

Pepper is the ubermom. She wouldn't leave her baby with Jack, even if he is baby crazy, without a damn good reason. I mean it is, after all, a bike shop. Normally Nick wouldn't

count as a good reason for such an out-of-character decision. It would have to be a crisis, such as last night's melt-
down where she told me she was afraid Nick was mixed
up in something dangerous. Had she confronted him again
and learned that the danger was imminent?

Don't give up on favorite items with small problems:
An inexpensive sweater defuzzer can give
new life to pilled sweaters, tops, and pants.

11

Was it my fault for telling her that Nick was out there, upset and worried about some danger?

"Okay, good, Jack," I said. "Carry on."

As I left the bike shop, I asked myself what to do now. I knew that in normal circumstances the right thing was to call the cops. I had learned that the hard way over the last few missteps, shall we say. But Pepper and Nick *were* the cops. Therefore, it wasn't like I was not working with the cops. I could have contacted Tierney, of course. But what would that do for Pepper and Nick? Would it damage Pepper's career when she returned to work if every one of her colleagues knew she'd been weepy and hysterical? My guess was yes.

And of course, it would get Tierney pissed off at me. This had turned into a crappy situation. I wasn't going to be able to relax until I found out what was going on.

I needed to find either Pepper or Nick. Then if there was something to be worried about, I'd have a better sense of what to do. Nick had been hanging around Hank's today, someplace I would have thought he'd outgrown. But then he'd always seemed happy there. Where else had he been happy? A couple of minutes of serious thinking and I thought I might have an answer. Nick had always been happiest making out. That was probably still true. For some reason, I felt compelled to check. Perhaps because the image of Nick's face, so full of fear, kept flashing in my brain.

I squealed away from the curb and headed for the only place I could think of that meant something to Nick. Bakker Beach. I use "beach" in its broadest sense as there is no sand, only rocks, trees, brush, and a bumpy track off the nearby county road. At least there was a view of the Hudson, which was particularly spectacular during a full moon. Bakker Beach was far enough out of town to be a fine and private place for making out. It was a twenty-minute drive from the edge of town. Nick had collected panties from half the graduating girls in St. Jude's, if you could believe his claim. Of course, that had been before Pepper got him in her sights. They'd had their own Bakker Beach moments.

Twenty minutes later, my heart soared as the Miata lurched down the bumpy track and crested the slight hill at the end of the line. Two vehicles were angled on the ragged grassy slope. A squad car was idling, door open, although Nick was nowhere to be seen.

I stopped at the top of the incline to the beach and hopped out of the car. I didn't want to get stuck on the sandy uneven track.

Pepper's new red Ford Edge was parked straight on, doors closed. I paused midstep. What was she doing here? What if I was about to interrupt a romantic moment between a married couple? I stuck my head back into the Miata and gave a short blast with the horn. I waited to give them time to adjust their clothing if necessary and then stomped over toward the car.

I felt like giving the two of them the kind of old-fashioned talking-to that you hear about. I also felt like letting the air out of their tires. Nick was going to be in trouble at work, not that I cared. But overprotective Pepper had left her baby in a bike shop. How crazy was that? As I reached Pepper's car, I could see she was resting her head on the steering wheel. I knew she was tired, but this was ridiculous. You would have thought the blast from my horn would wake her up. I was surprised her own car horn wasn't blaring with her head in that position.

I knocked on her window. She didn't move. I hammered loudly. Nothing. I tried shouting. Still nothing.

"Pepper!" I pulled at the door handle in a panic.

Locked.

I banged on the window again.

I raced to the front of the vehicle, intending to pound on the windshield. I raised my fist and gasped. Pepper's face was squashed against the steering wheel, a jagged gash showed on her forehead. There was far too much blood.

I don't know why I thought screaming "Pepper" would do any good. I tried screaming for Nick, and that failed utterly, too. It crossed my mind that whoever had done this might still be in the vicinity. I whipped my cell phone out of my pocket to call 911.

Great. I must have been in one of the few pockets without cell phone service in the entire county. I moved to the other side of Pepper's vehicle and tugged at that handle. She was bleeding quite a lot. I thought if I could staunch the flow, I could drive us to the hospital, or at least to meet an ambulance.

Of course, it was locked.

Pepper always kept her doors locked. She wasn't the trusting type. But she wouldn't have locked the doors against Nick. That didn't make sense. Unless Nick was the person who'd injured her. I couldn't allow myself to think that Pepper might have been dead. I hunted around for a rock big enough to break the back window without getting Pepper hit by glass. The rocks I tried were pathetically small.

I hated to leave her, but I didn't have any choice. I turned to head up the hill to the Miata when a movement caught my eye, from the brush by the side. Naturally, that movement was between me and my car. Who was it? The person who'd injured Pepper? Nick? A bear?

I didn't wait to find out. I jumped into the idling police car and slammed and locked the door. The key was in the ignition or it wouldn't have been idling. Lucky for me it hadn't been idling long enough to kill the batter. I tried my cell again. Still no signal. I stared at the police radio equipment. How did that work? No time to find out. Out of the corner of my eye I could see a dark shadow approaching. I wasn't the only person in the world who would have grabbed the wheel, slammed that cop car into reverse, and stepped on the gas.

The squad car rocketed backward toward the Miata, and I jerked the wheel in time to miss it. I zigzagged backward up the road, practically standing to touch the pedals. No way was I taking the time to adjust the seat.

As I approached the county road, I slowed until I found a segment wide enough to turn around. With one eye on the back window, I managed the U-turn. I tried again with my cell phone. Still no service.

I shot forward in the car and drove to the highest spot of the hill.

The little bars were back on my phone. Four!

I pressed 911 and gasped for breath.

"Oh hi, Charlotte," the familiar voice said. I'd known Mona Pringle since high school at St. Jude's, although lately all our interactions seemed to be through 911.

Mona said, "Do you have a cold or something?"

"Emergency, Mona. No time for banter. Pepper Monahan has been badly injured. She's at the entrance to Bakker Beach. She's in a locked vehicle, bleeding. Her husband—"

"Nick the Stick?"

"Nick's car is on the site with the door wide open and there's no sign of him."

"Any sign of the perp?"

"No one else that I could see, Mona. I think you should say "officer down" or something to the police, so they realize how—"

"Don't worry. I know how to do my job, Charlotte."

Everyone's a prima donna these days, even the unflappable Mona. I said, "They need to know that Pepper's keys are inside of the locked car and Nick may be hurt, too."

"Got it. Hold on, I'm calling it in."

I tried to hold it together as I shouted, "And Pepper's lost a lot of blood. A whole lot."

"Stay on the line," Mona said.

I sat and got my breathing back to normal after stating my case. Had I told her everything? Had I made sure they knew they were going to have to open the door of Pepper's car? Would they realize how serious it was? Would they have the right tools?

"Charlotte?"

"Yes."

"Where are you?"

"I'm on the county road near the entrance to Bakker Beach."

"Stay in your car. Keep it running with the doors locked, and move down the highway away from the entrance. Do you hear me, Charlotte?"

"Yes, Mona. I hear you."

I may have glossed over the fact I was driving an official police vehicle. And one that appeared to be involved in a crime. I had planned to park it back by Pepper's car after I made the call, but even in my state, I could see that wasn't a good plan.

"There's a problem, Mona."

"Beside the officer down and the missing officer?"

"Yes. I'm actually in the police car."

"Of course you are. I don't know why I didn't think of that myself," Mona said. "That's a good one, even for you."

"It was empty and the door was open and I realized that my car was up the road and when I saw that Pepper was injured, I knew I had to get help. And— Oh crap."

Mona said, "What now?"

"There goes *my* car!"

"What?"

"My Miata. It's racing down the highway toward town. He must be doing a hundred and fifty."

"Who was driving?"

"I don't know. I couldn't see. But whoever it was, he's got plenty to feel guilty about."

*Inexpensive over-the-door shoe racks keep
shoes visible and the closet floor neat.
Don't keep more shoes than you can store in view!*

12

I took a minute to call Tierney. My hands and voice shook, but there was no point in him getting the information third-hand from some snickering colleague. It was getting close to our date time, although that wasn't going to happen now. Tierney arrived shortly after the ambulance and the fire department.

I had to admire those firefighters. I took a chance and followed them in Nick's police car after they all shrieked past me. They were prepared for anything. The firemen apparently have special tools for getting into vehicles, something thin and yellow called a glass punch according to the smart young cop I remembered from a previous encounter. He was one of the first on the scene and took the time to check if I was okay. Why couldn't they all be like him? Normally he was friendly and concerned, and even better, he wasn't so tall that I had to strain my neck to look up to him, like so many men in my life, Jack and Tierney included.

Six more police cars arrived in chaotic short order but had to be moved so that the ambulance with Pepper could

scream away to Woodbridge General. A tall, awkward guy
with a hangdog face stepped out of the last cop car to arrive. Tierney chewed him out for blocking the road. The
latecomer's seventies-rock-musician mustache almost quivered. Serious face or not, in my opinion having a mustache
like that proved he wasn't nearly as intelligent as the crisp,
clean-shaven junior officer. For one thing, he had the look
of a cartoon dog and he seemed to be walking in circles.

"Move your sorry butt, DeJong," Tierney added to the
cop with the mustache, before he ambled by me, jingling
his keys. To me, he said, "I thought you were going straight
home to get ready."

I braced myself for a blast. "Something that Pepper said
on the phone alarmed me. I wanted to reassure myself. I
went looking for them."

"We're the police. We would have found them."

"You would not have found them. Don't even pretend.
You are so new to Woodbridge, I bet you'd never even
heard of Bakker Beach. And another thing, do you expect
me to believe that your colleagues would have looked for
a married couple, both police officers, here in make-out
mode before dinner? Because that wouldn't happen."

"Eventually, they would have been found."

"Eventually wouldn't have been soon enough. Pepper
could have died here. All alone."

"Tell me again why you thought to look here?"

"I checked out places that Nick liked to go when we
were kids. This was the first location I tried. I figured he
was keeping a low profile."

He scowled and paced back and forth, glowering at Pepper's vehicle. "Explain to me again where the squad car
was."

"I think it was right there." My hands were still shaking
as I showed him how Nick's car had been parked. "I could
put it back if you want. The door was open and the keys

were still in the ignition. The engine was idling. I needed to get away."

"Okay. And the person who took your car?"

"I don't even know if it was a man or a woman. I saw a dark shape. And I was out of there."

"Could it have been Nick?"

"I can't believe that it was Nick. How could he leave his wife like that?"

"Why did you think you'd find Pepper here?" I figured I knew what he was doing. Typical cop stuff. Asking his questions in a disjointed way, seeing if I'd stumble as I told my bizarre story.

"I was looking for Nick."

"Why?"

"Because I knew Pepper was also looking for Nick. Being Pepper, she had a good chance of finding him. If I found Nick, I'd find Pepper."

"Why did you want to find Pepper?"

I hesitated. I would be violating a confidence. But it was the right thing to do. Pepper had been making up her own rules and look where that had gotten her.

"She was almost hysterical, worried about Nick. She even left her baby at Jack's cycle shop."

"That's hard to believe."

"Hard for anybody to believe. Except for Jack, of course, who thought it was the most normal occurrence in the world. And Little Nick, who was having baby fun."

But Tierney didn't want to talk about Jack. "What was she worried about?"

There we were, at the moment of truth. I could connect with Tierney, who I knew to be a decent person, or keep Pepper's secret, whatever it was. I thought about Pepper and her terrible injury, and I thought of Nick, missing.

"She thought Nick was frightened of something, that he might have stumbled on something dangerous."

"And you didn't see fit to mention it to me? We were talking before you drove out here."

"It was too vague for one thing. I didn't even know if it was true, or if . . . You know, it can't be easy being married to Nick Monahan, so it seemed possible that she was overwrought, exhausted from the baby and Nick's usual hijinks. But I did track Nick down and talk to him earlier today."

"And?"

"And I didn't learn anything. I could tell he was scared, though there was no clue what he was frightened of. He acted as though he was afraid for Pepper, too. I wondered if he'd been gambling and lost a pile of money or experimenting with drugs and he was afraid she'd catch him and leave him. I suppose in either case, there could have been people after him. I even considered the possibility of a jealous husband. That's all I know. But Pepper was worried about him. But before you chew me out, I'm pretty sure you wouldn't have gotten much out of him, either."

Tierney gave me a hard look.

I said, "And being Nick, he could have been afraid of embarrassing himself in front of his co-workers. He's as dumb as a post, but he's not crooked in any way."

"Embarrassing himself? How?"

"I don't know. Maybe he's losing his hair. You know how vain he is." I was surprised to find that I felt a smidgeon of guilt over trashing Nick in front of his superior officer. It wasn't that I didn't care about Nick, although he was like having a badly behaved little boy around. That reminded me of Pepper.

"We shouldn't be wasting time here. I want to go to the hospital and see if Pepper's all right. Maybe I should call Sally. Her husband's a doctor and—"

"I've met Sally and Benjamin, remember? At Margaret's after wedding party?"

"Sorry. I forgot. I'm rattled by all this. Can I go? Do you think I can help here? Do you want me to look through the woods for Nick? Because—"

"I would ask you to, but you're wearing the wrong shoes for it," Tierney said.

"What?"

"Of course I don't want you to look through the woods for Nick. You saw Pepper's injuries. She's a trained police officer and look what happened to her. You are a civilian. And a tiny, unpredictable, utterly obsessive civilian at that. You have a handbag as a weapon. Oh wait, you don't even have that with you. It's in your car, I bet. So. Do I have your assurance that you'll call me if you have an idea? I mean any idea remotely connected to Pepper and Nick? I'd like to know that you won't run into another dangerous situation because you are too stubborn to call me."

"You don't need to use that tone."

"But you *do* need to keep in touch with me on this."

I still didn't see what choice I'd had. And while I did agree that keeping in touch with Tierney was a good idea, I couldn't imagine going on a date after what had happened to my friend.

"I guess our dinner's off. You'll be tied up with . . ." I gestured around at the squad car and Pepper's vehicle.

"We'll be doing a search for Nick. We have to get as much covered as possible before it gets dark."

"Will you keep me in the loop about Pepper?"

He paused and nodded. "If I can." I was pretty sure he was bending some rule and I appreciated it. "I don't imagine they'll let anyone see her for a while. She'll need to be examined. That kind of head injury is going to require tests."

I had to admit that was true. "I should get over to CY-Cotics and help Jack figure out what to do about Little Nick before I go to the hospital. I hope Pepper left everything the baby needed. She didn't expect to end up in emergency."

"Good idea. And Charlotte. You've been friends with both of them for a long time."

I blurted out, "Pepper's been my friend almost all my life. We went to school together. We used to call ourselves the misfits. Along with Sally and Margaret and Jack."

"But not Nick?"

"Oh no. Nick wasn't a misfit. He was always a cool guy. We were spectacularly uncool."

Tierney's mouth curved in a smile. A cool smile. "Pepper and Nick are a strange couple. And from what you said earlier it sounds like they'd been having some issues lately."

"Lately? They always have issues. Nick loves to chase women. He doesn't usually catch them. But the chasing, that's an issue in itself."

"I get where it would be. So my point is, do you think that Nick would have hit Pepper?"

"No."

"Hear me out. Maybe he backhanded her to keep her from screaming at him? Didn't mean to hit her that hard. Then he panicked and—"

"No!"

"People are often in denial about what others are capable of doing. We don't like to think that one of our friends could beat his wife. But it happens and we have to face up to it. Do the right thing."

"No argument here. I don't think that Nick would do that. For one thing, he's not an angry person. He's not struggling with rage or control issues. He loves Pepper. In his own stupid way."

"A lot of guys beat the women they think they love."

"I understand what you're saying and I'm trying to get my head around that, but the fact is, Nick is scared of Pepper. She's in charge. I could believe that she'd clobber him before I could see it happening the other way around. But at the same time, I don't believe she would hit him. Oh God, I hope I'm right about all of this." I stared at Tierney.

"I hope you are, too."

I stood there chewing my lip. Pepper had grown up in an abusive home. She'd had the bruises to prove it, although she always denied that. Her dad had been a cop, too. Had she found more of the same with Nick? A pattern repeated? Had I missed the signs because I was too caught up in my own images of what kind of people they both were?

I felt shaky about the entire situation. "Can I go now? I'd like to go see her. And I need to find out if Jack's all right, too."

"You know something, Charlotte. You've had a shock. You've been in a bad situation. Why don't you go home and go to bed. Or take a bath or something to relax. Everything in the world is not your responsibility."

"Maybe that's true. But my friends are. Pepper is. Nick is my friend in a weird way. How can I go home and take a bath when we don't know if Pepper's going to be all right or what's happened to Nick?"

"Okay, okay. I'll get one of the officers to take you by the bike shop and then to the hospital. We're on the lookout for your car."

"Thank you. I'm sorry tonight didn't work out."

"There will be other nights."

"Let's hope you find Nick and he's all right."

Tierney nodded grimly and stared out over the Hudson for a long minute. I had no idea what he was thinking. Half of the uniformed officers milling around kept their eyes on him. I understood this was serious business, two of their own.

The smart young officer drove me to CYCotics, his dark intelligent eyes lacking the humor I usually saw there. No sign of his quick wit, either. He seemed distracted by the seriousness of a situation that couldn't have a good ending.

I was, too, and forgot to ask his name. I figured I should find it out as he kept showing up at crime scenes that involved me. Something in common and all that.

———✦———

I don't know why I'd been so concerned about Jack. He had Little Nick rigged up in his one office chair. He was using his foot to gently jiggle it up and down as he did a bit of paperwork standing at the cash desk.

A grin creased his face. "Hey, Charlotte. This is a boys' club, but maybe we'll let you in. I'm almost finished here. We had a ton of customers around the time we should have been closing, right, little dude?" He glanced behind me at the young officer with the serious face. "What's going on?"

"Pepper's been hurt. She's at the hospital with some kind of head injury. I'm going over there now. I needed to know if you were all right and managing."

"Why wouldn't I manage? Never mind. What happened to Pepper?"

"We don't know." I glanced at the cop, but he had ambled to the other side of the shop to examine a particularly seductive racing bike hanging on the wall. Jack would have cheerfully sold it to him for less than ten thousand. He wasn't paying any attention to us.

"That's bad," Jack said.

"And Nick is missing," I hissed.

"What?"

"Shh. Do you think it's possible that Nick could have injured Pepper? Hit her? Have I been wrong about him all these years? Is he worse than merely a vain and vacant pretty boy?"

Jack scratched his head. "I don't know, Charlotte. Pepper would have sent him flying through a window if he'd even thought about something like that. But—"

"But what?"

"People in abusive relationships hide it. The abuser wants to get away with it, and the person who's being abused may be frightened and ashamed. Might be afraid to be left alone."

"I understand all that, Jack, as upsetting as it is. I'm wondering if that's what we have here."

"Nothing to do but ask Pepper, I suppose. She'll probably be furious if you even try."

"For sure. But trust me, the cops are going to ask her. I'm getting in there first. Let's hope that she's able to answer questions." My voice wobbled. "Oh, Jack, there was so much blood."

Jack wrapped his long arms around me. I needed to be held and comforted in this terrible situation. He whispered, "Did you see the wound?"

"I saw an awful gash on her forehead. She was lying against the steering wheel."

"Everything happens for a reason," Jack said.

"It's good to have a tame philosopher around in these challenging times," I muttered.

The smart young officer cleared his throat. I had forgotten he was even there. I supposed he had things to do. I said, "Jack, you'll have to take Little Nick home. Better put him upstairs in my place."

"Why?"

"Because if for any reason they send a social worker around to check on him, your house is furnished in bike parts and there's no food in the fridge. No fridge at all, unless you bought one yesterday."

"But you don't have food in your fridge," Jack said.

I heard the cop clear his throat again. I raised an eyebrow, and Jack turned and stared at him.

He said, "No, ma'am, but it's a nice place, well-decorated and clean, and obviously a home. You're right. It will make a good impression."

I told Jack not to let any social workers look in the fridge until I stocked it up. "Call Sally," I added. "She'll know what to do when you run out of anything that has to do with babies."

—✦—

"What is everybody talking about?" Pepper said. "I can't remember anything, and the questions these so-called doctors ask are absolutely ridiculous. How did any of them ever get through medical school?"

At least she wasn't in the intensive care unit. And she hadn't required surgery. It was bad enough though that she was surrounded by mysterious equipment and equally mysterious hospital smells. Still, Pepper lay in the hospital bed, pale, wan, and even feistier than usual. The bandage on her head covered part of her hair. "I hate it here," she added with a grimace. "I don't want to be in a place like this without getting to carry home a squirming bundle of joy at the very least."

She made eye contact with the tall, dark-haired police officer who'd been assigned to guard her. Of course they knew each other from work. He was expected to guard her from me at this point, apparently. I recognized him in the crowd of milling officers at Bakker Beach. He didn't seem to recognize me. I thought that was a good thing.

His name was Officer DeJong, but Pepper called him Roger. As in "Go ahead, Roger. You can take a coffee break. I need to talk to my friend in private. She's okay."

From the intense look on his face, I figured he probably carried a torch for our Pepper. He was a bit too young and she was too married, and there was the matter of his bad mustache, but I was happy that someone beside her misfit friends appreciated Pepper. He flushed, too, when she spoke to him. He said, "I'll be right outside. You just have to call for me." He shot me a look, equal parts unfriendly and suspicious. I supposed that was in case I turned out to be a danger, being a magnet for murder and all. Didn't bother me. I was happy she was guarded by someone who took the job seriously.

I said, "And speaking of squirming bundles, Jack still has Little Nick. Oh, Pepper, don't try to sit up."

"Why is Little Nick with Jack?"

"Come on, Pepper. I said not to sit up. Now look."

She leaned back and closed her eyes. If anything, she was even paler than before. I wouldn't have thought that was possible.

I said, "They say you have a concussion and a hairline fracture, so please don't make any sudden movements. Don't you want to get out of here and back to Little Nick?"

"Answer the question."

"Jack has Little Nick because you dropped him off at the bike shop. You had something to do. I believe that something was to go looking for your husband who was under the impression that he was in danger and that he might be putting you in peril as a result."

"That can't be true."

"It was. And I guess it still is."

"I mean about the baby. The bike shop? With all that dust and grease? And sharp objects? Oh my God."

"If it's any consolation, that's the best part of all of this. First of all, Little Nick is getting valuable work experience in the sale of high-end European bicycles. And he and Jack are bonding."

"He can't stay there."

"I believe they're now at my place where they'll be simulating normalcy in case child protection workers drop in."

"What's he going to eat?"

"Sally is dropping by with supplies. Little Nick's in good, if somewhat eccentric, hands."

Pepper was lying there, eyes closed. "Jack should have his own kids. He's made for fatherhood. Did you ever think of that, Charlotte?"

"What difference does it make whether I think of it? What happened at Bakker Beach, Pepper?"

"I can't remember anything. I can't even recall being there. I don't even know if it's true I was found in my vehicle."

"It's true all right. I found you there, unconscious, locked in, bleeding." I didn't mention that the shiny new red crossover vehicle would be somewhat worse for wear between the cops breaking into it and the blood from Pepper's injury. The Monahans get very attached to their cars, and I didn't want to make Pepper feel any worse. "Do you remember driving around town looking for Nick?"

"No. They told me I may never remember what happened. That happens in head injury cases. So where the hell is Nick? Why hasn't he come to see me?"

This was going to be tricky. "We don't know where he is, Pepper."

She opened her eyes and fixed me with a poisonous glance. "What do you mean, *we*?"

"I don't. And the police don't. But he was at the beach."

"He couldn't have been."

"His squad car was there. This is hard for me to ask, but does Nick ever hit you?"

She sat up, jerking her arm sideways and sending a glass of water plummeting to the floor. "Are you out of your freakin' mind, Charlotte Adams? What kind of dumb-ass question is that?"

Officer DeJong shot back in the room so fast I knew he'd been listening at the door.

"A legitimate one."

"Are you insane?"

"I had to ask."

"You did not have to ask that. Nick didn't do this to me. You know how you can tell that Nick Monahan doesn't hit his wife?"

"How?" the young cop said. I swear he had a spasm in his jaw.

"Because he's still freakin' alive. That's how. You should know that, too, Roger."

I was glad to hear her answer. But I didn't have the heart to say that I hoped like hell Nick was still alive.

Hang all jackets—even suit jackets—together in color order. Do the same with pants, skirts, and shirts. Discover new combinations and new outfits without spending a cent.

13

I left the hospital after Margaret arrived to spell me off. To my surprise, Tierney showed up at almost the same moment, keen to talk to me.

"We've found your car. Abandoned in a downtown lot."

"Great. Was Nick—?"

"Nope. No sign of him anywhere. Don't worry. We'll find him."

"So is my car here?"

"We'll need to keep it until forensics has a go at it. We need to know who was in it. If it was Nick, there will be traces. Someone else, same thing."

"But—"

"Sorry. That's the way it goes. I don't imagine they'll keep it all that long. This is a serious case, though, and we're not taking any chances. Maybe you can borrow one or rent one for a couple of days. I'll take you home now."

He gave me a minute alone with Margaret. Margaret is the least demonstrative person I know, but even she managed to produce a hug. "I'm glad to come in and stay with

Pepper. I couldn't sleep anyway. Frank is off with every other cop in town trying to find Nick," she said in the hallway as I prepared to leave. "They're all badly shaken by this."

Officer DeJong gave us a look that said he didn't trust either one of us as far as he could throw a gurney.

"I'm not surprised. One cop's been attacked and another one is missing. In a small force like this, they must be reeling."

"No one will be booking time off until they find him."

"Fingers crossed, Margaret. Take care of Pepper. I don't think she realizes how bad this looks for Nick."

She nodded. "I sure hope he didn't do it."

I wasn't under any illusions that Tierney's offer to drive me home was romantic in any way. He wanted something. I figured I knew what. As we drove, I tried a preemptive strike. "She doesn't remember anything. She got very angry at the suggestion that Nick might have hit her."

"I heard."

"You heard how? Oh. I knew that Officer DeJong was a spy. I believe that she doesn't remember. And I also believe that Nick wouldn't hit her. So the point is, who did?"

Tierney kept his icy blue eyes on the road ahead. "You may be surprised to hear that we, the police that is, are asking ourselves the same thing. And we are also wondering if a man who supposedly never hit his wife tried to kill her, would she find that too traumatizing to remember?"

I fought back tears. What the hell? Pepper and Nick's marriage was strange at the best of times. Why was I feeling this way?

"Want a tissue?" Tierney said.

"I do not need a tissue." I sniffed. "I am fine. A bit tired. And worried."

"Probably hungry, too. Do you want me to order you a pizza or something else?"

"No thanks. I have stuff in my freezer." I didn't mention it was all variations on the ice cream theme.

"Just asking. When this is all over, we'll try our dinner out again. If you're still speaking to me."

"Maybe you won't be speaking to me."

"I will be," he said.

———————

Jack and Little Nick were asleep on my bed, both making soft guzzling noises. Sally had dropped off enough equipment for a squad of babies. A portable crib, toys, formula, bottles, diapers, baby wipes, a couple of new soothers still in the package. Even a book and a little music box that played a lullaby. That must have been what knocked Jack out. I moved Little Nick to the portable crib that was taking up quite a bit of space in my bedroom. He continued to sleep angelically as I tucked him in. He had a lovely clean baby smell so I figured Jack must have managed to give him a bath. I checked the bathroom, and the puddles on the floor and water droplets all over the walls confirmed that. Never mind. It had to be done. I tiptoed back through my bedroom and covered the exhausted Jack with a cozy quilt before I ambled into the kitchen to forage for food.

To my surprise, I found some. Sally must have tossed in a bag of groceries as well because I spotted eggs, milk, orange juice, and salad fixings in my fridge along with what looked like a whole chicken, uncooked. I found cereal, jam, and wheat bread elsewhere. That was enough to fool any snoopy child welfare worker.

Truffle and Sweet Marie followed me into the kitchen and stood there with their legs crossed. When I took them out, they barked at me to let me know that the new state of affairs with a baby in the house didn't suit them in the least and I'd better make other arrangements on the double.

"It's purely temporary," I said. "Get over yourselves."

I guess it worked because they stopped barking at me and turned their attention to my neighbor's silky black cat.

Back inside, they settled down on the sofa in a sulky fashion as I rummaged through the freezer. Luckily Jack had been too occupied to steal the rest of my New York Super Fudge Chunk. Two tubs remained. The perfect late-night dinner. The other stuff would keep. I guess the faint scent of chocolate must have awakened him, because he stood yawning in the entrance to the little galley kitchen as soon as I popped the top off one. He scratched his bed head and said, "That little guy is pretty good company."

I filled him in on Pepper's status, handed him one of the tubs, and opened the other. I got a second spoon from my silverware drawer and savored the cold metal and its contents.

Jack said, "I think Truffle and Sweet Marie will come around and get to love him."

"I hope they won't have to. If all goes well, Pepper will be home soon and Nick will show up and tell us who did this."

Jack plunked down on the sofa and stuck his spoon into his ice cream. "If you say so. By the way, your mother called," Jack said.

I joined him. "Speaking of not good."

"Maybe you shouldn't talk about her that way. She is your mom. I wish I still had my mom. Remember all the good times we used to have when my parents were alive?"

"Do I ever. I'll never forget all the delicious meals your mom served your misfit friends. Your parents were wonderful. And the reason I remember them so well is because I was here in your house every chance I got. You had a home. Your mom was a mom. Your dad was a dad. My dad didn't exist, and my mother instructed me to call her 'Esme' from the time I could talk."

"I guess so. But still, she's your mom."

"Trust me. I know that. I do love her, but I'm not so sure I like her. I don't know if there's much I can do about it."

Jack said, "Whoa."

I said, "My memories. Don't get me wrong. I love to meet Esme in New York or London for an afternoon of shopping or in Florence to do the Uffizi. But it's not exactly a normal relationship. If she'd put in an order for a daughter, I wouldn't have been the result."

Jack's the best listener. So relaxed and calm and as a rule nonjudgmental.

I continued. "It doesn't matter. I have Truffle and Sweet Marie for unconditional devotion, provided I do what they say. I was never allowed to have a pet. I have wonderful friends, even if they're a bit nuts sometimes. Especially you, Jack. You're the best friend a girl ever had." I glanced over to see if he appreciated the sentiment. But of course Jack was snoring softly. I resisted the urge to whack him with one of my designer pillows.

Maybe I should have asked him what my mother had wanted before I went on my tirade. Too late now.

I made my To Do list, left Jack flaked out on the sofa, crawled into bed, and slept until Little Nick woke up screaming at three. Truffle and Sweet Marie were startled into barking long and loud. Jack slumbered on.

— ‡ —

"Man." I yawned as I staggered back upstairs after walking the dogs in the morning. "I don't know how parents cope. Did you get back to sleep, Jack? Silly question. Of course you did. You snored all night."

"Mmmf," he said. He was balancing little Jack on his hip and squinting at the can of formula. "I think he misses his mother."

"Don't we all? I think I'll find out what's happening there."

Before I could check with the hospital, Sally called. "Oh boy. Have you seen the news yet today?"

The news would mean Todd Tyrell, my least favorite announcer, and my answer to that question was always the same: "No."

"Don't turn it on."

"What?" Sally has had a crush on Todd Tyrell since we were fifteen. She never misses Todd on television and expects me to share her enthusiasm. She always thinks I should watch him. "Why not?"

"Oh boy."

"Is it Pepper?"

"They're exaggerating on the news, but it's not good."

I slumped on the sofa and rubbed my left temple. "What's happened?"

"Apparently there's bleeding on the brain. They're doing their best, but it's worse than yesterday."

"Bleeding on Pepper's brain?" I must have yelled that because Jack was at my side immediately.

I thought back to my conversation with Pepper when she'd sat up straight after being told to keep still. Did that contribute to this?

I whispered, "What's the outlook? Does Benjamin know?"

"He says it's guarded." Sally's voice was breaking.

"Guarded?"

"Could go either way."

"My God. That's terrible. I can't believe it. I'll go over."

"Don't bother. They won't let anyone who isn't a close relative in to see her. She's in ICU. Charlotte?"

"Yes," I whispered.

"Take care of yourself. This is awful for you, too."

I croaked, "What about you?"

"I've got a houseful of kids to keep my mind occupied.

You'd better keep your brain busy, too. And tell Jack he can drop Little Nick off here for the day or until Nick the Thick shows up. What's one more?"

I glanced at Jack. "All right. But I'm not sure he'll be willing. In fact, I don't know if he'll give him up without a fight."

"Whatever. We're all here in play central and the door's open. Well, we'll open it if he knocks."

I filled Jack in on Sally's call and watched his face fall. I decided to bite the bullet. I took a deep breath and turned on WINY news. "Let's see what they're saying officially." As usual, Todd Tyrell's giant teeth filled the screen and his grating voice scratched at my brain. I shuddered.

"And update on the crime wave sweeping our community—"

"Just the facts, you jackass," I said bitterly. "If you try to make entertainment out of what's happened to Pepper, I will go over there and make you eat those teeth."

Jack said, "Are you talking to the television set?"

Little Nick said nothing.

Pepper's wedding photo flashed across the screen. She was beautiful, shining, white veil flying high, strapless wedding dress revealing toned shoulders and arms. The best day of her life if you went by her face.

Todd Tyrell's face returned.

Police are continuing to comb the woods on the out-side of Woodbridge for Nicholas Monahan, a third-generation Woodbridge police officer. Monahan, who was demoted this year from his position of act-ing detective, is considered a person of interest in the attack on his wife, Detective Pepper Monahan. Detective Monahan is clinging to life at Woodbridge General Hospital. Stay tuned to WINY for breaking news.

A shot of the woods and police officers combing the area flashed across the screen.

I pressed mute to dim the sound as the phone was ringing again.

Tierney.

"Don't watch the news," he said.

"Too late. Why didn't you let me know what was going on? Is Pepper clinging to life?"

"I'm letting you know now. The next twenty-four hours will be crucial. We're all rooting for her."

"Me, too."

"I know this is hard for you, when you reconnected and everything."

"Yes. What about Nick? Is there any sign of him?"

"Nothing. Nowhere."

"Connor?"

"Yes."

"I thought of something. Nick couldn't have walked out of there."

"We had already thought of that. The main road is busy enough so that he would have been seen."

"So either he's still in the woods. Or he hitched a ride. Or—"

Nick's handsome face flashed across the screen. This shot was from the wedding album, too. He also looked happy. Maybe to be getting married. Or being Nick, maybe from squeezing one of the bridesmaids.

Tierney didn't let me finish. "That's right. But don't think about that stuff. We're hoping to find him."

"Alive, you mean."

"That's the plan. It looks like he was in your car."

"Are you sure?"

"We found traces."

"Well, actually, he was in my car. He stopped me

yesterday—was it only yesterday?—and pretended to give me a ticket. He got into the passenger seat briefly."

"What?"

"He—"

"I heard you, actually. That's so far removed from procedure that it caught me by surprise."

"I told him it wasn't the way to do it. But it might explain why you'd find a strand or two of his hair and maybe fingerprints."

"Maybe."

"Lots of people ride in my car: Jack, Lilith, the dogs. . . ."

"We didn't find fingerprints from anyone else in the system. We're not expecting to find your friends or pets in AFIS."

"Well, yeah. What about Margaret? Is she still at the hospital?"

"They sent her home when Pepper went into surgery. She's probably still sleeping."

"What happened?"

"According to Officer DeJong, who was guarding the room, around eleven o'clock, Margaret decided to walk up and down the corridor, to stretch her legs. Pepper was sleeping. While she was gone, DeJong heard a thump and opened the door. Apparently Pepper had gotten out of bed and then fallen. Luckily he was able to press the help button and a doctor and a nurse got there in seconds. He was pretty shook up."

I didn't ask if Tierney had slept. Something told me he hadn't. "Wait a minute, if there's no sign of Nick, who authorized the surgery? Was Pepper awake?"

He paused. "I believe her parents are on their way from Florida or wherever they retired to. They must have okayed it."

Pepper's parents? Things were dire indeed.

Tierney interrupted my thoughts. "Think positive. I'll try to keep you informed about Pepper. I know that she's the one you're close to."

After he disconnected, I stared at the screen. A trailer for a coming movie. I thought about Tierney's words. Pepper was my friend. And Nick had been in my life for years, too. I even cared about him in a weird way. Had he actually left his wife to die and me at the mercy of a would-be killer?

Jack interrupted my thoughts. "Pepper's parents. Whoa. This is out of control. What about Little Nick?"

"Let's hope his own parents are going to be all right."

"Both of them."

"Both of them."

I knew one thing for sure and that was that Pepper would not want her child to live with the same man who had left her bruised every week as a child.

I could have used a great big Jack-hug at that low moment, but he had turned his attention back to Little Nick.

That left me to worry about Pepper. Why had she gotten out of bed? What had she remembered?

*No matter how long the dress you wore to the homecoming
dance stays in your closet, it cannot make you eighteen
again or bring back the night. Find a new home for it!*

14

Sally was right. Sometimes the best thing when you can't
help is to keep going. The To Do list I'd written the night
before seemed so innocent now. It didn't have *Grieve for
friend.* It didn't have *Save Little Nick from evil grandparents.* It did have two closet appointments and a trip to the
library, a bit of dog training, and routine business development and office chores. Somehow, none of that held much
interest for me at that moment. But still it was something to
do as the hospital had said only family visitors for Pepper,
bizarre in this case.

Jack also had a full day ahead of him.

He declined Sally's offer and took Little Nick to the
bike shop with him.

"What if he cries and disturbs your customers?" I still
had trouble adjusting to the bike shop as day care.

"They can find another bike shop. Babies are part of soci-
ety. The little dude likes it there. People have to learn to—"

"Okay, okay. I guess he'll be all right there. It's not like
a typical nursery, that's all."

"Why not? We have music and bright colors on the bikes and nice things to look at. Plenty of objects to help develop his muscle control. He'll be more than all right. It's not like he's walking yet. He wants someone to smile and play a bit. Did you see him smile at me?"

"Fine. I concede defeat."

I helped Jack cart out the mountain of gear and jiggled Little Nick on my hip as he set up the car seat in the Mini. Little Nick looked around for Jack and reached for him, but I didn't take it personally. The kid was making a wise choice. Jack double-checked the car seat that Sally had dropped off and tucked the gurgling baby into it. I thought the boys looked pretty happy as they headed off to business. Was it my imagination or did Little Nick smile at me, too?

Whatever. It felt good, even as I felt a wave of fear for him and what his future might hold.

Jack's ancient Mini was only big enough for the boys, so I checked with my insurance and called the car rental company they recommended. I sat tight until that office could drop off my replacement vehicle.

Unfortunately that gave me a lot of time to think about Pepper and what had happened. It wasn't enough time to have any of it make sense.

⸻ ✦ ⸻

Harry opened the door and blinked at me in surprise. "I didn't expect you."

I blinked back at him. "But didn't we make an appointment?"

He glanced behind him. "We did, Charlotte honey, but I've been watching television and isn't that your friend who—?"

"It is. And I have to keep busy or I'll go nuts. The only thing is that if something . . . dramatic happens, I may have to leave."

"Naturally, you would have to. We'd understand completely. Some events take precedence."

Of course, the Beauchamps would understand. I lowered my voice. "Did Lorelei see the news? That would be terribly upsetting for her so soon after your daughter's accident."

He shook his head. "Don't worry about that, honey. She never watches the news. Never listens to the radio. Doesn't want to know. Just wants silence. She won't even have music playing."

"Maybe that's a good thing today. Considering."

"I suppose you're right, but it is terrible about Pepper Monahan. I remember her as a child, too. I'm sure I first met her at your mama's place. I can't believe her husband would do such a wicked thing."

"*If* Nick did it," I said as evenly as I could. "We don't know exactly what happened yet."

"Humph. Well, let's hope she makes it through her surgery. Then maybe she can tell the police what he did. I hope she has a guardian angel because she's been dealin' with a devil."

I had to think that this outburst was very unlike Harry, who was usually the most courtly of southern gentlemen. Well, for all I know of the species anyway.

"Do you think Lorelei will be up to seeing me? Is she . . . ?"

"Yes, honey, she sure is. She's up and she's dressed and lookin' gorgeous. We're finishing our coffee. Care to join us for a minute? Since it's a beautiful day, we thought we'd have our breakfast in the conservatory."

For sure coffee was a better start for me than champagne cocktails. I followed Harry, sniffing the aroma as we went. The conservatory had even more glass than the rest of the house, but it had only two plants. I wasn't sure, but I thought the ficus looked like it might be silk. Never mind. Who am I to talk? I don't even have a single plant in my sunniest window.

Lorelei was stretched out on a chaise, ignoring a plate with a muffin and some apple slices and a few grapes on a small side table. She seemed puzzled by their presence.

"I just made a fresh pot of coffee, Charlotte honey," Harry said.

"It smells heavenly," I said.

"That's our house blend. I do a mix of Kona and Guatemalan and a hint of dark roast, in case we need a boost."

"I need a boost for sure."

"Well then, I'll bring it in the biggest mug we have."

I wasn't sure if one mug would be enough to get me back to normal, but if it tasted half as good as it smelled, I'd be happy.

Lorelei was lovely in a casual printed silk tunic, the background color the pale corn silk of her hair and a lovely azure blue as a contrast color. Her hair was pulled back in a loose knot. She had on slim chinos, and her feet were bare. It was a very unstudied look, perhaps the Beauchamp version of casual country, but I knew better than to believe anyone looked that good by happenstance. However depressed she might be, Lorelei still kept up her appearance: fresh soft highlights in her hair, a well-kept pedicure, eyebrows recently done, too. Good, very subtle jewelry, pale brushed gold earrings winked in her ears.

"Maybe today's the day," I said, taking a seat on a matching chair.

I hadn't done a great job with my wardrobe that day. For one of the rare times in my life, I'd grabbed the first thing I saw in the morning. I was lucky both shoes were from the same pair.

"Maybe." She smiled.

"I have an idea." My main job was to get this show on the road. Otherwise, I'd be dropping by every day to stare at the water with them. The Beauchamps might pay thousands of dollars of services without a blink, but that didn't mean I could take advantage of them with a clear conscience. She raised one of her pale sculptured eyebrows.

I said, "Seven closets seem a bit overwhelming for me."

She nodded. "You could be right."

"So why don't we start with one and take it from there? This is something you want to do to improve your life, not to bring stress."

"I think that's a good idea."

"Good. You should pick the one you'd like to begin with."

She actually frowned, two tiny lines marring the perfect forehead.

I soldiered on. "Would you like to start with the one that's giving you the most trouble?"

She shook her head. "That's my main closet. It's the largest one. You've seen it. No, I'm not up for that."

"Fair enough. Is there another one that you'd like to try?"

"Well, darlin', we could always do—" Harry had arrived back with a pot of fresh coffee and their largest mug, which was about the size of my smallest cup.

Lorelei whirled, a move that was anything but languid. She said, "No, we can't."

"Of course not. I shouldn't have suggested it."

I felt a bit like Alice in Wonderland trying to figure out the coming reactions of the Queen of Hearts. As Harry poured my coffee, I decided that the closet he shouldn't have suggested must have been Anabel's.

"How about the one with the Christmas decorations?" Harry was determined to be helpful. But I could have told him that one wasn't going to fly.

"Not Christmas." Lorelei folded her arms in front of her. "Not Christmas. Too many memories."

"Christmas would be too difficult. I agree. Do you have one closet specifically for winter clothing?" I said, keeping my voice cheerful.

"Two actually," Lorelei said with a twitch at the corner of her mouth. "Harry spoils me, you know."

I did know. I wondered how much of her behavior was acting spoiled for the fun of it and how much was genuine misery. Of the two, Harry seemed to be the most heartbroken by Anabel's death.

"We could start with one of those. Make space for new purchases in the fall. What do you think?" I asked.

"Perhaps that could work. We can see."

An awkward silence hung in the air. Harry broke it up. "How is your mama, Charlotte?"

Getting past the idea that anyone would ever think of Esme as "my mama," I grinned.

"Maybe someday you three gals can get together again," Harry said. "That might be fun, wouldn't it, sweetheart?"

"Yes, it would," Lorelei said with a smile that didn't come anywhere within a long block of her beautiful eyes.

"Sure," I said, imagining Harry and me witnessing as Lorelei and Esme tossed verbal bombs at each other, leaving us splattered with the resulting damaged egos.

"We could have a party?" Harry's eyes lit up.

"Absolutely no parties," Lorelei said.

"A dinner, darlin', not a party per se."

"There are no visits planned," I said, hoping to put an end to it.

After all those years of being a captain of industry, Harry must have been desperate for things to keep him busy and yet still leave him time to dote on his fragile and difficult wife. An imaginary visit from my mother for instance.

Lorelei said nothing, got to her feet, and led the way. Two minutes later all three of us were standing in front of the closet in a third bedroom on the second floor. This one seemed to be a room given over to clothing. There was an oversize ironing board and a Rowenta iron, as well as a steamer and a huge three-sided mirror. I couldn't imagine Lorelei steaming anything herself, but surely she had people to do those things for her.

She sat in the upholstered chair and waited. I opened the door. As in the bedroom, clothing was jammed inside. Everything in there would have required steaming the minute it came out.

Harry said, "More coffee?"

We both shook our heads. I was finally going to do what I'd come for.

"Tell me, Lorelei. Do you wear all these clothes?"

"Of course."

I could clearly see price tags still dangling, so I knew this wasn't true. "Do you think you will wear them this coming fall and winter?"

"I'd like them available in case I want them. They all have some value to me. I don't think I'll give any of them away."

I nodded.

"And I don't want to sell any of them."

"Right. So are you happy the way things are going here?"

She jerked her head to stare at me. "What do you mean?"

"Perhaps the closets suit you the way they are? Maybe you just need more closets or racks to hang things so they won't be crushed. That would be very easy to do, and it wouldn't take any time. This room might be perfect for a few racks."

"I never liked racks."

"I can understand that. They have a very temporary feeling to them."

"Worse than that. They remind me of modeling. You

know, this whole thing is giving me a headache. I have to go back to bed."

Harry watched helplessly as she left the room, graceful yet listless. Every move a slap in the face.

I said, "I am sorry, Harry. I don't think Lorelei's ready for it yet."

"You're probably right, Charlotte honey. It's frustrating, but I can't think what to do anymore."

"Well, maybe she needs more closets built. You could get in a good carpenter and line the walls with them. Maybe use mirrored door on some so the room doesn't get too claustrophobic. Lorelei would have to agree, of course."

I was actually hoping the project would end at that very minute. I could get on with my life and not have to come here and feel the energy sucked from my mind and heart.

"We'll try that. I know this is hard on you and I know you have troubles of your own, but I think it is helping." He flashed me an appreciative smile. "Would you like to have a look at Anabel's room?"

No, I thought, *I don't want to see Anabel's room. It's going to be a shrine to her and another totally strange manifestation of this family.*

"Please," he said. "I'd love to show you. We'll give Lorelei a minute to settle in before we go."

I figured that meant time for the next sedative, if that's what Lorelei was on, to take effect. Lorelei's door was closed, no light showing from under it as I followed Harry along the long, softly carpeted hallway. I realized that while the first floor was all polished stone, wood, and glass, the entire second floor was buffered in this pale silver carpeting.

Harry led the way. "It's at the end of the hallway. I said 'room,' but it was more like a suite, designed especially for her. It had a separate entrance so she could come and go like any adult. Her own bath, of course, and a dressing room like her mama's. Well, maybe not like her mama's, but you get the picture. Then she had a little sittin' room and her bedroom. Perfect little apartment. Lorelei never understood why she didn't live here for the rest of her life. But Anabel always wanted to be useful, and she felt she had to be out in the world to do that."

That gave me pause. Anabel hadn't gone far away, or so I'd thought. But I didn't know that much about her.

"Where did she live when she left, Harry?"

"She got a little condo downtown, practically on the river. She had a trust fund from my daddy. She didn't want us to help her, thought she should make it on her own. But it had to be by the river. Both my girls like to see the Hudson. Anabel loved the water even more than her mama does."

He opened the door and the light made me blink. I suppose I'd been expecting a dim and quiet space like Lorelei's. Anabel's face glowed from a collection of photographs on a wall montage. Her graduation photo showed a wide smile, a square jaw, and honest, serious brown eyes. She was all Harry, sturdy and sensible. I could see nothing of Lorelei about her except the soft blond hair. Not a girly girl, not a clothes horse, not a flirt. Just a nice young woman who wanted to be useful. And maybe she'd also wanted a life.

I stepped forward to stare at a shot of Anabel in hiking gear, and another one of her in a sea kayak. I stared at a group photo in the inside of a bar or a restaurant. Anabel was in the middle, laughing. Dimitri was clowning around for the camera. Gwen wore a forced smile, and to the far side was a striking dark-haired girl with a nose ring. She looked steaming mad. Jewel?

Harry said, "I put up a lot of these photos after she . . . I wouldn't want you to think she was vain. She wasn't at all, and she never would have kept all these around in frames. I found a lot of them in her condo when I went to close it down. It was a side of Anabel that we didn't get to know. I think we should have. But I wanted to see them. Her mother can't bear to see the pictures yet. She doesn't come in here."

I waited until his voice settled. He said, "We still keep her things. That's why Lorelei wouldn't want you to clear them out. We have to wait until she can at least look at them. I should never have suggested that you take care of Anabel's closet."

We have a mantra in the business: The artifact is not the person. That scarf is not your mother. The recliner is not your father. The pearl choker is not your grandmother. There are many strategies to help people deal with what someone else has left behind. It's also the hardest part of organizing. People don't want to let go.

Harry knew that if Anabel's clothing went to someone who could use it, it would enhance her memory, not diminish it. From what I knew about Anabel, she'd want to share. Of course, the decision no longer rested with her.

Even so, that wasn't why he'd brought me there. He wanted me to see how much he'd lost. How much they'd both lost. I was beginning to understand, even though I didn't have much room in my heart for extra pain on that particular day.

After a long moment of silence, Harry closed the door and we walked slowly side by side along the corridor, down the remarkable stairs and to the front door. As I said goodbye he squeezed my hand. "I do not know what to do," he said.

"Neither do I." I returned the squeeze.

I am an organizer, not a clinician. I can help them improve their homes and their lives, sometimes even their marriages and careers. But there was not a damn thing I could do to help Lorelei Beauchamp. Or Harry.

I used my cell to check with the hospital. Pepper had been moved from ICU but still was not allowed visitors. I glanced at my watch. I decided to catch Ramona before lunch. I started up the rental and burned rubber to the library. I spotted a streak of blue in the reference stack and pounced. Ramona whirled, making her latest dangling silver earrings clink.

"I'm sorry to hear about Pepper," Ramona said. "I know you two go way back."

I nodded.

"Nick, too. Even if he is a rotten little jerk."

Again, nodding seemed appropriate.

She said, "Of course that is my own personal view and does not reflect the views of the administration of the Woodbridge Public Library. As you can see, we are up to our patooties in not taking a stand."

I could hear a rustling of raised eyebrows among the denizens of the reference department.

"I have your clippings about that other matter. Everything I could think of that might have some connection, and some stuff that might never make it online. I made copies so you don't have to sit here with people breathing down your neck."

"Thanks," I said. "And I want to ask you something. You're plugged into the community resources. I'm interested in finding out what's available for women who've been physically abused by their husbands. Do you have—"

"Sure do. Got a brochure, got some contact names. Have some social workers to contact and a shelter. I'm assuming it's not for yourself unless those dogs of yours are getting out of hand."

"Not for me. And in fact, maybe not for anyone. I'm not convinced that abuse is the issue at all. It's pretty awkward, but I can't stand around and do nothing in case it is."

"I hear you. It's a tightrope. But we still have to do the right thing. I'll get that information for you."

I felt a bit better taking a step forward. Normally I
would have discussed something like this with Pepper, gotten an "off-the-record" answer. For obvious reasons, that
approach wouldn't work in this case.

"Let me know," Ramona said, "if you need help or support in that other matter. You can count on me."

I thanked Ramona and headed home to read the clippings about the death of Anabel Beauchamp.

I knew she meant it. And I figured she was well aware
that I was enquiring on Pepper's behalf.

—◆◆—

One of the best things about running your own business is
having flexibility in your schedule. As much as I missed having the normal weekends that other people enjoyed, I did like
the fact that I was in charge. And lunch didn't mean gulp-
ing a protein bar one-handedly at my desk while working
spreadsheets with the other. I might make a lot less money
as a one-person business and I might actually work longer
hours, but I always made a point of putting *Friend Time* on
my To Do lists. I always made sure I had *Dog Time*, too, as if
Truffle and Sweet Marie let me get away without that.

As I pulled into the driveway to give the dogs a quick
walk, a cuddle, and a seat-of-the-pants bit of training, I
spotted Jack's bicycle near his front door. I realized he was
at the shop with a most likely wailing infant and I hadn't
given either of them a moment's thought. I am, after all, my
mother's daughter. I took care of Truffle and Sweet Marie,
said to hell with the barking training, and tore off to CYCotics to see what was needed. This particular "friend time"
wasn't on the list and it didn't need to be. I was headed
there anyway. No point in phoning as Jack doesn't always
answer. Part of that laid-back cycle shop thing. Must come
from the same place as the Hawaiian shirts.

I puffed into CYCotics carrying a container with three

panini sandwiches—prosciutto and Asiago, to be exact—
and two large cups of coffee. My cell phone was vibrating
as I struggled to open the door, but I didn't have a free
hand to answer it. I had the envelope from Ramona in my
briefcase. I don't know why I was expecting a tsunami of
diapers, overturned equipment, a squalling baby, and a
frazzled Jack. I felt vaguely disappointed by the air of calm
and quiet. There were even a few male customers quietly
drooling over some special type of alloy wheels in the corner. A woman accompanying one of them appeared to be
drooling over Little Nick.

Jack hung up his phone and gave me a startled look
when I arrived. That was followed by a whispered, "Shh,
just got him down for his nap."

Huh.

"What's going to happen, Charlotte? Did you hear the
news?"

Of course I hadn't. I'd been busy rushing about. I set out
the sandwiches on the desk and then asked, "What?"

"Maybe it's not the right time to talk about it. Margaret
just called. She was looking for you, but you didn't answer.
Frank told her the police believe that Nick was the person
who did this. Pepper's injuries are consistent with being hit
with a baton. They've found Nick's with his prints on it and
traces of . . . Pepper's blood."

The full horror of that showed in Jack's eyes and I am
sure in mine, too.

Jack continued. "He's no longer a person of interest.
There's an actual warrant for his arrest now. Pepper hasn't
regained consciousness yet, but she's out of surgery. Her
parents will be arriving from Florida to take Little Nick.
Pepper wouldn't want that. She doesn't have anything to do
with her parents. So we can't let that happen."

"You're right. She'd never want him to live with the
same man who gave her regular beatings when she was

growing up and the woman who let it happen." I'd already lost interest in the food. "I'd better call Margaret."

"Already done. That's why I was talking to her," Jack said. "I remember Pepper's bruises. I know how she grew up. I couldn't take a chance."

"I can stay here with you, until Margaret shows up."

"Never mind. She'll be looking for the best way to postpone handing over Little Nick until Pepper is able to speak for herself. She'll find an interim solution. Nick's parents would be better. No one made his life miserable when he was a kid."

I thought back to Nick's mother, a bighearted, bigarmed, booming woman. No one would ever give her a hard time, and no one gave her kids a hard time, either. She and Nick's dad had retired to North Carolina, and I knew their health wasn't great, but I was betting that they were also on their way back to Woodbridge. But considering that Nick was under suspicion, I figured there wasn't much chance the child welfare authorities would hand over Little Nick to them. And they would be concerned about finding Nick, too.

"I know I won't be able to keep looking after him," Jack said. "Much as I'd like to. Even you don't believe this was a good spot for a baby. Margaret says I should take him to Sally's and she'll apply for an interim custody arrangement. Seeing as there are four healthy happy kids there and Benjamin's a pillar of the community, she's confident that might happen. Especially as she can document that Pepper's estranged from her parents."

"What a tough situation. But if it's any consolation, Jack, I've had second thoughts about the wisdom of taking a baby to a bike shop. I just had to open my mind and my eyes."

"I appreciate that. Are you going to eat any of those sandwiches?"

I always plan ahead for Jack's voracious appetite. "Go ahead. I'm not hungry. I'm going to look over these clippings about Anabel."

"What's the point of that? You don't still think there's something suspicious about it, do you?" Jack asked before chowing down on one of the panini.

I turned to the clippings I had brought in with me. "I believe Nick knows something and whatever it is has him falling apart."

Jack said, "Can you do me a favor later?"

"Sure."

"I have some extra blankets at home in my closet, and I thought it might be nice if I could put the little dude down on the floor and let him work on his crawling technique without him getting splinters from these old wooden floors. Can you drop them off to me if you have a chance? I don't want to close the shop when business is getting better. I think the little dude is a good luck charm."

"I am going to try to see Pepper, but I'm glad to bring them afterward if you're not in a big hurry."

At that moment the door jingled and sure enough another young couple strode in. They looked like they knew exactly what they wanted in an overpriced bike. Leaving Little Nick happily burbling at colorful bike parts, Jack ambled over to help them make that happen. I turned my mind to the clippings again. I had only a couple of minutes to peruse the articles. The file from Ramona was what I would have expected: an obituary for Anabel, an article about her accidental death from the local paper. A lot of coverage that resulted for her famous mother. But there were also pieces about the work she was doing prior to her death. A couple of newspaper photos and a printout from a website with her photo. In the newspaper she was wearing a plaid shirt and jeans and grinning as a new grant for the youth program was announced by city officials. Even subtracting the genius of newspaper photography, here was someone who enjoyed what she was doing. She was glowing. I shuddered when I turned over a photo of the watery foundation where she'd drowned. It reminded me of huge, gaping jaws.

I reminded myself that overwrought reactions were useless. I needed to have an unbiased, unemotional understanding of what had happened. My eyes widened as I spotted something that might help. A clipping from the local paper contained a familiar name and a new bit of information: Brad Dykstra had been one of the paramedics who had tried to save Anabel.

*Consider your quality clothing in a new light. Can you
update items by shortening them or taking them in?
Factor in the cost of simple alterations to see if they're worth it.*

15

My attempt to talk my way past hospital staff to check on
Pepper ended in failure. The regular WINY updates didn't
help. So I was in need of a smile when I pulled up at Wendy's
place. But I wasn't expecting the dress that provoked it.

"She'd hidden it," Lilith shrieked. "Can you believe
that?" She pointed to the object in question first and then
to Wendy, who was sitting on the bed doing her best to
maintain her good nature.

One look at the yellow dress with its eighties sleeves and
full skirt and I could indeed believe that someone would
hide it. Of course, Wendy was the client, and I thought I
might be a bit more discreet than Lilith. Comes with age
and having a business.

"Her own son ratted her out!" Lilith was having a good
time.

Wendy wore a sheepish grin, but was she having that
much fun?

"He did," Wendy said. "I'd hidden it in Seth's closet, and
he found it and brought it back. He was greatly incensed."

Hmm. I had a feeling that Seth might have been less incensed over the startling dress and more inclined to want to see Lilith up close.

"Did he have a comment to make?" I asked, wondering if he had tripped over those size fifteens as he arrived.

"Too overcome with shock," Lilith said, still laughing. "Maybe it's the bright yellow. Maybe it's the beaded top. Or the puffy sleeves."

Wendy said, "I loved that dress and I had a lot of fun wearing it, and I don't want to get rid of it. I'm digging my heels in on that."

"Special events?" Lilith said. "What? Costume parties? Were you going as Big Bird? Wait! It has everything *but* feathers."

I decided at that moment that Lilith and I needed to agree on a verbal code that signaled "give it a rest," "chill," or maybe plain "shut up."

"Laugh all you want. The dress stays."

Lilith wiped the tears of laughter from her face. I thought Wendy showed great restraint in not mentioning that the time would come when Lilith's bright spiky teal hair and piercings would be passé even with disaffected youth. Wendy and I knew that even if Lilith didn't yet.

"Oh well, I guess memories are good. We got rid of everything else with hardly any hair being pulled," Lilith said. "We're still tight for room, and Wendy's going to need some new stuff, so I'm pushing for it to go."

"And as for the dress, Wendy, if you want to keep it as a souvenir, perhaps a photo of you wearing it might do the trick. Put it on your bedroom wall. Better than hunting in the back of the closet for memories."

"Especially if it's in Seth's closet," Lilith interjected.

"That photo technique is not a bad idea, and Lilith suggested it for a couple of other items. I think I'll do it for the Christmas sweaters. I made them for all of us when the boys were little, and we do have photos of them."

"None for this?"

"Oh sure. Brad is always big on photos. But the thing is, I love this dress. Even if it's out of style and I'll never wear it again, although it still fits."

"What do you like about the dress?" I asked.

"I have to hear this," Lilith teased.

"The color. Isn't it happy?"

"Yes. It's like wearing a happy face," Lilith said. "Round and . . ."

I shot her a look. She caught my expression and said, "Oops, Charlotte thinks I've gone too far. Sorry, Wendy. I was just having fun."

"Pfft," Wendy said, with a wave of her hand. "Me, too. With a house full of men and boys, I can take a little teasing."

Lilith looked relieved, and I certainly felt it.

I said, "So the color?"

"And the fabric. It feels so good, light and filmy, yet solid and substantial. If I ever found something made out of fabric like that again, I'd buy it, no matter what it was. I have a wedding to go to and I'll never find anything I like as much as this. In fact, the way I'm going, I'll never find anything, period. Especially on my budget."

Lilith couldn't contain herself. "Promise me you're not even thinking of leaving the house again in this dress!"

Wendy said, "I'm silly and sentimental, but I'm not planning social folly."

Lilith clutched her chest, indicating that she might have missed a career on the stage. "What a relief."

I stepped over to the dress and touched it. Wendy had a point. The fabric did feel silky. It would be lovely next to your skin. That's something to think about when you get dressed up, the sensuousness of the clothing you're wearing. And the color was spectacular, even if a bit overwhelming.

"I have an idea."

"Please, tell me you don't," Lilith again, back in play mode.

"I do."

Wendy looked up expectantly.

"Lilith, what exactly is wrong with this dress?"

"We already talked about the color."

"Yes, but we all like the color."

"Not an acre of it. You could erect a tent with less fabric."

"What else?"

"Are you kidding? Do you not see those sleeves? In the circus maybe."

"So far so good. And then?"

"What are those? Rhinestones? It's like a kewpie doll dress." Lilith couldn't hold back.

"Those were the times," Wendy said.

I said, "But not the skirt?"

Lilith tilted her head. "The skirt's okay. It's a nice classic shape."

I reached over and picked up the dress. I tucked the overwhelming top inside the skirt. I laid the "skirt" on the bed and peered into the closet. I didn't find what I was looking for, so I snatched up a long-sleeved navy tee and displayed it on top of the skirt.

"Wow," Wendy said.

"That rocks, Charlotte!" Lilith did a little dance to illustrate approval.

"Right. Bright gathered skirts are very useful items for a wardrobe. What I suggest, Wendy, is that you ditch the top, put on a waistband and shorten the skirt, and you can wear it with a plain neutral top. All you need is a good dressmaker. Although you should try it with the top tucked in before we get too excited."

Sometimes you get it right. The outfit was going to be spectacular on Wendy, although maybe not with her sneakers and cotton socks.

Wendy said, "I'll find a dressmaker."

Lilith said, "Hold the phone, lady. I can do those alterations for you. I get all my stuff at the Goodwill. I hope you don't think I can afford to go to college *and* get my clothes altered."

"Talk about a full-service package," Wendy said, then added, grinning, "although I know that extra charges may apply."

"Problem solved," I said. "We'll take a look to see if you have the right shoes for it and the right purse and—"

"She does. Remember? The shoes and purse were classic and fine," Lilith said. "Although she could still benefit from a trip with you to shop for something more fashion forward."

"Oh boy. I couldn't wear anything like that." Wendy pointed at my sling back pumps. "Hey, I owe you two so much. You're going far beyond the call of duty. I don't know how I can make it up to you."

Lilith said, "We're taking your hundred dollars. Don't forget that."

"Listen, I mean it," she said.

I hesitated. "We're not even finished yet, Wendy. We still have to set up your storage systems."

"I will still be grateful."

"Tell you what, I would like to speak to your husband. I have a question that pertains to his work. Would you ask him to give me a minute or two?"

"You can have Brad for as long as you want him." Wendy heaved herself out the bedroom door. "I won't let you keep him, but I won't be counting the minutes. Seth, where's Dad?"

"He's in the kitchen packing his lunch."

I headed downstairs to talk to Brad out of hearing of everyone else. I thought as I spotted him that he was the perfect partner for Wendy. He was almost as mellow and even more unshakeable, I guessed. He was the face you'd want looking down on you if you were lying incapacitated on the floor of your kitchen or if you were trapped in a car that was about to catch fire. No question about that. I found myself wishing he'd been on duty on the too frequent occasions when I'd found myself in an ambulance.

"How can I help?" he said.

I admired the trim insulated carrier and the matching drink container.

"It's a bit awkward."

"Go ahead. Try me. You've made Wendy very happy."

"It's about Anabel Beauchamp."

He blinked. "What about her?"

"I understand you were at the scene of her terrible accident."

The smile slid from his face. I got a flash of how a tragedy like Anabel's must haunt emergency personnel; then, just as quickly, he assumed his public expression. The casual friendliness was gone, too. "It was terrible. I don't know what information I can give you."

"I'm sorry. I realize it must seem like a very insensitive question, and I'm sure you don't want to revisit something like that. But Anabel's mother keeps insisting that someone killed her. I don't know what to say. I'm not looking for the gruesome details. I thought perhaps you could reassure me that didn't happen. I can try to help her mother deal with it. I suppose it's grief, but this idea is certainly ripping her apart."

Brad's face was calm, impartial yet sympathetic, a useful expression in his line of work. "It would sure rip me apart if it had been one of mine."

I nodded. "So you can confirm what the police are saying?"

He looked surprised. "What are the police saying?"

"That there was no indication of foul play."

I didn't interrupt as he concentrated. "We don't look for signs of a crime. We're all about the injured person. Although we do look around to see what might have happened. But I didn't see anything to indicate that she'd been attacked."

"That's a relief," I said. "I don't want to be giving her mother false reassurances, but I've been hoping that she wasn't murdered."

He shrugged. "I asked myself that at the time. How could she have fallen right there? Why didn't anyone see or hear or come to her aid?"

I nodded encouragement.

He said, "Where were her co-workers? Didn't people on the street hear anything? What was she doing there in the first place?"

"So you suspected something was wrong?"

"It's not my job to suspect. It's my job to keep people alive. God knows, I wanted to keep that girl alive. But she was definitely gone before we arrived."

"Do you think it was not an accident?"

His knuckles were white on the handle of the lunch pail. "An accident seems likely, but I don't know how the police or anyone else could possibly feel confident making a statement that it definitely *was* an accident. The site was so churned up by those first two cops on the scene, there wouldn't be much hope of finding any evidence, footprints or anything like that. The second guy was all right, but the other was a total loose cannon. A panicky jackass. I think he's the one they've got a warrant out for now. Now I wonder if he wasn't involved in Anabel's accident, too."

"Wait a minute. There were two cops?"

"Yup."

"One was Nick Monahan. He'd be the panicky jackass, I guess. But who was the other one?"

Brad shook his head. "I don't know their names. I knew them both to see them, that's all."

"You said they churned up the site. But the paramedic team was there, too. You would also have tramped in the mud, no?"

"Sure, and the firefighters were on site, too, but we focused on our jobs. And we didn't tramp all over everything. We didn't walk all around the perimeter or pace in the mud. There wouldn't have been much left for the cops to find."

We stood there silently after that, looking at each other.

"Thank you," I said. "I appreciate your candor."

He shrugged. "You ask me. That and three bucks still won't get you much of a sandwich in this town."

<hr/>

I had a lot on my mind, but I needed to drop by Woodbridge General to see how Pepper was doing. First I made a flying trip to Kristee's Kandees to pick up some of Kristee's black-and-white fudge. I actually think that this fudge might be a wonder drug. I bought a gift box for Pepper and a couple of miniboxes in case I needed a bribe.

I knew the nurses wouldn't tell me anything, and I'd gotten Sally's voice mail when I called. I'd had a half-baked idea that I might locate Benjamin and badger him for information. He also has a weakness for black-and-white fudge.

First I decided to check at the information desk. To my relief I was given a room number for Pepper.

"That's good. I was worried she might have been moved back to the intensive care unit," I said.

The smiling volunteer behind the counter assured me that Pepper was still in the regular unit. That was good news. It probably meant the injury was less serious than they'd thought. I already felt well disposed to people who volunteered their time to the community that way and flashed her my biggest smile. I stopped at the hospital gift shop and picked up some magazines for Pepper to go with the fudge. Nothing useful. Nothing practical. Nothing motherly.

More good news. I recognized the cop who was stationed at the door of her room. Luckily it wasn't the bright young officer who had driven me home. He would have been tricky to get past, even with a bribe of fudge. No, this one was DeJong, the overgrown, awkward, and not-so-smart guy with the mustache that made me want to reach for a razor. I remembered him from Bakker Beach. Of course, I'd seen him on guard duty at the hospital as well. I was counting on him remembering me, too, and thinking I had a right to be there.

I smiled up at him and said, "Sorry, I'm late."

He frowned at me. Didn't like the sound of late.

"I couldn't help it," I said. "I was held up. Why don't you check with Detective Tierney?" Given the tone that Tierney had used with him at Bakker Beach, he would eat crushed glass before he followed up on that.

"Well," he said with great and totally unmerited dignity, "don't let it happen again."

I wasn't sure what he thought I was late for. Or why he wouldn't have been informed. It was a good thing that I didn't intend Pepper any harm if this was the person they had protecting her.

Even so, I handed him one of the two miniboxes of fudge. "I hope this will save my reputation."

I slipped into the room and blinked at the flowers. Someone could have opened a florist's kiosk just from the blooms Pepper had received. I found myself smiling at the thought of how many people cared about her. Making the news would get the word out, too. My smile faded when I got a look at Pepper. She lay there, pale as old milk, her head bandaged. The entire area around her eyes was as dark as if she were wearing a cheap Halloween mask. Her nose was twice its normal size, and one eye was almost swollen shut. If her original injuries hadn't been bad enough, now she had a nasty cut near her mouth, the dark stitches shocking against her dead white skin. I gasped before I caught myself.

The eyes popped open.

"Did I hear you gasp?" she whispered.

"No." Sometimes denial is the best policy.

"Did."

"Just a sniff. I have allergies." I sat down in the visitor's chair. "Must be all the flowers. You opening a shop, Pepper?"

"Funny. You don't have allergies. Liar."

"Okay. You're bruised and it took me by surprise. I think bruises get a bit more colorful day by day. It's to be expected after what happened to you."

"What did happen to me?"

"I was hoping you remembered."

"My colleagues are, too. Freakin' relentless bunch. Remind me to be more sympathetic when I grill someone in future."

I grinned. "What did you tell them?"

Her voice got a bit stronger with every word. "I told them I don't *know*. Are you not listening to me?"

"Now you know how the rest of the world lives."

"The rest of the world doesn't have a face like this. I need you to be straight with me, Charlotte. How bad is it?"

I would have had to be out of my mind to tell Pepper the

truth. I thought fast seeking reassuring but not obviously false descriptions. "Sure, I'll be straight," I lied.

"And?"

"Sorry?"

"Knock it off. What do I look like?"

"Well. Like you walked into a door or something. But it's getting better. I'm sure by next—"

"Give it a rest. How bad?"

"Hard to describe. There's a lot of bruising, as I said, but it will subside soon and you'll be yourself again. If you don't mind me saying, I think your head injury should be your main concern."

She closed her eyes. "Worse than I thought."

"You don't look that bad." I spoke with feigned confidence, glad that there was no mirror within sight.

"Bullshit," she said.

I decided to change my tactic. Pepper was tougher than any nail. "Fine. You're pretty beat up. You were hit with something in the face, and then apparently you fell and injured yourself again. You cut yourself a bit more this time. You're a cop. You've seen people after accidents or beatings. You must be aware of what that would look like."

"Oh crap," she said.

"Forget about it. It's purely temporary. You're alive at least. What have they told you about your head injury? The rest is merely . . . window dressing."

Despite the swollen eye, she shot a poisonous glance in my direction. "As you're such a vain little creature, Charlotte, how would you feel if this was your face?"

If there was an upside to this conversation it was that Pepper seemed to have regained not only her power of speech but also her natural sense of authority.

Even so, I felt stung. "What do you mean 'vain'?"

"You know perfectly well what I mean. And speaking

of vain, where the hell is Nick? Why hasn't he been in to see me?"

"I don't know." Less true. I did know why. Nick was on the lam. I didn't know where. Distraction was called for. "Little Nick's fine."

The one good eye opened wide. "Oh my God. I left Little Nick with Jack. How long ago was that? What is the matter with me?" Pepper tried to sit up.

I grabbed her hand. "He's still with Jack. He spent the night in my apartment. They're having a great time. I believe Jack is using him to lure unsuspecting customers into CYCotics. Little Nick wears down their resistance, and Jack sells them a nine-thousand-dollar bike. You should get Jack to give you a cut of the profits."

"He's safe?"

"Of course."

"Then where's his useless father?"

How could I tell her the truth? While I was grasping for the right weasel words, Pepper uttered a strangled gasp.

I jumped up from the chair. "What is it?"

She said, "Oh my God. What if Nick is dead?"

*Invite a friend to help you de-clutter your closet. The buddy
system can keep you strong and decisive. Friends don't let
friends keep junk. Promise to return the favor.*

16

I glanced at the door, expecting to see a cop with a
chocolate-covered face shoot into the room. "I don't think
Nick is dead."

"But he might be?"

I considered my answer. How would I want to be treated
if I were lying there? Would I want people humoring me?
Lying to me? Treating me as incompetent? I said, "I hope
not."

"You hope not?" She gripped my hand so tightly it
hurt.

"Did you see Nick at the beach, Pepper?"

"I don't remember. I think I saw his squad car." She
loosened her grip on my hand.

"Are you able to recall what happened to you? Who attacked you?"

She said softly, "I can't tell what I remember and what
I've been dreaming. Everything is mixed up. I think Nick
is dead. I hope that's a dream."

The door opened. I whipped around to see Connor Tierney giving me the kind of look that you never want to see on the face of a man you're planning to date. Judging by the expression, the dating thing was now a no-go.

"Hi, Connor," I said brightly. "I thought I'd pop in and see how Pepper was doing today."

I felt icicles form on my nose. My imagination, perhaps. Those glacial blue eyes can give that impression.

I prattled on. "Yes. All her friends are worried."

"We, that's we the police, are worried, too. That's why we have a police guard at the door."

"Of course." I smiled brightly, glad I'd reapplied my lipstick before arriving at the hospital. "Officer, um, knows me."

But Tierney wasn't finished. "Officer DeJong. That would be the police guard you deceived to get in here. At least get his name right."

"I know his name. But deceived? I wouldn't go that far."

Pepper said, "Cut it out, Tierney. You, too, Charlotte. I want to know what's happened to Nick, and I don't want any more bullshit. From either of you."

We both inhaled and exchanged glances. What would that information do to Pepper?

Finally, Tierney said, "We are looking for him."

"You haven't found him?" Pepper demanded. I could tell what she meant.

Tierney said, "No."

Pepper exhaled. Perhaps she'd thought Tierney was bringing her the worst news she could ever receive.

"He could be at work. He's on days this week."

"No."

Pepper didn't appear to have heard. "It's one of the things he's good at. Going to work, I mean. He loves the uniform."

Tierney lifted an eyebrow. That was the kind of gesture

that I took to mean he hoped if he ever had a wife that she'd
be able to find more to praise.

Pepper said, "Charlotte, did he call anyone we know?"

"Sorry, Pepper. He didn't call me or Sally or Margaret."

"What about Jack?"

I shook my head.

"So he didn't even check with Jack to see if Little Nick
was all right?"

"Jack's a bit careless about picking up messages."

"Find out. Maybe Nick did call. We might be being un-
fair to him."

"Did Nick know the baby was with Jack?"

"I don't remember if I told him."

"Is that why you followed him to—"

Oops. I caught another one of those icicle glances from
Tierney. Those suckers can sting.

Tierney said, "We don't know where he is. He hasn't
been seen since you were found on Bakker Beach."

Pepper said faintly, "I think he was there when I drove
down the road. I saw the squad car with the door open. Unless that was a dream."

Tierney turned to me. "I think you'd better wait outside, Charlotte. I need to speak to Sergeant Monahan in
private."

Pepper said, "No way, José."

"What?" Tierney's jaw dropped.

"I'm sure you heard me. Charlotte is my best friend, and
in the absence of my family, she's going to stay with me
while you question me."

"I'm not questioning you, Pepper," Tierney said. "I'm
trying to share information and get a bit back in return."

Even I, not even remotely a cop, recognized the first-
name ploy that is commonly used in interrogations. "I am
not going anywhere," I said, folding my arms across my
chest to accentuate my position.

"Ask your questions," Pepper said. "Maybe if I find out what's going on, I can give you some useful answers."

"All right."

I said, "Are you sure she's up for this kind of police treatment? She's badly injured and she has a head wound and—"

Tierney glared at me. "Just so you know, I spoke to the doctor in charge and she says that Sergeant Monahan is well enough to be interviewed."

"Interviewed, sure," I said. "Grilled, I don't know."

"I am not planning to grill her. I do have ask some questions. No choice. I'll be as gentle as possible."

I managed not to snort. Pepper didn't.

Tierney said, "We don't know where Officer Monahan went after he left the area."

Pepper said, "Have you put an all-points bulletin on his vehicle? Maybe someone carjacked it. That would explain it."

Tierney seemed to have trouble meeting her eyes. "No APB on the car, Pepper. We have that."

I was chewing my lip through all of this. How was Pepper going to react? I reached out and took her hand. I gave it a good squeeze. A "Misfits rule!" kind of squeeze.

Tierney said, "The squad car was still there when we found you. Actually, Charlotte found you and called it in."

Her eyes widened. "Bakker Beach is in the middle of nowhere. Where could he have gone without the squad car?"

"Someone hijacked my car," I said. "I couldn't see who it was."

Tierney glared at me. "We found Charlotte's car abandoned in town. There was trace evidence that indicated Nick had been in it."

Pepper said, "I'm surprised that Nick would even get out of his car at Bakker Beach. It's surrounded by miles of brush land and marshes, too."

"That's why it was such a good make-out spot," I said.

Pepper uttered a strangled laugh. "Exactly."

Tierney said, "This is going to be painful, Pepper, and I'm sorry. But it was as you say a make-out spot. Nick didn't know that you were going to follow him. Is it possible he was . . ." He paused and cleared his throat. "Meeting someone?"

"You mean a woman?"

Connor Tierney wisely made no reference to Nick's hobby of chasing women. "Yes."

"I don't know. Old habits die hard."

I felt Pepper squeeze my hand. A signal not to screw things up. I decided to keep quiet.

Tierney said, "Did you think it was Charlotte?"

"What the hell?" I yelped.

"You want to stay here. You have to hear the uncomfortable questions."

"I knew it wasn't Charlotte."

"Okay. Did you have any clue to who it could have been?"

"No. Is that all, Detective? I feel like I've been struck by a train."

"It's not all. Someone at that site hit you very hard. The two prevailing theories are that you stumbled across an assignation and either Nick's lover hit you or Nick did."

"Not Nick."

"Then—?"

"I don't remember! Do you think I wouldn't tell you who hit me if I knew?"

I decided to change the topic. "Why did you go to Bakker Beach, Pepper? Were you following him? Or . . . ?"

She shook her head and flinched. "I have no idea."

I hesitated. There was another possibility. What if she *had* followed him unaware that Nick had been lured by someone who was not expecting her to show up? What if

Nick had been murdered before she arrived? It would explain the open door of the patrol car and the fact that Nick couldn't be found, as well as the attack on Pepper, a possible witness. Maybe Nick was lying on the bottom of the Hudson. Perhaps subconsciously Pepper knew that. It didn't explain why there was no extra car. But what if the murderer had been in the car with Nick? Holding him at gunpoint. No way could I give these theories an airing in front of Pepper. Why wouldn't the police have considered this?

I said, soothingly, "Of course, memory loss is to be expected. You were very badly injured and in a locked vehicle. I couldn't even get in to see if you were dead or alive."

"Locked? I must have locked the car." I could tell she was struggling to remember what happened. "But why would I lock it after someone hit me?"

Tierney said, gently this time, "I'm hoping you can tell me."

"I don't know."

"Was it Nick?" There was the question, slippery as a snake. Oh, Tierney, shame on you.

"No."

"Who then?"

"Listen to me. I do *not* know. But it couldn't have been Nick. He's never raised a hand to me. Ever."

I stared at Tierney. I wished I shared Pepper's absolute certainty that Nick hadn't hit her or worse, tried to kill her.

"I'll have to check in again. I hope your memory will start to come back."

"What did the doctor say?" Pepper asked.

"Maybe, but don't count on it."

"And in the meantime what are you doing to try to find Nick?"

"Ground searches of the area. We've had the choppers out. We have an all-points bulletin out for him."

"You're assuming he's hiding. But what if he's injured? Or worse?" The panic in Pepper's voice was unavoidable.

Tierney said, "I'll be back. And, um, by the way, you won't need Charlotte as your stand-in relative much longer. Your parents are coming to take care of the baby."

"What?"

"They're on their way from Florida."

"Who contacted them?"

Tierney blinked. "I don't know."

"Must have been one of Dad's old buddies from the department," Pepper said. "I suppose it could have been anyone."

This time he shrugged. "They're coming. I thought you'd be happy."

He wouldn't have thought that if he'd known how Pepper grew up, but as we liked to point out, he was new in town.

"Well, they're not getting my son. I can tell you that."

"You are going to need help."

"Listen, Detective. You don't get a vote in my son's well-being. Charlotte, I want Margaret in here right away. I want to make sure that Little Nick is taken care of if something happens to me." She inhaled. "Or to his father. I want that in writing and I want it now. I need to have someone reach them and tell them not to bother. And I don't want them in this room, either."

Tierney practically needed to pick his jaw up off the floor.

She said, "Talk to the chief, Connor. Tell him I said that, and make sure they don't show up here. I mean it."

I let go of her hand and headed for the door. "I'll call Margaret right now. I know she's already been talking to Jack. I think there's a plan to give Sally and Benjamin temporary guardianship. But now that you're conscious again, you can make that decision. It will be better."

Tierney gave me a tight nod and passed me, heading

down the corridor, keys jingling. I hurried after him. "I'm sorry things are working out this way, Connor."

"Working out this way? You mean *you* doing whatever you can to make this more difficult than it already is?"

"Pepper wanted me to support her. We go back a long way."

"And half the time you've been at each other's throats."

"Well, not this time."

"What's that about her parents?"

"Long story. Miserable childhood."

"Can I have more detail?"

"You'll have to ask her. It's not my story to tell. But you know Pepper. She means it."

"I do know Detective Monahan. It doesn't take twenty years to pick up on what kind of person she is. There's a very good chance that Nick Monahan tried to kill his wife on that beach. Got that?"

I rambled off my theory that Nick might have been killed and the killer interrupted by Pepper.

"Contain your imagination, Charlotte. And don't do anything else to make this situation more difficult than it is." He strode off, keys jingling even louder, back ramrod straight. I stood there to catch my breath. Officer DeJong watched, mouth open. I might find it harder to trick him the next time.

I walked back to Pepper's room.

"Is he gone?" she asked as I stepped inside.

"Yes."

"Are you sure?"

"He went . . . I'll double-check." I stuck my head out the door and glanced down the corridor. I could see Detective Tierney turn the corner to the elevator bay.

"He's gone," I said.

"Good. Now here's what I want. Don't argue. Don't do anything but listen."

"Okay."

"Nick's in big trouble. I can tell."

"I'm sure—"

"Don't interrupt, particularly don't interrupt to lie. He's in trouble, and he's not smart enough to get out of it on his own."

I kept my mouth shut.

"They think he did this. I can tell. I know our techniques. And they'll find him. He's not bright enough to stay hidden, and he'll do something impulsive or idiotic. He'll be killed, if he's not dead already. So, Charlotte . . ."

"Yes."

"I need you to find him before they do."

*Play classic rock when you are cleaning out
your closet! The catchy tunes will help keep
you energized, positive, and moving fast!*

17

The problem was, I agreed with Pepper. Nick was quite likely to do something that would make things worse.

I tried calling Tierney without success. I had decided to push my idea that someone might have taken Nick. Of course, that didn't quite match up with Pepper's fear that Nick would do something stupid, even if he wasn't guilty of anything. Tierney was a pro. He could decide which theory made sense, once I had a chance to explain my views to him.

I was chewing my lower lip as I crossed the Woodbridge General parking lot. Still, I thought, I had found Pepper at Bakker Beach. The police hadn't. That was because I knew Nick and had a pretty good idea of how he'd behave. There was no point in trying to figure out in which instances he was using logic. That didn't help much with Nick.

I sat in my rented Matrix and thought hard. What did I associate with Nick the Stick Monahan? Okay. Women, beer, cars, trucks, and bad decisions came to mind. Make-out spots, too.

I wasn't likely to figure out what women he might be

ogling, as it could be fifty percent of the population. He wouldn't hide out in a bar or a roadhouse. But cars and trucks. Now, that was a possibility. I drove by the house on Old Pine Street and up to the garage. Nick's prized 'Stang was parked inside. As was his shiny black truck. Naturally, the cops would have checked those out. Those license plate numbers would be flagged in the system.

Nick had the best security you could buy for that garage. I wasn't sure if he had video surveillance for his home, wife, and baby, but I knew he had cameras trained on those vehicles. The cameras would capture anyone approaching the garage, but the recording device would be in the house. There might be other information in the house, too. Maybe I could uncover something Nick had left, a clue to his whereabouts or what had frightened him. Maybe even footage of Nick sneaking home. The house, naturally, would be locked.

Just in case, I tried the door.

Good deadbolts front and back. A security system that would require a code. No way was I getting into the Monahans' house or garage.

—◆◆—

Before heading back to the hospital to see if Pepper could help with the alarm code and key problem, I popped home to check on the dogs and to pick up those blankets for Jack. I had almost forgotten them with all the drama and it was getting late in the day.

After Truffle and Sweet Marie had a quick walk, a snack, and a fast but halfhearted training session, they turned their tails toward me and went back to sleep on the sofa.

I headed downstairs to Jack's apartment to find the blankets. Jack hadn't exactly said where I'd find these alleged blankets. Most of his storage was for bike parts. I'd given up pestering him about it, even though I'd truly believed that once he had the shop, he wouldn't store quite so much bike junk in what was supposed to be his home. Still, I persevered and eventually ended up at the armoire in his bedroom where he kept his collection of Hawaiian shirts, baggy shorts, and scary Lycra racing gear. The blankets were folded neatly and stacked on the top shelf.

Of course, the shelf was too high for me to reach. Jack might be six feet and a bit, but I don't quite make it to five. I glanced around. Naturally, Jack did not need ladders. I checked my watch. I had to get going if I was going to accomplish anything with the rest of the day. I blame it on the stress of the situation, because I did what I always tell people not to do. I took what seemed like the easy way. Instead of heading back upstairs to my apartment where there was a perfectly good stepladder, I jumped up and grabbed the corners of the bottom blanket and tugged. It wasn't as if they could break, right?

Both blankets tumbled to the floor. That part was good, but the shoebox that had been apparently sitting on them tumbled, too. Crap. We all have stuff in our closets that we don't want anyone to see. That's my theory. Of course, I hadn't included Jack in this theory, because he is the most transparent person I know. Still, as the box hit the floor and spilled open, photos fluttered around.

I scrambled around to gather them up. There were old Polaroid photos of his plump, perfect parents. Shots of us misfits standing around the kitchen while Jack's roly-poly mum made cookies. Photos of us in Halloween costumes, also courtesy of Jack's mother. Nice images of Jack's dad and the gang on a sled on the toboggan hill. Pepper in pigtails, Margaret short of a tooth, me standing on a chair seeming to give orders. Good times. I gathered them up, feeling the ache of memory as I thought of the Reillys and the difference they'd made in all our lives, not only by adopting Jack, then a gangly boy with spiky hair, but also in the kind and nurturing way they had treated all us misfits. I hadn't realized that Jack still had these photos. I wondered why he'd never trotted these pictures out at one of our events. As I picked up the photographs one by one, glancing at each, I came upon my graduation photo. "Charlotte" was written on the back in Jack's casual scrawl. Then the shot of me leaving Woodbridge to head to New York City, the first big job. A blurry print of me on campus during the early college days. Then next to the Miata. There was one of me at Margaret's wedding party months earlier, and another one, I guess you could call it candid. I was asleep on my sofa surrounded by wiener dogs, my mouth open, drooling, with an empty bowl of popcorn on my chest. I didn't find any shots of Sally, Margaret, or Pepper, but I found dozens more of me.

I had no idea what order the photos had been in before the box had fallen out, but I straightened them up in what seemed to be a Jack-like arrangement. I headed back up the stairs, got the stepladder, brought it down, and replaced the box on the shelf. I closed the door and took the stepladder back upstairs again. I loaded the blankets into the rented Matrix and headed out. I didn't let myself think much more about the photos, because I couldn't figure out what the hell that was all about.

—＊＊—

I dropped off the blankets to Jack and Little Nick. The baby was happily gurgling in Jack's arms, distracting Jack from a couple of guys who were vying for his attention. Apparently they were desperate to order DT Swiss wheels, whatever they were. I didn't want to break up that happy scene, so I left the blankets and went straight to the hospital. At this rate, Jack would need to bring his part-time repair guys in for more hours and put them to work in sales, too.

Luckily there was a new cop guarding the room, an officer I recognized from the crime scene. He looked to be a few years past retirement, one of those guys who didn't want to give up the job. He let me through to visit Pepper on her say-so, although I knew he was keeping a fatherly eye.

"Pepper," I said brightly knowing the cop was listening. "You asked me to pick up your toothbrush and a few toiletries, but I couldn't get into the house."

She opened her swollen eyes and said, "What? Oh, right. I'll have to give you my key."

"Great. I'll go pick up whatever you need and bring it right back."

She blinked. That looked painful. "I don't know where my keys are."

"The keys were in your vehicle. Oh hell, Tierney must have them."

"I'll have to ask him to bring them in," she said.

First I said, loudly, "Yes, maybe do that tomorrow." Then I leaned forward to whisper in her ear, "I don't want him to know that I'm going there."

I didn't mention that we had no idea where Nick's house keys were. Did the police have those, too?

"Right," she mouthed.

I fished a piece of paper out of my purse.

Pepper wrote, *Mavis Morley. Cleaning lady. And CODE 7622#. Front and back doors.*

Of course, Pepper had someone clean her house when she was working. She scrawled the name, address, and telephone number. She scribbled, *You distract him*—she stopped writing long enough to point to the hallway—*and I'll call her and tell her to hand them over. Pass me the telephone.*

I complied, then grinned and stepped into the hallway.

"Excuse me, Officer," I said, beckoning him away from

the door. I lowered my voice. "I don't want her to hear me."

He glanced toward the door and said, "I can't leave my post."

I whispered, "You don't need to. Step away so that she can't hear us. Keep your eye on the door."

"What is it?" he said when we'd moved a few yards down the corridor.

"I need to know what you've found out about Detective Monahan's husband."

"I can't tell you that," he blustered. "That's up to the brass. They'll make a briefing."

"We've all been friends since we were kids. I am worried about her. Do you think he means to harm her? I mean would he come in here and—?" I gave him my best expression of alarm.

Oddly enough, I thought this guy wasn't buying the idea of Nick as the deranged husband, either. I said, "Because if it wasn't him, it was sure somebody, and I need to know what kind of person you're looking out for."

"You actually need to mind your own business," a voice said behind me. I whirled to find Tierney, back again. Didn't the man have any work to do? "This officer is far too experienced to fall for your cheap tricks."

"Guess you're right," I said, sheepishly. "Sorry. You can't blame me for trying. By the way, Pepper's wondering where her keys are. She's hoping I can go over tomorrow and pick out some toiletries."

"I could send a uniform," Tierney said.

I shook my head. "Too personal. Whenever you're ready to give up the keys, let me know. I'll say good night to Pepper now."

Pepper gave me the high sign as I left, and then she turned an anxious eye toward Tierney. Tierney didn't think I should stay on to hear whatever he had to say.

Mavis Morley's kind face was full of questions, but she handed over the key without a fight. "I sure hope Mrs. Monahan's better soon."

I nodded. "Me, too."

"It's hard to believe that Mr. Monahan would do such a thing," she said, shaking her tight gray perm. "There was never any sign of anything like that."

"No," I said, "there wasn't."

"I don't hold with that at all, wife beating. I didn't think he was the type. Her, neither."

"We'll wait and see what the police turn up. They haven't proved that he did it."

"But they're looking for him."

"Yes, but I'm not convinced, and his wife's *absolutely* not convinced."

"The poor thing. But that's often the way, isn't it? They can't accept that it happened to them."

I pulled up in front of Pepper's house and noticed the unmarked car parked two houses down the street. My favorite bright young officer was sitting in it looking alert and on the ball. I was pretty sure he'd already spotted me, too. So much for checking out the Monahan house surreptitiously. I got out of the Matrix and walked back to his car, hoping for a chance of picking up some new information.

"No luck yet?" I said.

"No sign of him." I imagined he was thinking, *This is Nick Monahan. Anything's possible.*

I added, "I don't suppose he'll come home when there's an APB out for him."

He shrugged. "Or if he saw me talking to you for that matter. That might scare him off."

"You're right. You guys could do better in the camouflage department."

"Tell me about it," he said with a quick grin. "I'm only a foot soldier. I don't get to make those strategic decisions."

"Nice to see you," I said. "Gotta go now. Good luck with your assignment."

"You, too," he said with a wide grin. "Watch out for Tierney. He's on the warpath."

I hoped that meant he wouldn't let Tierney know that I'd been cruising down Old Pine Street.

I made a quick call to my friend, Rose Skipowski, to check how she was doing and to ask a big favor. She was doing fine and she was happy to help. That left me at loose ends. I headed home to Truffle and Sweet Marie. We had a walk, they had some food, and I tried a bit of training. When the dogs took their hourly nap, I sat at my little desk and made a list of the things that were bothering me.

Top of the list was Where's Nick? followed by:

+ *If he's still alive, what is Nick afraid of?*
+ *Who hurt Pepper? And why?*
+ *Will they try again?*
+ *Why did Pepper go to Bakker Beach?*

The issues about Anabel Beauchamp, her tragic death, and her mother's obsession would have to go on a separate list. There was so much to worry about that it put my little no-barking project with Truffle and Sweet Marie into perspective, that was for sure. The worst part was that there wasn't much I could do to find answers to any of those questions.

18

I took an ice cream break before I picked up Ramona's file to have another look at the information there. Reading it in CYCotics hadn't been ideal for concentration. I had stopped reading closely in the excitement of spotting Brad Dykstra's name as the paramedic who'd been first to the scene when Anabel died. Now, I took my time and read closely and carefully. Nick Monahan's name appeared in one of the articles as one of the officers at the site. I decided it was worth it to try and find the name of the other officer so I could ask him or her about Nick's behavior. In the third clipping an Officer Dean Oliver was quoted. *Got him now*, I said to myself. I wasn't sure exactly what I'd be asking this Officer Oliver, though, so when I finished checking through the files and clippings, I decided to take a little trip. There was still plenty of June evening before it got dark. And the time was right.

Truffle and Sweet Marie were quite happy to come along with me and try a walk in another neighborhood. We piled into the Matrix. I parked two blocks away from the construction site, took the doggies and the roll of brightly colored poop bags, and set out. "No barking," I admonished.

It was a soft and fragrant evening, the end of a beautiful sunny day that I hadn't enjoyed at all. The old lilac trees here and there were at their peak, and the scent was wonderful. The warm days and convenient heavy rains in the middle of each night had been great for the greenery. Woodbridge was in bloom. I noted a small but steady amount of traffic in the area. The man I'd seen previously with the jaunty straw fedora whizzed by on his motorized scooter, setting off a blizzard of barking from my canine companions. He tipped his fedora at me and seemed to find the dogs amusing. That was more than I felt as the dream of therapy dog success continued to fade. As we sauntered along, we passed an elderly couple out for a stroll. Luckily they didn't have a dog for Truffle and Sweet Marie to bark at. A police car drove slowly down the street, and a man in a leather jacket melted away before it did its slow roll past. I could tell from his shape and movements that he was young. Dimitri? I couldn't be sure. We strolled past the point where he had disappeared. I saw there was a dingy alley leading to nowhere that could be any good.

As we approached the construction site, I slowed, pretending to wait for the dogs to sniff every pole. A yellow pickup with the construction company logo was parked nearby. It was exactly the kind of fence that the misfits used to hurl themselves over for the hell of it, when we weren't in Jack's basement watching slacker movies.

I stopped and stared as the gate to the site stood open. I couldn't believe my eyes. How could this company be so careless after what had happened to Anabel? I reminded myself that the truth was, I didn't know what had happened to Anabel. I stepped closer to the door and let Truffle follow his twitchy black nose into the opening. I followed and found myself staring at a pair of work boots. I glanced up and met the eyes of a scowling man with a yellow hard hat. Make that two men in hard hats. The second one grinned and pointed at Truffle and Sweet Marie, who had joined him.

"Oops," I said. "The gate was open and the dogs pulled me in."

"It's a dangerous spot, miss," the second man said. "Especially for wiener dogs." He bent down to let Truffle and Sweet Marie sniff his hand. They might bark at babies and little old ladies, but they wagged their tales at this huge, scary individual. Not barking? Maybe that was good news for my training project.

"Isn't this where that terrible accident took place?" I asked. "It is dangerous. I'm surprised the door was still open."

The first man said, "That gate was open because we're here to check out something in the site. It's not open to the public, and I have to ask you to move back onto the sidewalk. We have insurance issues."

"I'm sure you must," I said.

"The project is about to go ahead again. And we'd like everyone to stay alive. The mud is real slippery," the second man said, standing up again. "You need to have boots with grip."

"Of course," I said, glancing at the foundation, which had even more water in it than the first time I'd peeked through the slot. "Come on, Truffle and Sweet Marie. This isn't a place for us. Remember what happened to Anabel."

Was it my imagination or did the two men exchange that cliché known as meaningful glances?

"That was tragic," the second man said. Mentally, I thought of him as Mr. Friendly, while the other guy had become Mr. Grumpy.

Mr. Grumpy said, "Yeah, and it was brought on by her being in a place that she didn't belong at a time she shouldn't have been here."

I said inanely, "I don't see how she could have fallen into that foundation."

Mr. Friendly said, "But the fact is that she did. And we wish to avoid liability for—"

Mr. Grumpy jumped in. "Idiots who get into places they don't belong."

"Don't mind us," I responded with a smile. "We're on our way. I imagine you'll be getting that foundation pumped out soon."

There were still people around on the street as I exited. Granted it was now June, and Anabel had died in March. But it would still have been light enough at that time of year. After daylight saving starts in March, if the weather's nice, people are happy to step out for a bit in the evening after the dreariness of winter. How could no one have seen or heard Anabel?

Brad Dykstra's comment echoed in my mind. It could have been an accident. Had I exaggerated the doubt in his voice? I stared back toward the site. I knew the wooden formwork around the foundation hole was muddy and high, with nowhere to get a grip. There was still enough water to drown in easily. I could see how the police, never looking to boost either the murder rate or the unsolved rate, would consign it to the "accidental" category.

What the hell had Anabel been doing behind that fence in the first place? The dogs chose to bark at something across the street, and I turned to look. The fedora man zipped by on his scooter again. He waved up at someone in the apartment building. I noticed a figure appear by a row of plants in a second-floor balcony across the street. Did those people worry about the lonely death of a young woman practically under their own windows? Did any of them ask themselves, *If only I had glanced out or chosen to water my plants at the right time, could I have prevented that tragic death?*

———

At nine o'clock I settled the dogs in and headed for Rose's place. I was wearing a pair of running shoes, black yoga pants, a stretchy tee, and my jean jacket with a jaunty scarf. Comfortable enough to jump a fence. Rose was happy to comply with the favor, which was to lend me her car.

"Do you want me to come with you?" Lilith asked.

I shook my head. "In case there's any issue, I'd like to keep you out of it. You don't need the cops on your back. Not that I'm doing anything illegal."

Shortly after ten, it was finally dark enough. I cruised down Old Pine Street. I didn't see any signs of the unmarked car. Maybe they were getting smarter. I parked around the corner and sneaked across the backyard, dodging moonbeams and hoping none of the neighbors spotted me. Luckily the mature trees in Pepper's backyard were in full leaf, so I was probably safe.

The key worked, the code worked, and I was in. I locked the door behind me, in case the smart, young police officer came back and gave it a try.

It was a beautiful night with an inconvenient full moon. I reminded myself that I had Pepper's permission to enter her house. It was not in any way a crime scene, and I didn't have to worry much about the police. Still, I didn't want Tierney knowing what I was up to, even if it wasn't illegal. I didn't turn on the lights. At this point, the full moon came in handy. There were no signs that Nick had been around, although who knows what those signs would be? Based on my theory that everyone has a secret in their closet, I was hoping to find Nick's.

The bedroom closet was full of Pepper's clothing. No surprise. The second bedroom was the nursery.

I tried the closet in the third bedroom. If I had my geography right, this one was right over the front porch. I took

a peek out the window. No police car in view. That was
good. This was Nick's playroom all right. I found workout
gear, weights, and a treadmill set up in front of a television
with a DVD player attached. Lots of action DVDs stored
underneath. I ran my finger over the equipment. Even in
the pale moonlight, I could tell it was dusty. Pepper had
said that Nick had been distracted lately, so no great surprise. I opened the closet and found it full of men's clothing. Nick's spare uniform and his neatly pressed shirts,
long and short sleeved, were hanging there as well as a lot
of casual clothes, neatly hung up, shirts together, casual
shirts folded on a shelf, jeans neatly positioned. I found
a stack of men's magazines. Nick probably thought Pepper wouldn't touch those, so that he would feel that was
a good place to hide something, if he had something to
hide, which being Nick he would have to have. Pepper on
the other hand would be well aware of the fact that Nick
would have something to hide and Nick would think she
wouldn't check the men's magazines. I shook them all out,
but nothing suspicious fluttered from their pages. So much
for my complicated thinking. I felt around the back of the
walls and on the shelves about. I stuck my hands in the
shoes. Nada.

Was Nick capable of finding an unusual hiding place for
anything? I was somewhat hampered by the fact that I had
no idea what kind of secret item I might be looking for. I
had nothing more than my lame theory.

I jerked my head back out of the closet at a sound. What
was that? A scrape? The sound came from downstairs. Had
the police officer watching the house spotted me entering
the back door? But I'd locked that door behind me. Had a
neighbor seen me and alerted the cops? A wave of panic
washed over me. Why hadn't I reset the alarm? Where
could I hide? The closet seemed a possibility, but it was
way too small for me and Nick's clothing.

The scrape had turned into a slight bumping noise, then a soft *thump, thump, thump*. I have spent enough time with Jack Reilly to recognize that as sock feet on the stairs. I gasped, whirled foolishly, and dived into the end of the closet. I pressed myself to the far wall and did my best to get my breathing under control. I thought I sounded like a locomotive pulling out of a historic station. I stayed slumped in that corner and hoped if worse came to worse that I'd be hidden by Nick's Levi's. Minutes passed. Or possibly hours.

I jerked when the closet door opened, barely surpressed a gasp. I held my breath as somebody rapidly whipped through the clothing. Whoever that somebody was, he was breathing hard. And he was also in desperate need of a shower. Sometimes your deodorant isn't up to the job, and this guy was having one of those days. A cop? I didn't think so. Whatever you can say about them, cops are well groomed, proud of their appearance. As the last pair of jeans shielding me from view shifted, I squeaked in panic. Not that my would-be attacker heard because he screamed. A familiar voice.

I said, "Shh."

"Charley?"

"Nick?"

"What are you doing here?"

"I might say the same for you."

He decided to brazen it out. "I live here."

"Yeah and there's an APB out for you."

"That's a mistake."

"I'm sure it is." I crawled out of the closet and managed to hold my head high.

Nick said, "Why were you in my closet?"

"Hiding, of course. Why else would I be there? I'm here to get some stuff for Pepper and I didn't want the cops to see me and—"

Nick burst out, "They say she's in the hospital. I heard it on the radio. They say she's badly hurt and she may not even—" To give him credit, his voice rose in anguish.

"She's a bit better. She can talk. But she's been horribly injured."

He ran both hands through his hair, speechless for once.

"They're saying that you did it, Nick."

His eyes were wild, like those of a panicked horse, handsome but doomed. "Ah, Charley, you don't believe that, do you?"

"You are connected somehow. So you'd better tell me what the hell is going on."

He let out a long wail. "I don't know."

"Pull yourself together. What happened at Bakker Beach?"

He shook his head. In the pale light in the room, Nick Monahan looked like death not even warmed over. He smelled pretty revolting, too. "I wasn't there."

"Your squad car was there."

"They took it. They took it, and they must have tricked her into meeting me there."

"Who are 'they'?"

Nick slumped against the wall. "I don't know who they were. They got behind me somehow and must have knocked me out. I guess they took the squad car and got Pepper somehow."

"Nick, no one is going to believe that. It's too crazy."

He whispered in his best little boy voice, "But I need you to believe me. I was out cold. By the time I came to, it was night. I had to hitch back to town. Losing the squad car like that is the worst thing that could happen to a cop."

"Not the worst thing, Nick. I'd say what happened to your wife beats being embarrassed about losing the car."

He hung his head, still a bad little boy at heart. "You're right, Charley. That's the worst thing ever."

His cell phone rang, and he reached into his pants pocket, pulled it out, and flicked it open. He closed it. "Tierney, trying to psych me out. They all keep calling."

"Why do you keep it on?"

"In case it's Pepper."

Well, Pepper had instructed me to find Nick. At least he was alive. That would be good news for her. The fact that he didn't make sense was a blip. And of course, his story could be true. Not even Nick was dopey enough to make this up.

"Okay, let's go over it. Where were you when this happened?"

"I was on routine patrol about two o'clock when I got a text to meet Pepper behind the storage units out in the old industrial park. Remember we all used to make out there?"

"Speak for yourself. And you didn't think that was strange?"

"I thought maybe . . . I don't know what I thought, but you know Pepper, when she wants something, she gets it. I went."

"Where did the text message say Little Nick would be?"

Nick goggled at me. "It didn't."

"You don't think that Pepper would have mentioned that?"

"I guess so. But my mind wasn't on him at the time. I don't ever have to worry about Little Nick. Pepper does that."

I decided not to comment on that. "Did you call her?"

"No. I drove out to the industrial park."

"All on official time?"

He shrugged and grinned sheepishly. "It was a quiet day."

"You must have called in something."

"Don't get mad at me, Charley. I was having trouble concentrating."

"Because you were afraid of something or someone?"

"Pepper sounded like she was in the mood."

"Huh. So, okay, so while you were unconscious in the industrial park, someone must have tricked your wife into going to Bakker Beach, then driven your squad car out there, attacked Pepper, and left her to die. And guess who was set up for that?"

"But Charley—"

"Listen. You have to give yourself up, and you absolutely have to tell the police who and what you are afraid of. Obviously you have a good reason to be afraid. And it's not just you. Think of your family."

"I told you, I don't know."

From downstairs I heard the sound of a door splintering.

I whispered, "Aren't the police supposed to call out a warning before they kick the door in?"

Nick said, "You have to make sure nobody kills Pepper. You're the only one I trust."

"What?"

There was no answer from Nick as he flung open the window and vanished through it, scrambling over the porch roof to God knows where, leaving me to face whoever was thundering up the stairs. This time it was too late to hide in the closet.

19

As much as I'd been avoiding Connor Tierney, I was sure glad to see him and his pounding feet this time. I had an emotional wave of relief, which was understandable but not convenient. A large part of that relief was because none of the officers had shot Nick Monahan. He was just lucky they hadn't known which room we were in and had checked out the downstairs before thundering up.

"Don't think these are tears," I said to Tierney. "I'm suffering from spring allergies."

"Who asked?" Tierney said. He had led the charge up the stairs, a couple of armed uniformed officers following behind, weapons drawn. He also switched on the lights and took a hard look out the open window through which Nick had apparently catapulted.

Tierney turned back from the open window and said, "Who went out there? Was that Nick?"

I opened my mouth but no sound came out. But I knew I had to tell him the truth. "Yes."

"Where did he go?"

"I have no idea."

Tierney shot me a poisonous look. "Did you arrange to meet him here?"

"What? Of course not."

"It sure looks that way. You made sure the officer on guard didn't see you. You didn't turn the lights on. Why was that?"

"I didn't want a hassle about being here, if you must know. Pepper asked me to get her a few things."

"She didn't have her keys. I was dropping them off tomorrow."

I decided to brazen it out. I didn't want to be hauled into the cop shop. It had been a bad enough day. "That's a long time to wait for a toothbrush."

"Where's the toothbrush?"

"What?"

"You said you were getting Pepper's toothbrush."

"Haven't had a chance to get anything yet. There was someone in the house, remember? I didn't know it was Nick when I heard him come up the stairs, so I hid in this closet. But I'd better get her stuff now."

As I headed to Pepper's room, Tierney followed. "Are you sure you don't know where Nick went?"

"I wish I did," I said. That was true, too. But at least I could tell Pepper he was alive and pass on the bizarre story of the message to meet him. I had to tell Tierney, too. I relayed Nick's tale about being tricked into going to the storage area in the industrial park and knocked out and having his squad car stolen.

The young officer popped his head into the room at that moment. From the look on his face, neither he nor Tierney was buying Nick's version of what had happened. They exchanged glances, and I felt like a dope. If Tierney hadn't been there, I would have asked the young cop his opinion of Nick's possible guilt, but I didn't want to do that with those icy blue eyes watching.

I said, "I'm passing it along, but for the record, I don't find it any harder to believe than the theory that Nick would attack Pepper." I located a small rolling suitcase in Pepper's closet and picked out toothpaste and other basics from her en suite. I couldn't tell who owned which tooth-brush, so I decided to buy a fresh one for Pepper. I rustled up a pretty nightgown and a change of clothing, including underwear. I assumed she wouldn't be able to shampoo, and I tried to find hair products that would help. I took my time picking out a flattering outfit. I figured Pepper would be coming home soon and it might cheer her up to have her clothing ready to go. I added a photo of Little Nick to the lot. I tried not to think about where Nick would be in that little family.

Tierney watched me as I worked. I tried to ignore him as I moved on to Little Nick's bedroom. The room was better furnished than most people's living rooms, with bird's-eye maple crib, dresser, and changing table as well as a match-ing rocking chair with a cushioned seat. I got my bearings and gathered up a few extra items I thought Jack might need until Pepper got out of the hospital. Of course, while I can pick out what a woman would want in the hospital, I wasn't so sure I got all the right stuff for Little Nick. I took a package of diapers and some little outfits. I stepped over to the crib and picked up the blanket and a giraffe and a blue cow. They must have been favorites to get the prime crib real estate.

Tierney said, "I can tell when you're lying. Your eyes move the wrong way."

Another thing to worry about, the way my eyes moved. Lucky for me I was telling the truth. I couldn't even guess where Nick had gone. I slumped on the rocking chair and blurted out, "Fine, arrest me. Ruin my night. I don't know where Nick is. Let me take this stuff to Pepper first."

Tierney glanced behind him, but his uniforms had headed off to search the foundation shrubs and backyard for Nick before fanning out into the neighborhood. "It doesn't look good for me, either, you know, to be dating someone who gets arrested."

I said peevishly, "It was only one date. You didn't call me back, remember?"

"I had a good reason, which you know, and there was almost a second date, although fate seems to be conspiring against it." Tierney sighed, then said, "So where has he been?"

"Didn't get that far. He never said. He is totally stressed out. He said not to let anyone kill Pepper."

"Why would anyone want to kill Pepper?"

"Let me remind you that someone did try to kill Pepper. I was about to explore that idea with him and was trying to get him to turn himself in. I was making progress until you kicked in the door and came thundering up the stairs and he went flying out the window."

"Where did he—?"

"I have no idea. That is true, so stop badgering me."

"He didn't give any clue?"

"Well, I can tell you that wherever he's been, they didn't have a shower. I think he wanted to come home and get showered and change into some clean clothes. He sure didn't smell great."

"Did he get any clean clothing?"

I looked around and didn't see articles of clothing lying around. "He picked out some clothing, but I couldn't make out what."

Tierney said, "Now, that wasn't so hard, was it? You should try cooperating with the authorities more often."

"If you weren't so difficult, maybe I would. The main

thing is that he couldn't have attacked Pepper if he was knocked out behind the storage units."

Tierney laughed a bit longer than was absolutely necessary. "I can't believe you fell for that one."

"I believe him."

"Who could have known that was a special place for them? Who would have known his number? Who would have—"

"Are you kidding? Nick has such a big mouth. I think every one of my friends knew about that spot. We all knew about Bakker Beach, too. We all grew up together here in Woodbridge. There aren't many well-kept secret make-out spots among teenagers."

"Maybe one of your friends *was* involved."

"You can forget that idea. By the way, if you guys hadn't splintered the door, Nick wouldn't have jumped out the window and I might have found out something useful. I can't believe that you think—"

"Stop saying that."

"What?"

"That we splintered the door."

"Well, you did. You didn't yell a warning, either."

"We didn't."

"But I distinctly heard that back door being broken down."

Tierney shrugged. "We heard that, too, and that's why we rushed the house. I took the back, and I can tell you that door had already been kicked open."

"But I used keys and I locked it behind me. Nick must have had an extra set. Most people do. Anyway, he was already upstairs with me, and we both heard the door being kicked in. I thought it took you long enough to get upstairs."

Tierney stared at me, apparently not quite ready to accept this latest revelation.

I said, "But that means there was someone else in the house. Someone who was following Nick perhaps. Or me. It could be the person who attacked Pepper."

"I doubt that was the case."

I said, "Well, I realize you think Nick attacked her, but I don't. Plus I know what I heard here. And if that intruder didn't go out the back or the front door, then he might still be here. That's the person who's after Nick and who injured Pepper."

He glowered at me and left the room to call out to the uniformed officers. I could hear him instructing them where to look. I thought I heard him say, "Humor her," but I could have been wrong. I was glad he'd left the room, because I hadn't given up on the idea that, like all of us, Nick would have some secret in his closet. And I'd had an idea of a good place for Nick to stash something. I stuck my hands into the pockets of his spare uniform and came up with a small rectangle of paper, thickly folded. I slipped it into my own pocket and went to find Tierney again. I'd already decided I'd fill him in if it proved relevant to the investigation, but not if it turned out to be some kind of confession or private note to Pepper.

Call me sentimental.

When I bumped into Tierney, he announced that the search showed no one hiding in the house. I said, "Tell me, how did you know I was here?" I didn't mention that I'd been careful to dodge the squad car out front on my second visit.

"We got a call."

"Really? From whom?"

"Apparently someone called 911 and said there was a break-in. Must have been a neighbor. Of course, we had a uniform keeping an eye, and he figured Nick must have gotten into the house. And look at that, we nabbed you instead."

"Just lucky," I said. "So no idea exactly who called 911?"

"I don't have any idea, but if I did, guess what?"

"Well, only a minute or two elapsed between the splintering of the back door and your arrival. So it couldn't have been that 911 call."

"Charlotte, let me make this clear. You are not a detective. I am. You should stop looking for clues and perpetrators and let us do our job without interfering. Do you understand that? I hope so, because I mean it."

"No need to be nasty," I said.

There was no more talk of dates, and that was fine by me as I left, head as high as I could hold it, rolling the suitcase behind me. As I walked through the front door this time, one of the cops shouted out from the back of the house. "Looks like whoever it was got the security tapes. Didn't want to leave an image of himself." I wasn't sure which cop was talking. I wondered briefly if Nick had taken the tape. After all, what did he have to lose by being on the tape? No, my money was on someone else.

Tierney was right behind me. The key jingling was truly annoying by this time. I had just opened my mouth to suggest that the tape must have been taken by the person who kicked the door in, when he said, "By the way, did Nick have his cell phone with him?"

I blinked. "Yes, it rang and when he saw it was you, he turned it off."

He said, "So he has that phone? Good. We have evidence that a text was sent from Nick's phone to Pepper's twenty-five minutes before you found her at Bakker Beach. That's about enough time for her to drive out there, get attacked, and have you arrive. Still think Nick didn't have anything to do with that?"

‡

Of course, there was no way to get into Pepper's hospital room at that time of night. And it was too late to bring back Rose's car and collect the Matrix. I drove home, tired and worried. To my surprise, Jack was heading up my staircase with Little Nick in tow. "We've been watching the full moon in the backyard until the little dude fell asleep. It was awesome."

The baby's eyes popped open at the sound of Jack's voice.

"We dropped off to see the little dude's mom, didn't we fella?" Jack said.

"How is she?"

"Glad to see us. And maybe not quite herself." Jack paused. "Little dude reacted a bit to her face. Those injuries were horrible. How could anyone do that to Pepper?"

"I have no idea how. Or who."

"Did you know she's trying to make sure someone locates her parents to tell them not to come to town? I can't imagine doing that."

"Think back, Jack. It will all make sense. Contrast your wonderful childhood and her horrible one."

For the first time, I asked myself if that was why Pepper valued Nick: He didn't hit her, he didn't physically intimidate her or put her down. He was no prize, but maybe he was what she needed. But what do I know?

Jack said, "Oh right. I guess it's hard to understand what it was like to grow up in her family."

"Yes, and by the way, you have some kind of green baby food in your hair," I said helpfully. "I'm not sure that's a good look for you."

"All part of the package."

"What package?"

"The practice daddy package. Babies are complicated. I think I needed more training, but we're keeping afloat. Aren't we, little dude?"

The child did seem happy enough. But how long would that last? I wondered if Jack would be cured of his baby fantasies by the time Pepper got home.

I said, "I ordered pizza. You need to keep your strength up if you're going to keep doing this."

"Why wouldn't I keep doing it? I love this little dude, and it's mutual, in a nonverbal way. I'm here as long as he needs me. I rearranged CYCotics to make it a bit more baby friendly."

"Huh," I said.

"And I thought of a new product line."

"What?"

"You know if I had one of those baby trailers for my bike I could take the little dude to work without stuffing him into the car. So I ordered them for the shop."

"Let me repeat. Huh. Oh wait, there's more. If Pepper ever got wind of you driving her baby through the streets of Woodbridge in a canvas-sided conveyance on the back of a bike, you would have to find Nick and join him in hiding. I would then have to start hoping that you were alive, too. Don't you think I have enough to worry about already, Jack?"

"I'll let you worry about that. I'm going to try to attract young parents in, try the family promotion. Expand a bit from the racing and mountain-biking crowd. It still needs work, but we'll get there."

Luckily the pizza arrived and ended that conversation. I told myself that tomato sauce was a vegetable and anchovies were fish and so Jack and I were on the right track. I watched Jack reading to Little Nick from one of my shoe catalogues. He was making up a pretty good tale about Mr. and Mrs. Shoe and all the little sneakers. I let my mind wander. Truffle and Sweet Marie had gone from apprehensive to jealous to bitter and were ignoring me, although I was totally available to them. My mind drifted back to

Pepper. How had it come to be that we had her baby in my apartment in the care of the two most unparent-like adults I could imagine? And even more worrisome, what would happen to Pepper? What *had* happened to her? And on a less important note, what were all those photos of me about?

I reminded myself not to dwell on the box in Jack's so-called closet. I had bigger issues to worry about.

Eventually Jack conked out on the sofa, which came as no surprise. Little Nick fell asleep beside him and didn't wake up when I placed him gently in his portable crib, safe from any territorial behavior by the pooches. I placed myself in the bathtub with a large capful of jasmine-scented bath salts and a new mix on the iPod. I tried to let the strains of the day slip away.

I should have known better. Lounging in the bathtub always triggers buried thoughts. Sure enough, they rose to the surface. Pepper was so badly injured, it was highly unlikely she could have locked the doors of the Edge. The person hit her but didn't shoot her. Why? Crime of passion? Impulse? Or just didn't have a gun? How had the person gotten close to her in the first place if it wasn't Nick? Was Nick right, that the purpose of this attack was to get Pepper? If so, I figured there was a second purpose and that was to frame Nick for the attack. I had no clue who would want to frame Nick, but I was pretty sure that same person had kicked in the door of Pepper and Nick's house. I couldn't imagine any woman I'd ever met striking Pepper that way. And most women wouldn't have the physical strength to kick in that door. But this was playing the odds. I had no idea who the attacker was. But this would-be killer knew Pepper and Nick and must have had something to gain by harming one or both. An angry husband perhaps? Someone who might want revenge for one of Nick's poaching parties? I couldn't rule this out. Or a criminal? There would be great satisfaction in bringing down two members of Woodbridge's foremost police families. Something else struck me: That person saw me arrive at Bakker Beach and stole my car. Did he or she think that I might be a witness? My address was on my documents in the glove compartment. Was I in danger, too? In that case, was Jack? Or Little Nick? What should I do about that?

I glanced at the clock. Should I mention this latest series of brain waves to Connor Tierney? It was close to midnight by this time. How would he interpret a phone call from me? And would he take it seriously? Or would he have it all figured out by this point?

I got out of the bath less relaxed than I went in. Jack was still snoring on the sofa, and I didn't want to wake him up, although that's not so easy to do at the best of times.

I prepared my To Do list for the next day and then chose my outfit for the morning, making sure it would be practical enough for Wendy's project yet sufficiently elegant for the Beauchamps and—though I hated to plan for it—also suitable for television, in case I made Todd Tyrell's news and commentary. I picked charcoal pants instead of a skirt, a fine cotton cardigan in cream, and a pair of medium heels in bronze with gladiator details.

I exfoliated my face, took care of toothies, slathered on body lotion, straightened up the living room (not including Jack and Little Nick), and found myself wide awake. I have a personal rule about not working at night, a holdover from my former job where that was the normal state of affairs. So no work. I looked around for something that needed dealing with. My apartment consists of a living room, a spacious bedroom, which includes a small office space, a tiny galley kitchen, and a vast bathroom. I am only one person and I keep it under control.

What to do?

I decided to get ahead of schedule on the routine maintenance. I packed away the last of my cool weather gear and my early spring outfits in labeled containers. I took out the rest of my summer clothing at the same time. I put aside items that wouldn't make it another season, planning to take them with me on my next trip to the women's shelter. I washed and pressed what needed to be freshened up.

After an hour of this, I went to bed. Every sleep trick in the book wasn't enough to let me have a good night's rest. My mind was whirling. I saw Pepper. I saw Nick. I saw poor Anabel. I saw people from my past, the dead and the dangerous. When I finally fell into a deep sleep somewhere around four, I was awakened by a siren. I sat up and gasped. Were we on fire? I raced into the living room, sniffing for smoke and tripping over a pair of panicked dogs.

I shrieked, "Where is it? Call 911!"

Jack sat up and yawned. "What?"

Turned out that Little Nick has quite the set of lungs. Could have fooled anyone. I guessed he'd been saving it all up for the middle of the night.

"It's the baby, Jack. I don't know how you could have missed hearing him screaming."

Jack said, "The little dude? Okay, that's all right then," and immediately fell back to dreamland. It takes more than loud noises to bring him to full consciousness. I picked up Little Nick and tried to make soothing sounds. What had I seen Sally do with her babies? He howled as I prepared a bottle for him, desperately trying to remember how it was done. Why hadn't I paid more attention? It all looked so natural, even easy, but apparently there are techniques.

Truffle and Sweet Marie joined us in the kitchen and barked. I took that as a suggestion that they, too, could be calmed by warm milk.

It took an hour of feeding and burping, interspersed with howling, before Little Nick settled down. In another five minutes, Truffle and Sweet Marie got their groove back. I crawled back to bed wondering how mothers do it. And why.

———✦✦———

Shadowy figures crowded my dreams, making trouble and noise. *Go back*, they exhorted in their shadowy way. *Go back*, total strangers cried. My mother flitted through, her arm linked with an elderly French count. *Go back*, she ordered. Even Pepper had a cameo appearance. *Go back*, she whimpered. *I can't!* I kept shouting. Naturally, all night long it was impossible to go back.

Tierney showed up in my dreams toward dawn. "Don't even think about going back," he said before fading into the woods at Bakker Beach.

Attach an inexpensive double-hanging rod to your existing closet rod to dramatically expand your space for hanging tops, shirts, jackets, and pants.

20

In the morning, Jack and I were tied for worst-looking human being in New York State, but Little Nick was ready to party. I stumbled back from walking Truffle and Sweet Marie, shaking my head and trying to dislodge the clinging shreds of dreams. It's not like me to be groggy and inept in the morning. I hated it.

"You were sure making a lot of noise in your sleep last night," Jack said, rubbing his spectacular bed head and actually making it worse, although I wouldn't have thought that possible.

I glared at him. "In the greater scheme of things, how does my so-called noise stack up to your sleeping through a screaming baby opera and, might I add, with your mouth open and drooling?"

"You're such a kidder, Charlotte. The little dude didn't scream."

I rolled my eyes. "Before you get too deep into this daddy daydream of yours, you might want to work on the graveyard shift part of it."

"What's gotten into her this morning? Little dude's an excellent sleeper, aren't you?" He picked up the baby.

"Whatever."

"We're off to work right after breakfast. We know where we are appreciated and where we're not. But do you mind keeping an eye on him while I have a shower, Charlotte?"

I didn't argue. It wouldn't have done any good if I had. And I thought a shower would definitely improve Jack's public persona. I did my best to rustle up some grub for the baby and shovel it into him while the dogs eyed the child and the food. If I read their expressions correctly, they were not at all pleased to see the interloper still on the property.

As for Little Nick, he thought it might be fun to pull their ears. I put an end to that before there was an incident involving fingers.

Luckily Jack and the baby were gone before long, leaving a residue of pureed pears that was quickly hardening to cement on my coffee table. At any rate, I knew they'd end up having a good time at CYCotics while I was struggling with the junk in my head and the dream images I couldn't shake.

Go back? What was that all about? My dreams never make much sense, but they usually involve sorting things out. Striving to put things right despite the resistance of nightmarish dream clients. There is no going back in my dreams. I hate going back. I am all about moving forward, getting things done.

Tierney had been in those dreams and that reminded me. I picked up the phone and gave him a call. I noticed with a bit of surprise that I knew his number by heart. I left a message to the effect that, although he thought Nick was the bad guy, I knew he wasn't and Nick had been worried about his family. I suggested that Tierney might consider protecting Little Nick as well as Pepper.

After wasting too much time pacing, I pulled myself together and turned my attention to my To Do list. It did not have *Go back* on it. It didn't have anything about watching television, either. I clicked over to WINY and caught a blinding from Todd Tyrell's chompers.

> *Woodbridge Police continue their hunt for rogue police*
> *officer Nick Monahan. Monahan is suspected of hav-*
> *ing inflicted life threatening damage on his wife, star*
> *detective Pepper Monahan.*

Nick's boyish features splashed across the screen followed by a shot of Pepper in all her pre-pregnancy glamour. A lovely image of the two of them at their wedding followed. Todd yattered throughout.

> *Monahan is considered armed and dangerous.*

"He doesn't have his gun, you jackass," I shouted at the television. "And it's Nick. How dangerous could he be?"

I was scowling as I went back to the To Do list. Up until now, the day had looked simple enough:

+ *Take suitcase to Pepper*
+ *Pick up and deliver organizing tools for Wendy*
+ *Wendy wrap-up*
+ *Decision re: Lorelei*
+ *Dog training—bark project*

I stared at my list and added, *Go back?* I don't usually let my dreams dictate my waking hours, but I couldn't get this phrase out of my head.

I found a trusting young officer on duty at the hospital, and I was able to talk my way into Pepper's room with her suitcase. I was grateful but didn't predict a stellar career for him.

Pepper opened her eyes and glared at me, if it was a glare. It was hard to interpret her expression with all the damage to her face.

"First things first." I took the framed photo of the baby out of the suitcase and put it on the small bedside table. Pepper's expression softened, and I spotted a trail of tears trickling down each cheek. I said, "I know you must be worried, but Little Nick is still with Jack and still in good shape. He has slept and eaten and been bathed. They have bonded, and I imagine Little Nick will have a part-time job in CYCotics after his first birthday. He is apparently very good for business. Second, I have a change of clothing for you, some fresh nightgowns, and some toiletries. I brought your hairbrush and a few other things. When they let you out of bed, I thought that would cheer you a bit."

"You know what would cheer me? Knowing where my husband is."

"Me, too," I blurted.

"I told you to find him."

"I almost did. I checked your house under the guise of getting you these things. Nick turned up. He must still have the keys."

She sat up abruptly. "He's always misplacing his so he keeps a couple of sets hidden here and there. Where is he now?"

So much for my key theory. "Take it easy, Pepper. It's a long story, but when Tierney showed, Nick jumped out the bedroom window. But before that, he was all right, if you don't count sweaty and hysterical."

"Jumped out the window? Was he hurt?"

"It was the one in the room where he keeps his clothing. The porch roof must have worked in his favor. He must have shinnied down the post. Look on the bright side. He hasn't been found, so he couldn't have been injured. All the cops were in the house, so I imagine he got away without a problem."

Of course, Nick's problems were getting worse, but I was conscious that Pepper was not at her best for dealing with this.

She narrowed her eyes in that dangerous way she has. "What were you doing in that room?"

"Hiding." I sat down on the visitor's chair so I could make better eye contact with her. "I heard someone moving around and I hid in the closet. Nick came in to get some clothes, and we almost scared each other to death. But he's all right, and if you can convince Tierney not to pursue him in the media, I think we can keep him safe until—"

"Until what?"

"We find out what's going on. Pepper, you need to know this. He told me that someone sent him a message that he had to meet you behind the storage units at the industrial park. He was attacked there and his gun was taken and his squad car stolen."

She stared. "We haven't been there since we were teenagers. Who would do such a thing?"

And was it true? I wondered.

She said, "Did you tell Tierney?"

"I thought he needed to know how this attack could have happened and to see how Nick could have been set up."

She nodded, although that was probably painful. "Yeah, that Tierney. There's something about him I don't trust."

"You don't trust him?"

"I do not. He came from a big city force and he thinks he's a cut above everyone. I will be senior to him when I go back and I think he resents that. We'll be in competition for promotions, only I have the better connections. Also I think he's jealous of Nick."

If I hadn't been sitting, I would have fallen down at that. "Jealous of Nick?" I said weakly.

"Yes. I know you don't think Nick is very bright. Fair enough. That's not where his strength lies. I admit that, Charlotte. But everyone likes him. Even you, even when you're upset. He's irresistible."

I supposed she was right. Why did I even bother with Nick? He was always hitting on me, he was a less-than-perfect husband, and he was far less intelligent than my microwave oven. Of course, I was convinced he hadn't done what he was accused of. This belief was strong enough for me to drown out the warning voices in my own head.

Pepper was still ranting. "And he's always been a popular guy on the force."

No wonder everyone's so tense about the APB. They're hunting one of their own, I thought.

Pepper continued. "Tierney doesn't fit in and he never will. Ever!"

"Do you think that's important to him? He's a senior officer, seems pretty independent. Does he care if the boys don't ask him out for a brew when Nick gets to go and get his back slapped?"

"Believe me," Pepper said. "He is no friend of the Monahans."

I took my time and helped Pepper check out what I'd brought. She said, "I apologize for yelling. Thanks for everything, Charlotte. I appreciate what you've done. I don't know when I'm getting out of here."

I said, "I am so sorry this happened to you, Pepper. I'll drop in as often as I can. Leave me a message if you need anything. Anything at all."

She said, "I need two things: Give Little Nick a big kiss from Mommy. And I still need you to keep trying to locate Nick before anything else happens."

"I'll do my best," I said, not at all sure what else I could do.

I nodded to the cop on guard as I left, but my mind was on other things as I hurried down the hall on my way to my appointment.

Pepper didn't trust Tierney.

Could I?

⁕

Next I returned Rose's car and picked up the Matrix. Somehow I ended up with a new container of Toll House cookies in the process. I always profit from a visit to Rose's even when I don't deserve to.

Wendy's project was now on top of this list and close to being finished. Even though Wendy was my preferred client, I needed to make a living and it was time to move on. I checked Lilith's list of inventory. As usual, Lilith had done a great job. If I ever expanded my business, I would snap her up as a full-time assistant. I knew I was lucky to be able to squeeze a few hours from her now and then. I fine-tuned the list of what we needed: hanging cloth shelves, clear shoe pockets to hang on the door, and a double-hanging rod. From my earlier checking, I knew the cloth shelves were heavily discounted that week, and I had a coupon that would lop ten dollars off the double-hanging rod. After quick stops at the dollar store, the hardware store, and the container store, I was soon on my way.

I was smiling as I pulled into Wendy's driveway. Brad was working on the lawn and he gave me the high sign.

"I'll be out of your hair soon," I said.

"Are you kidding? You can move in. You've made Wendy real happy. Where's your assistant?"

"Her part is done. I'm on my own."

"Someone will be disappointed."

Ah yes, Seth. I grinned. "She's at her other job. She hasn't moved out of town."

"Might as well be on the moon, that boy's so shy."

"Sometimes these things work out. It's not that big a town."

Wendy was waiting with chocolate milk and short-bread cookies. She ushered me and my parcels in through the side door. As usual the house smelled wonderful. Something tantalizing was simmering in the large slow cooker, and a number of saucepans were bubbling on the stove.

"Expecting an army?" I said.

"Pretty much. Aaron and Jason, my other boys, are working in Albany during the summer, but they'll be home for the weekend. Forewarned is forearmed. I'm cooking up a storm. They'll eat through the house like a plague of locusts, and I want to have care packages for them to take back. I can't stand the thought of them living on pizza and takeout and submarine sandwiches."

I made a noncommittal sound. She had curled a moth-erly lip at my regular food choices.

Wendy said, "And candy bars. You can imagine."

For sure, I could.

Once we were in the bedroom, I parked my chocolate milk on a small dresser with a coaster and went to work.

"We'll use these hanging cloth shelves to divide the space between you and Brad. You can fold cotton tops and sweaters and store them there. Although now that two of your boys have moved out, I wonder if Brad could take over one of the other closets?"

Wendy said, "Oh, I don't know. I hate to ask him that."

"Do you mind if I do? I know other couples who man-age quite well." I would never have held up Lorelei and Harry or Pepper and Nick as model couples in any other ways, especially as Wendy and Brad seemed so affectionate and compatible. But the separate closet approach had a lot to recommend it.

Wendy said, "You can sound him out. Couldn't hurt. He might not like to change. And that will be all right with me."

"I'll go ask him now," I said.

"Too late. I think he left."

"He can run but he can't hide," I said. "I'll get him later."

I attached the double-hanging rod to the existing rod and said, "Show me the blouses and jackets you wear most often."

Wendy pointed to the items that Lilith had stacked and folded and stored on top of the bins. I tucked the chosen batch of tops into the middle. "Most often used, most accessible." We went through the other piles until the sweater "shelves" were filled.

"Keep your wardrobe simple, and keep getting rid of what you don't use. It will allow you to maintain a useful cupboard."

"Like magic," Wendy said. "I've seen those cloth shelves, but they always looked so flimsy that I couldn't imagine them working like this."

More magical moments. Before we began to rehang her clothing, we changed the mismatched and mangled wire hangers for the sturdy new plastic ones.

I slung the bargain clear plastic shoe pockets over the door. The shoes slid into the shoe pockets in a flash. I rolled up her collection of scarves and tucked them into the top pockets, clearly visible and easy to access. I stood back to admire the closet. Almost done and looking good.

I bent to pick up the bin with clothing to donate. "I'll get this out of the way so you won't be tempted to dive in and rescue anything."

Wendy kept saying, "Wow!"

"Not completely finished yet. I know Lilith has a last-minute surprise for you."

"What a sweet girl. That reminds me, I have some chili to send to her and Rose. There's plenty for you and a friend, too. Oh wait, before you take away that stuff, I keep forgetting to check the pockets. What do you bet I find some change and five of my front door keys?" Wendy quickly inspected all the pant pockets and came up with about twelve dollars in change and, as she had suggested, three extra copies of her front door key.

I said absently, "If you have one placc for your keys and you always put them there, you'll be able to find them."

Wendy laughed. "I know the theory. It's the practice that comes up short."

Even as I smiled at her, I was distracted by a pocket thought: how had I forgotten about the paper I'd taken from Nick's uniform pocket? There was way too much happening in my life, too many hospitals, police, and unknown malefactors. It was interfering with my priorities. But even so, I felt like a doofus. I whipped out my notebook and penned in a reminder to do that ASAP.

I grinned at Wendy. "One more visit and you'll be done with us and free to enjoy your wonderful closet."

Unfortunately, I was off to face the Beauchamps.

It may sound simple, but keep the items you use most often in the easiest spot to access. This will save you time and aggravation when you're getting ready in a hurry. Reserve top shelves and out-of-the-way places for rarely worn or out-of-season clothing.

21

Yes, I was aware of the evils of procrastination, but I didn't have an appointment with Lorelei until three. I headed for CYCotics with a large insulated container of Wendy's chili and rolls, plenty for Jack and me, too. Wendy couldn't have shown her gratitude in a better way. Jack had been overrun with midday customers, and I offered to distract Little Nick for a few minutes while he ate an early lunch in case the noon crowd overwhelmed him. His part-time repair guy was also run off his feet. I would have changed the baby's diaper, too, but that had all been taken care of. Jack was hitting his stride rather than losing interest as I had hoped. I reminded myself that he'd never lost interest in rescuing dogs and fund-raising for WAG'D. Apparently babies were just as fascinating, if not more so. He didn't seem to require any more assistance, so I dashed home to let the dogs out. Left to their own devices they will sleep until I arrive. This time was no different. There was no sign of gratitude when I woke them up and took them out. They were back busily dreaming in minutes. That reminded me, *Go back*. My own dreams had instructed me to go back.

———**✦**———

Shortly after, I sailed down Long March Road. I had plenty of time. It was just after noon as I headed down to Friesen Street.

Go back echoed in my head. "This is not going back," I said out loud. "This is merely checking something." I slowed in front of the apartment building across from the building site and stopped. I looked up. There was no one in the window with the flowers, but a woman was peering out the door to a second-floor balcony with a thick row of thriving plants. An elderly man shuffled slowly into the building.

I locked the car and hurried through the front door at the same time. He turned and held it for me. He held the interior door for me, too. So much for security measures. I reined in my inner bossy boots and refrained from telling him not to let strangers into the building. You can't go by appearances. However, it was convenient for me. I figured the second floor was the place to start. I headed to the end of the corridor where I assumed the occupants would have windows and balconies overlooking the street and the construction site. There was no answer at the first door. If my guess was right, the second door would probably be the unit with the balcony plants. I knocked on the door and waited as a tapping sound came closer. An angular woman who would have been tall if she hadn't been quite so stooped opened the door and asked in a quavery voice what I wanted. I put her somewhere in her late eighties, still going strong and elegant in her periwinkle silk blouse.

"My name is Charlotte Adams. I would like to ask you a few questions about the construction site opposite. Are you comfortable talking to me?"

A chuckle followed. "Well, you're no bigger than a minute. I think I'll be safe enough."

This presented another opportunity to warn about judging people by appearances and how that can be dangerous for older people. But, she got it right: I am not very big and she'd be safe with me.

I stepped inside a tiny apartment, stuffed with enough furniture to fill a two-story house. I like to help people who are in that situation, but that wasn't why I was there.

"I am Thalia Waverman. Please have a seat," she said, gesturing around to the two oversize sofas and the cluster of chairs.

She moved with a slow, arthritic gait. It didn't dampen her mood, though, and I got a whiff of Chanel as she limped past me.

I said, "I'd love to see the plants on your balcony. They look quite amazing from the ground floor."

She brightened. "Why don't we talk out there? Spring and summer are too short. We should enjoy them while we can, although you probably have a few more years than I do ahead of you. You'll need to carry an extra chair, though. I can no longer manage that."

"Happy to." I selected the nearest dining chair and carted it to the outdoor space.

She glanced down as the man in the fedora scooted past on his motorized scooter. Across the street and down, people came and went from the Hope for Youth at Risk office.

I said, "I thought that the construction site would be visible from here. But I see it's obscured by these plants."

She nodded. "Hibiscus. I put them there because I didn't want to look at it."

"I can't blame you. What was there before? Familiar buildings?"

"It's not that," she said. "They were derelict and boarded

up. A danger to our neighborhood. People were afraid to walk past them."

"Did people in the neighborhood resist the redevelopment?"

"If they did, it's news to me, dear," she said, picking a nonperforming leaf off the nearest hibiscus.

"Oh, well. I must be mistaken. The reason I am here is that my friend was killed on the site and—"

"A friend, was she? How sad." She patted my hand kindly. I felt bad at lying to this lovely woman. Anabel had not been a friend, although I'd known her since she was a child.

"It was very sad. I wondered if you happened to see her the day she died?"

"Oh!" she said.

"I am sorry to ask you to revisit that day. It must have been upsetting enough talking to the police about it."

"The police?"

"Yes. They must have asked you questions after the accident happened."

She shook her head. "They didn't. I would have been happy to talk to them. I don't get that many visitors up here, you know."

"Maybe you were out when they came around?"

She shrugged. "I don't go out that often except on my balcony. This was, let me see, back in March? I have no idea what I was doing then. The days do blend together. I might have had a doctor's appointment, I suppose. Or gone for groceries. I could check my calendar, but I'd have to find it first. Silly me, I didn't even offer you a glass of water or a cup of coffee. I still make good coffee. I spent enough time in Europe to learn how to make a decent brew."

I accepted that. She turned down my offer of help, and I stayed on the balcony watching the car and foot traffic below. When she teetered out with a tray, two cups, and a steaming little Bodum of wonderful smelling coffee, my heart was in my mouth. I gave myself a mental talking to. After all, I couldn't even make coffee that smelled that wonderful.

Once the coffee was poured, she said, "Yes, I had wondered about that, too."

Letting my cup pause in midair, I said, "Did you see anything?"

"I believe so. It had been such a rainy week, coming down in buckets for days and days. It was a Friday, I believe, because there was no one left working on the site. Then the sun finally came out, very late in the afternoon, and for a short time it was beautiful. In March we are desperate for a bit of sun. I came out to enjoy the last bit of warmth and plan a bit for my balcony in the summer. I like to ponder what to plant and what to buy and what containers to use."

"And what did you see?"

"I saw the young woman who died slip in behind the gate to the construction area. I wish now I had realized how dangerous it would have been after all that rain, so slippery. I could have called for help. It would have made a difference. And she seemed to be wearing a lovely swirly cream-colored skirt and pretty shoes, high heels."

"Can you see someone's shoes clearly from here?" We were on the second floor.

She chuckled. "Oh, you caught me out. I do have a pair of binoculars. I often take a peek at birds or people. Better than television. I'm old. Need a bit of diversion. I'm probably not the only one."

It was convenient that a witness had been using binoculars at the right moment. Of course, the fact that Anabel had been wearing dress shoes didn't do much more than confirm it would have been dangerous on that slippery site. I reminded myself that that was what I wanted to establish.

"She ducked in through the opening? Do you think she was meeting someone?"

"I couldn't tell. But I think that if she'd planned to meet somebody in *that* place, she wouldn't have been wearing a light skirt and those high heels."

I said, "Was the gate to the site open?"

"I suppose it must have been. She pulled it toward her and disappeared through it. I was surprised that she'd risk ruining those shoes. I don't think I'm much help to you if that's all I remember."

I smiled. "You're doing fine. And you're right. Most young women wouldn't go onto a site like that with their heels on. Wouldn't want to ruin them for one thing."

She said, "Well, there was a tall fellow in a blue coat, very odd-looking, with a hat, who seemed to be waiting for someone. The young woman was walking toward the youth center. When she saw him, she stopped and changed direction. That's when she ducked into the site."

"You think she was dodging him?"

"I thought it at the time, but now, well, I don't know."

"Did he follow her onto the site?"

"No, he didn't. He hung around for a while, then walked away. The next thing I noticed, the police were arriving. And then ambulances and fire trucks. Such a fuss. I didn't realize that the young woman had died. But at any rate, I didn't have much to add to the story. A terrible accident."

"Yes," I said. "And either she had had a brain wave about something and decided to stick her nose in and then slipped in just the wrong place or, more likely, didn't want to see this man and decided to dodge him." And drowned alone senselessly as a result.

"I suppose so. Such a tragedy."

"Do you think anyone else saw the man in the blue coat?"

"Somebody must have. There were other people coming and going. Friesen Street is always busy. The kids from the center, shoppers. I especially noticed your friend, because of her shoes, I suppose. One of my former neighbors thought he heard a call for help. He was out for a walk and he hurried home to call 911."

"Really? I'd like to talk to him."

"We all would. He was a lovely kind fellow, but he had bypass surgery in April and he didn't survive it, I'm afraid."

I said, "Here's my telephone number, Thalia, if you think of anyone else. And I suppose I'd better have yours, too." I handed her a business card with my cell phone number on it.

Thalia wrote out her phone number for me and pocketed my card. I took a couple of seconds to transcribe her number to my phone list. She said, "And you could ask Rudy."

"Who's Rudy?"

"He's the merry fellow on the motorized scooter. With the lovely fedora, just like the old days. You haven't seen him?"

"I have. In fact, he's tipped his hat to me more than once."

❦

When I left Thalia Waverman's place, I made a point of dropping into the office of Hope for Youth at Risk. Gwen spotted me and her beautiful face hardened. The person she was talking to continued to lean forward, speaking intensely to her. He twisted around when I approached, and I got my first really close look at Dimitri.

"I'm Charlotte Adams," I said, extending my hand.

He grunted. A shame. Someone that striking should be able to communicate.

Never mind. I'm capable of carrying a one-way conversation. I shot off with both barrels: "Anabel Beauchamp's mother has asked me to look into her death. She thinks it was murder."

Gwen rose and crossed her arms over her chest. "This conversation is not going to happen. Please leave."

I said as if I hadn't heard, "But I believe as you do that it was an accident. I need to have enough anecdotal information to help her mother accept this. I've been told that Anabel was wearing a skirt and heels when she entered the site. I've never seen Anabel in anything but very casual work clothing or sports gear. That sounds like she was going to a meeting or on a date—it's certainly not something you'd wear to a muddy construction site. Do you know if she was planning to meet someone?"

Dimitri turned away briefly. If that wasn't grief written on his face, then he should have had a brilliant career in acting. He had the looks for it, too. He faced me and said, "Yes, she was meeting me. We did have plans. Then she never turned up because she was dead. As you know."

After the grunt that I'd first heard, I was surprised by his voice, soft, gentle, and his words, which were a lot more articulate than I would have expected. There may have been a subtle trace of an accent, exotic for Woodbridge. Russian, I assumed. I could easily understand why Anabel was so taken with him.

I said, "I am so sorry for your loss. I understand you and Anabel were close. It must have been very difficult for you."

He swallowed and nodded. I was glad he didn't grunt again. He said, "You want to reassure her mother? Then you will have to work very hard to do that because whatever else, it was not an accident. I guarantee that. I don't care who says otherwise."

Gwen Jones widened her expressive eyes. "Dimitri, you know that's not true. As hard as it is to accept, Anabel's death was a terrible fluke."

"A fluke? She died and you call it a fluke? We were going to be married and you think she would take a stupid chance with her life? She was waiting for me. She didn't meet anyone. She would never go check out that site in her dress shoes."

Gwen snapped, "But she could afford a hundred pairs of designer shoes."

Dimitri shook his head. "She took care of her things. She was never wasteful. You know that, Gwen."

Gwen turned away, and Dimitri turned back toward me. "Somehow she was lured onto that site and someone killed her. We'll never find out what kind of monster did that until people like Gwen, who pretends to be so good, or the police, who don't want any bad statistics, or maybe her mother, who doesn't want any bad publicity, stop blocking the truth. You want proof it was an accident? You won't find it because it wasn't. It was murder. Everyone knows it and no one will do a thing."

Gwen sputtered, "That's not true."

I said, "Why do you believe it, Dimitri?"

His raised voice betrayed the barely contained emotions. "I just told you. Isn't that enough?"

Before I could counter that, he was out the door. I raced after him, but he had disappeared from view. Down that alley, I supposed.

Gwen said, "Thanks a lot. None of this crazy talk is going to bring Anabel back. Now, in case I wasn't clear before, I will be now: Do not come back to this office making trouble again."

—❖—

After the intensity of Dimitri's reaction and being tossed off the premises by Gwen, I sat somewhat shakily in the Matrix for a few minutes trying to figure out what was going on. Although common sense and official opinion told me it was an accident, a small nagging voice at the back of my brain insisted that if Anabel had been murdered, her killer had gotten away with it. Still, I found myself upset by the raw emotion behind Dimitri's outburst. I'd had an up-close view of how strong his feelings had been for her. And still were. There was no doubt in my mind that he truly believed that Anabel had been murdered.

But did Gwen honestly believe it was an accident, or was she trying to protect her vulnerable organization? Something I'd heard about the neighborhood buzzed in the back of my brain. What had Tierney said when we'd met him at Betty's? He'd talked about some badass types they were keeping an eye on. What else? Serious criminal activities in that area and they were working to keep a lid on them. Could they be connected to Anabel's death? Was there more going on and the cops were unwilling to admit it because it might compromise some other investigation? Let the Beauchamps suffer—who cared? I opened my handbag, extracted my notebook, and wrote *Gwen* and *Dimitri*. I gave Gwen a question mark. Under Dimitri's name, I wrote *Criminal activities?* Thank God for paper.

Paper.

That reminded me, why the hell hadn't I taken a look at the small folded paper I'd found in Nick's pocket? Where was it? I closed my eyes and thought. I'd left it on my desk that night, meaning to check it to see if it was a private note to Pepper or something relevant. I put that down to how upset I'd been about Nick flying through the window when Tierney and his team came in. That stirred up a few other thoughts. Tierney seemed to have made up his mind about Nick without considering any other options. He was determined not to listen to anything in his defense. Another thing: Tierney had insisted that the cops had done a door-to-door search on Friesen Street and talked to the people in the apartment building. But Thalia Waverman told me they hadn't. I believed her.

Was Pepper right and Tierney was not to be trusted?

I pulled myself together and edged the Matrix out into the street. I took a look at that alley at the same time. Not a place I'd ever walk. Where did it come out? It was a long shot, but I wondered if I might find Dimitri on the other side. I drove slowly to the corner, turned right and right again to Potter Street, which ran parallel to Friesen. The alley did indeed exit on Potter Street. I parked again and got out of the car. No sign of Dimitri, but as I said, that had been a long shot. Just then, Rudy whizzed out of the alley in his motorized scooter and tipped his fedora to me.

I waved to him and gestured for him to wait. I trotted over and introduced myself. "Hello. I need to speak to Dimitri. He got very upset about something I said and I didn't get a chance to apologize."

Rudy stared at me without blinking. I hoped he wasn't going to do a Gwen on me.

I added, "Do you know where I might find him? I thought he might be on this side."

Rudy said, "Not much happening here. All the action's on Friesen. There's only people on Potter, that's all."

I looked around and had to concur. The only two people on Potter at that minute were Rudy and I. The street was lined with aging triplexes with sagging roofs and front stairs you could break your neck on. I wasn't sure where Dimitri would have gone from there.

I said, "Does Dimitri live here?"

Rudy studied me.

I smiled, encouragingly.

He said, "No."

"Do you know where he does live?"

"Yes, I do."

I waited and then tried again. "Would you be willing to tell me?"

"Dimitri's had enough trouble. He don't need no more."

"I agree. I don't plan to give him any trouble. I want to talk to him about Anabel and how she died. He was upset when I repeated that Anabel's death was an accident. He insists she was murdered. I'd like to know why he thinks that. Maybe I can help."

"You don't mind me saying so, miss, but you don't look like you could help out much with no murders."

I raised my chin. "Appearances can be deceiving."

"Yeah, I sure know that, but I'm still not going to rat out Dimitri to you."

"Are you his friend?"

"I guess I am."

"He's lucky then that you look after his interests. Will you give him my card and ask him to give me a call? He can name a place to meet and leave a message if I can't get to the phone. I'd like to find out more from him. I will do my best to help him. I can write it all down if you'd like."

"No, miss," Rudy said, tapping the side of his head. "It's all up here, and I'll give it to him."

As he rumbled down the street I wanted to kick myself for not asking Rudy about the man in the blue coat. I chased after him and caught up panting.

"Do you remember an odd-looking man in a blue coat who was hanging around the day that Anabel died?"

He looked up and blinked.

I said, "He had a hat, too. Something like yours, I think."

Rudy thought hard. "You know, I would have remembered that. I pay attention to hats. Didn't see any guy like that, that day."

"Not that day, but some other day?"

He shook his head. "No, miss. Never seen a guy like that at all around here."

He was gone in a whir of wheels, leaving me feeling I hadn't asked the right question. Had Rudy seen such a man somewhere else? Why would that be relevant? Oh well, I'd pursue it the next time.

When I returned to the Matrix, I noticed the construction site fronted on Potter Street as well as Friesen. I walked toward it. The back side of the site had the same boards blocking the view of the fence, the same slot for viewing, and, this hit me, its own door, also padlocked. I stood on my tiptoes again and peered in through the viewing slot.

Had Anabel met someone on the site without being spotted by witnesses on Friesen Street? I figured someone with the right footwear could easily have made their way to the other side where Anabel entered without being injured. I was thinking of a man with boots with a good grip. But had that happened?

And who might have seen that from Potter Street? If the police hadn't taken the trouble to interview Thalia Waverman with her unobstructed view of the site, would they have bothered to ask the residents of Potter Street? I added that to my list of questions to ask . . . but ask whom?

Minutes later, I sat in the Matrix and took out my notebook. Under Rudy's name, I wrote:

Did the police talk to him?

Who does he know on Potter Street who might have been interviewed?

What does he think happened to Anabel?

I decided I'd like to ask Dimitri the same questions.

22

Truffle and Sweet Marie woke up and yawned when I
clumped up the stairs and into my apartment. As soon as
they figured out there were no treats coming, they curled
up under their blankies and went back to sleep. I checked
the pile of unfiled papers on my desk. What was happening to me? Papers not filed? That was a first. I located the
small, tightly wrapped rectangle of paper I'd found hidden
in Nick's uniform pocket. I unwrapped it. Inside I found a
familiar type of plastic hotel door key. I turned it over and
checked carefully. There was no identification on the key.
It was a bit of purple plastic with an arrow showing the
direction to insert. Could have been any hotel in the area.
No, that wasn't actually true. There weren't many hotels in
Woodbridge. We had mostly charming renovated bed-and-
breakfasts in our historic uptown and downtown areas. I
figured they weren't using electronic key cards. The hotels
were on the edge of town, the usual chains, a few middle-
of-the-road spots, and some dingy dives. Why would Nick
have a key card to any of them? That was the question. Of

course, anyone could have a forgotten key in his pocket, but, in this case, Nick had carefully covered this one in paper. Not a brilliant strategy, but consider the source.

I took a couple of minutes at my computer to print out a list of hotels and motels on the outskirts of Woodbridge and the bordering towns. Of course, I had no idea if this key was one that Nick had used himself or if he was keeping it for some other purpose. There was no ID on it, hotel or room, so I decided to assume the key was his. Why hide it otherwise? Pepper would have been instantly incandescent at the sight of a hotel key. That in itself would be a good reason to tuck it away in an unused spot. Was that what Nick had been searching for in his closet when the cops arrived? Well, you need some kind of hypothesis to proceed in any experiment or investigation. Mine was that Nick had this room key because he had a room.

If Nick had a room somewhere, he'd make sure it wasn't too close to town, in a place he might be spotted. On the other hand, it should be somewhere he might have a reason to be that wouldn't look suspicious. I checked my map and compared it to the list. I crossed out the higher-end chains. There were lots of business meetings held in those, and Nick might bump into someone he knew. That left a handful of motels in the mid- to lower-end range. I also figured that with all the media fuss, Nick would have changed his appearance a bit and would not be using his own name. I took a couple of minutes to find a clear recent photo of Nick. He'd changed quite a bit since his own wedding photo that was splashed all over the media. I found the one Sally had taken at Margaret and Frank's wedding dinner less than a year back and printed it out. I popped the key card into my pocket and put the list and the photo into my purse. I had one more thing to check out before I headed to the Beauchamps'. I thought I'd follow up on the motels later, and take my time, because I didn't know what I'd find. Keeping that in mind, I decided to walk the dogs early, in case it took me a while to get my hotel research done.

———◆◆———

It was my lucky afternoon when I spotted a familiar police officer passing slowly on patrol two blocks away. I hoped that Officer Roger DeJong would remember me gratefully as the kind visitor who'd gifted him the box of Kristee's black-and-white fudge, rather than as a source of trouble with Tierney. He wasn't the brightest light on the force, but he didn't seem to hold a grudge. I took a chance and waved. So far so good, I thought, as he pulled his patrol car over. I stepped out of the Matrix and walked over to talk to him. I tried to sound casual.

He nodded. Was it my imagination that he looked apprehensive? Maybe he still remembered the rough ride Tierney gave him whenever he had anything to do with me. I smiled in what I hoped was a sympathetic way. "Do you patrol here often?" I said.

He blinked and then nodded. I imagined he was wondering if Tierney would bite his head off for admitting this.

"I need to have a word with a young man named Dimitri. Do you know him?" I said.

"What's it about?" he asked.

Why are the police always so suspicious? If I'd said the truth, that I was following up on an idea I had about Anabel's death and local criminals, Officer DeJong would tell Tierney that I was nosing around. Didn't want that, so naturally I fibbed. "Well, I am involved with a charity. We visit older homebound immigrants and we need someone who speaks a bit of Russian to translate something for us for one lady."

All right, I admit that was a stretch, but it was the best I could come up with on short notice. I supposed under the right circumstances it might have been true.

DeJong stared at me assessing that story. I gave him my best wide-eyed smile.

He said after an unnecessarily long time, "He is an outreach worker at the youth agency. I don't think that's a full-time position. I heard he's also part-time at the bowling alley. If he's not at the agency, you might find him there."

"Thank you, Officer. I—" He drove off before I finished.

I trotted back to the car, checked the time, and decided to check out Dimitri after I saw Lorelei, yet again. As I pulled out to start the drive to the Beauchamps', my cell phone trilled. I pulled over and answered it. Harry.

"Sorry, Charlotte. Lorelei's not quite up to it yet. Can we make it four o'clock?"

"Sure thing," I said, glad of the extra time. "See you then."

I made a U-turn and drove to the only bowling alley in Woodbridge. I supposed I could have walked. I headed inside and glanced around. On this gorgeous June day, there was lots of action inside the vast bowling alley. Who needed sunshine and gentle breezes when you could have tenpin bowling? Amid the usual clatter of pins, cheers, and groans, I spotted Dimitri working the shoe rental. He seemed startled by my presence.

"I need a word or two. Do you have a minute?"

He nodded. "I'll ask my boss to cover."

The boss apparently agreed because he nodded and waved us away. This was a good thing, a sign that Dimitri was an asset in the alley. I waited until he beckoned me to a door in the back, and then we stepped outside on the side of the building. I looked around at the Dumpster and shuddered. I hate Dumpsters. He said, "Sorry, I can't smoke in the front and I could use one." He pulled a package and a lighter from his pocket, lit a cigarette, and leaned against the graffiti-covered wall.

"This will sound crazy," I said, "but I'd heard that there

were some dangerous people hanging around on Friesen Street, maybe getting too close to the kids. Do you think that may have had anything to do with Anabel's death? Could she have overheard something? She was fearless. Would she have told off the wrong person? Interfered with some transaction? Threatened to call the cops?"

He exhaled, shook his head. "She would never call the cops on the kids."

"I didn't mean the kids, but the bad elements who might have been selling drugs or . . ." I wasn't sure what the bad elements might have been up to, although there were a limited number of possibilities, drugs being high on the list, so I let it drop at that.

I could tell he was thinking hard.

"Small-time scum mostly. Dealers would beat up a kid who tried to pull a fast one. But these guys aren't going to kill a citizen on the streets of Woodbridge. So what if she saw them or even threatened them? Nothing's going to happen to them. They wouldn't need to kill her, just ignore her. It was up to the cops to stop them, and they never seemed to be able to get proof of anything. If they do get arrested, they can afford the good attorneys. Life's not always fair here in the land of the free."

"Who do you think was behind it?"

"I can't imagine anyone trying to hurt her for any reason."

Of course, I was no further ahead. I took a deep breath and said, "I understand your friend Jewel didn't like Anabel."

He narrowed his eyes at me. "Jewel is a confused girl, but she isn't going to hurt anyone. She was angry, and she let me know it. She's in California now. She wanted to be a tattoo artist. Lots of business there. She's over it."

"I'm sure you're right," I said. "Do you know if she ever comes back to Woodbridge?"

He stood up, tossed the cigarette on the ground, and stepped on it. "I don't. And I wouldn't tell you if I did. I thought you were trying to help, not bring more trouble."

I felt a shiver as he gave me a dirty look. What did I know about him anyway? I glanced around. While the inside was bustling, here I was alone with Dimitri. It hit me that Dimitri himself could have been the badass influence who was getting too close to some of the more vulnerable kids. I imagined Tierney's voice saying, *When will you learn?*

"I'm sorry," I said. "I didn't mean to upset you. I am ready to give up on this. Anabel's mother thinks someone killed her, and I thought you felt the same way. I guess it was a mistake on my part to ask around, and I'm going to tell her mother that. In fact, they're expecting me and I should go."

Dimitri stepped toward me and I stepped back. I felt a frisson of fear. I realized that it had been pretty dumb to let myself be alone in an isolated place with a man who might be very dangerous. Of course, up until that moment I hadn't thought he was dangerous, just a grieving boyfriend. I, of all people, should have understood that the boyfriend is not always what he seems. Still, I didn't get it. If Dimitri was implicated in any way, why would he have insisted that Anabel had been murdered? It didn't make sense. I straightened my shoulders and tried to figure how to get past him and back into the bowling alley. At that moment a squad car turned the corner slowly and drove past us. I felt like kissing the grouchy Officer DeJong, although I didn't think he'd appreciate the gesture much.

I waved merrily. He waved back grouchily. As the patrol car inched forward, I realized my knees were weak.

Dimitri melted back into the building as DeJong pulled up by my side.

"Are you all right?"

"Sure," I said. After all, Dimitri didn't know my full name or my address or anything else about me.

"Can I do anything?" he said. "You look like you've had a scare."

"I guess I have had."

"Maybe you shouldn't talk to lowlifes. I shouldn't have told you where to find this guy. I didn't think he was dangerous or I wouldn't have. Detective Tierney will have my head on a spike."

"Not your fault. Our little secret. And anyway I've learned my lesson. From now on, I'm only talking to police officers. Ha-ha."

He grinned, something that didn't happen often from what I'd seen. I took advantage of the grin to say, "Do you know Dean Oliver?"

He blinked. "Dean? Of course I know him. We're a small force in Woodbridge. Why?"

"Because the whole reason I wanted to talk to Dimitri is that I need to reassure Anabel Beauchamp's mother that her death was an accident and not murder. I was convinced it was an accident, and then all this stuff with Nick Monahan made me wonder. I read in the paper that this Officer Oliver was on the scene as well as Nick. I thought he might clear things up."

Officer DeJong's brow furrowed. He hesitated and stared at me. After a long pause, he said, "I didn't know he was there. But if it was in the paper, I guess it can't do any harm to talk about it."

"Exactly. What harm could it do?"

"Don't ask me. I keep getting everything wrong lately. Anyway, you already know Dean, I think. He was at Bakker Beach and at the hospital, too. Didn't he drive you home?"

"Oh." I barely stopped myself from saying, *He's the smart, cute one*. DeJong's day had apparently been bad enough without insulting his own intelligence or mustachioed appearance. "Of course. I'll look for him."

"Don't tell Tierney I told you anything," he said with another failed attempt at a hairy grin. "Dean's a golden boy. He can't put a foot wrong. So he won't have to worry about getting roasted."

"Thanks. And thanks for being here when I needed you, Officer DeJong. I appreciate it."

DeJong flushed. I guessed he wasn't used to being thanked. "Hey, be careful. Let the detectives work it all out. We don't know what's happening lately. Maybe when they turn up Nicky Monahan we'll get to the bottom of things."

"I'm not convinced he could have done these things."

DeJong shook his head sadly. "Doesn't make sense, does it? I've known Nicky since he joined the force. I can't figure what went wrong. That girl's death hit him real hard. He must have snapped. Lost his marbles. You ask me, he needs help."

"Maybe," I said with a sad smile.

––•––

Harry was waiting at the door when I arrived. He shook his head sadly.

I said, "Oh."

He shrugged. "The champagne cocktail today is ambrosia. Would you like one?"

"No thanks. I don't need anything, but I think we should talk."

He gestured toward the grand, stark living room, and I followed him in.

"It's not working, is it?" he said.

"Maybe when Lorelei has some closure over Anabel's death, she'll be able to take care of her closets. Right now, they're the least of her problems. Let it go."

"You're right, Charlotte honey. I suppose I am trying to distract her. But there's good news, though. She has decided to humor me, in turn, and let me pack away those winter coats in the front closet. We usually put them in the cedar closet. It's got a climate control so the fur trims are all right."

"I can help you with that," I said.

Harry wouldn't relax until I had ginger ale in a champagne glass. As I sipped, he said, "I keep hearing about this attack on Detective Pepper Monahan. It's a terrible story. She's a beautiful woman. I can't believe her husband could treat her like that."

"We don't know what actually happened yet."

After some casual chat and a plate of crackers and cheese, we headed to the crowded closet. We separated out those coats and jackets that needed cleaning. One beautiful silky trench in an unusual shade of amethyst was covered with splashes of dirt, and a cashmere car coat had a large coffee stain. A blue knit cape had some kind of unidentified grease on it. We laid those aside for cleaning, and Harry took an armload of coats. I did as well. "It's a small thing," he said, "but I have to feel I'm getting something accomplished."

We carted the coats downstairs to the cedar storage area, which was larger than most people's living rooms and lined with sturdy hanging rods. Another trip each with an armful and the coats were stashed for the winter. We did the same with boots, putting one gorgeous pair of buttery soft leather ones aside to have the lifts repaired and setting aside a pair of black patent leather platform boots, which Harry said he'd clean. Hats and scarves followed. I carried a black trilby, a poor boy cap, and a puffy fur number.

Harry said, "She loves hats. I think she prefers the rain and snow because she always has an excuse to wear one."

I knew that Lorelei would acquire a new wardrobe of outerwear when fall rolled around and she'd keep everything she had. I would have liked to see some of these items go to the women's shelter. Woodbridge winters are cold and damp, and genuine wool and cashmere would seem like a miracle to people who had nothing.

When we were finished, Harry said, "Thank you. I know it's been frustrating."

I said, "I hope to be able to put her mind to rest at some point."

Harry hung his head sadly. "I don't know if anyone will ever put her mind to rest, Charlotte honey. But I am glad you are here for us."

I decided to drop the items off at the dry cleaner's. That would give me a sense of doing something for Harry if not Lorelei. And another reason to go back to Friesen Street. First I checked in with Woodbridge General to see if I could visit Pepper. I got no answer in her room. A call to the nursing station told me she'd been taken for tests, whatever that meant.

I checked out the three motels within a short drive of the Beauchamps'. None of them had purple key cards. That would have been too easy.

<hr/>

I was back on Friesen Street and heading into the dry cleaner's minutes before they closed their doors at the unusual time of seven. I put the amethyst trench and the cashmere car coat on the counter, with the blue knit cape next to it. I realized that I had forgotten to check these pockets, something I am always telling my clients to do. There were a few unused tissues in the car coat and a torn envelope and a crumpled note in the pocket of the trench.

As the dry cleaner filled out the slip, I tossed the tissues and checked the crumpled paper to see if it was trash, too. The woman behind the counter looked up as I gasped. The note said:

Dimitri and I will already be married when you read this, Lorelei. No fuss, no big deal. The way I want it. I hope you and Harry will accept that and welcome Dimitri into our lives. Despite the way it seems, I do love you both, but I am going to live my own life on my terms.

Anabel

How had Lorelei reacted to that note? She'd obviously opened it and read it. Had Dimitri betrayed the love and trust that Anabel had promised him? My cell phone was bleating insistently. I answered it the third time it vibrated in case it was news of Pepper. Too late. Harry had left a message to call him. I thought this note was better returned to him and Lorelei in person, not discussed on the phone. As I always believed, every closet has its secret.

A strange and horrible thought crossed my mind as I stared at the coat. The lovely amethyst trench was covered with splashes of dirt. I snatched it back from the cleaner and said, "Sorry, I'll leave the other things. But I need this back."

I returned Harry's call. "Is it the coat, Harry?" I said when he answered.

"She's pitching a fit, Charlotte honey. I explained that you had only taken it to be cleaned, but you know what she's like."

I said, "Was she wearing it the day Anabel died?"

I heard Harry's intake of breath. "How did you know?"

I lied a little bit. "I know it was a dirty day. What was she wearing with it?"

"The black patent boots, I think, and the trilby. She looks wonderful in that outfit. Of course, she hasn't worn it since."

"Tell her I'll bring it back tomorrow. It hasn't been to the dry cleaner's yet."

Minutes later, I was across the street, ringing Thalia Waverman's door. I waited for the slow progress of her cane. She opened the door and smiled at me with delight.

This time she insisted on plying me with ice tea before she would talk what she called "business."

"Thanks, Mrs. Waverman."

"Thalia, please. We agreed."

"Thalia, do you recognize this coat?"

She shook her head. "No. It's very beautiful. Should I?"

"Think back to the day Anabel died across the street. You said you saw a man in a blue coat and Anabel seemed to be avoiding him. At first I thought it was Dimitri, a young man with a dark leather jacket."

Thalia snorted. "Dimitri?"

"Yes."

"Of course it wasn't Dimitri. We all know him. He's done a lot to make our little neighborhood safer."

Why hadn't I asked about Dimitri before and saved myself some trouble? Once again, a surprise.

I said, "Could this be the coat the man you saw wore?"

"Yes, but now, my dear, I see that this is a woman's coat. The person was far away and so tall, I suppose I thought . . ."

"A six-foot-tall model wearing three-inch heels and a hat with a crown might give that impression. Especially wearing a hat you might expect a man to wear."

"I should have realized. Men today don't wear hats like that, do they? Except for Rudy."

I hadn't asked Rudy the right questions. A woman in a hat? That might have done it. Even if I'd said "person," I could have saved myself some time and trouble. Now I had my information: Lorelei had been on Friesen Street the day Anabel died, although she hadn't gone to the construction site. Lorelei had read Anabel's note and gone down to stop

the wedding to the unsuitable young man, Dimitri. Anabel had not wished to deal with her formidable mother at
that moment, so she had dodged behind the fence in the
construction site to avoid a confrontation. While there,
she'd slipped on the muddy walkway in her unfamiliar
high-heeled shoes. Lorelei must have realized this in some
part of her disturbed brain. No wonder she was in such bad
shape. Of course she wanted to believe someone had murdered her daughter. Who could blame her for that?

23

Lorelei's predicament was not my only problem. I put in a call from my cell phone to Margaret to see if she'd been able to see Pepper today. I got her voice mail. The blessing and curse of our times. I couldn't concentrate on my business. I decided to knock off the rest of the hotels in the interim. I checked out two off I-87 and one near the south end of Woodbridge. No purple key cards in either case. Plus the staff of all three looked at me as if I'd lost my mind. It was tedious and it made me glad I hadn't chosen private detective as a job. I had the belated thought that perhaps a private eye would have called and asked.

Still, it was a positive action and it took my mind off waiting for Margaret to call me back, and kept me from wondering if I should get something in for dinner as Jack was bound to have worked up an appetite looking after Little Nick.

Most important, it kept me from dwelling on what Pepper had asked me to do, which was find Nick, and what I wanted to do, which was find out how Anabel had died.

I pulled over as my cell phone trilled. I was surprised to hear Thalia Waverman's sweet quavering voice on the line.

"I am sorry to bother you, but I was chatting with my friend who lives on Potter Street and I told her you were here asking questions. It's so nice to have a bit of news to share. At any rate, she mentioned something that she'd seen. I thought you might like to hear about it."

"Thank you, Thalia. What is it?"

"I'll put my friend on, will I? Turns out the police didn't come to her door, either," she said.

An even more quavery voice came on the line. "That's right," she warbled. "No sign of them. Asleep at the wheel my late husband would have said. This is Jane Cantley speaking. Thalia can't be allowed to think she's the only one who could ever come up with a scrap of news."

"I'm glad you're both on the job," I said with a smile in my voice.

"*I* certainly am. And I didn't see the person that Thalia described, but I wondered if the police officer wouldn't have seen everything."

"Which police officer?" I asked.

"Well, the one who went behind the fence, of course."

"Behind the fence at the site? You mean the first officer to respond? They didn't—"

"No, dear. I mean, the officer who was already there. He seemed to be meeting with someone that I couldn't see. It may have been your Anabel Beauchamp, but I don't think so. I had the sense of a large person. I didn't see the young woman because, naturally, the Friesen Street entrance isn't visible from my apartment. I could only see him entering."

"He must have been responding to a 911 call."

"Oh no, dear. I don't think so. It was ten minutes at least before there was the first hint of a siren."

"Thank you, Jane," I said. "May I have your telephone number if I need to call you again?"

"Oh, Thalia knows where to find me," she said as the line went dead. After that, I heard only the sound of things falling into place in my mind.

<hr />

Margaret arrived at my place seconds after I did. She seemed to be missing her usual air of cool, detached competence.

The dogs leaped off the sofa and raced to the door doing their best Rottweiler imitation.

"I'm glad to see you, too, pampered little pets," Margaret said to them as she walked in. They were all over her. I was in their bad books because of the training regime and the fact I'd hardly been home that week.

Margaret said, to me this time, "Do you think that everyone in the world has lost their mind lately? The whole idea of the guardians for Little Nick has me creeped out. I hate the idea that he might need guardians, although we have to accept the idea that brain injuries can be very unstable. I lost a client not too long ago after what looked like a slight injury. And there's a chance Pepper might not make it." Margaret ditched her lawyer suit jacket and flopped on the sofa. Truffle and Sweet Marie jumped up to snuggle. They love women. Soft, cuddly, and nice smelling. And in this case, worried.

I said, "I refuse to believe that Pepper won't make it, and I don't believe that Nick is behind her injuries. I understand why she wouldn't want Little Nick raised by the same people who made her childhood miserable. Isn't it good to get these things taken care of legally before rather than have a court battle if it . . . not that it will come to that."

"But we'll have to have everything nailed down to make sure he's the guardian. Both sets of grandparents would have a stake. The right lawyer could make the case that Pepper's decision was flawed by her head injury."

I said, "But her own father was abusive. Surely that would . . . what do you mean 'he'? 'He' who?"

"Jack, of course."

"What? Jack? The buddy who doesn't wear winter clothes in the snow? The guy who has bike parts stored in his oven?"

"Well, to repeat, she does have a head injury. Like I said, I don't know that any decisions she makes under these circumstances would hold up in court anyway. But is Jack such a surprise?"

"He'd be great emotionally. But you know, not the most conventional of homes. Someone else would have to be in charge of snowsuits and baking cookies for school events."

"I hear you and I think we'd have better luck if it was Sally and Benjamin."

"Who already have four kids of their own?"

"Doesn't matter. Stable. Respectable. House full of toys. Yada, yada. Not my decision of course. Pepper wants your name as a guardian, too."

I squeaked, "Are you kidding me?"

"It is pretty weird. You have a hard enough time raising your dogs. Discipline is definitely an issue."

I hoped that wasn't a growl I heard from Sweet Marie.

I said, "Margaret, what's going on? How can all these terrible things have happened to Pepper and Nick?"

"I have no idea."

"What does Frank say?"

"He has no idea, either, which is the main reason why I have no idea. You know cops, they clam up."

"What's the good of marrying one if you can't extract information from him? Have you never heard of pillow talk?"

"I hate to break it to you, but the police have cornered the market on investigating. You shouldn't make it one of your new business lines."

"But I have helped before."

"And you got hurt. Other people got hurt, too. Leave it to the pros."

"Why does everyone keep saying that?"

"Mainly because it makes sense. For a sensible girl like you, it shouldn't require explanation."

"Very cute. Of course, the police, that is to say, Pepper and Nick, are the ones in the messy situation."

"Well, whatever is behind it? You should steer clear. That's my advice as your lawyer and even more so as your friend. And don't bother sulking. I get enough of that from my parents. It rolls right off my back and trickles away."

"I'm not sulking," I said sulkily. I headed into the kitchen to get some treats for the dogs. Unfortunately, we were out of ice cream.

"Doesn't matter either way is my point."

"Where do you think Nick is hiding out? Ah, c'mon, Margaret, don't roll your eyes."

"Huh. I'm amazed that you can see that from the next room. You're very good, Charlotte."

"Okay, never mind Nick. Listen to this: Lorelei went to Friesen Street because she'd had a note from Anabel saying she was getting married. I am almost certain it was her. She was seen. I think that Anabel ducked behind the fence to avoid her mother and she was wearing girlie shoes and lost her footing."

Margaret stared. "That would be the most awful thing that a mother could ever deal with."

I nodded. "But there's another wrinkle. One of the women in the neighborhood says that a police officer was already behind the fence. And that he was meeting with someone else who entered on the Potter Street side."

"What?"

"There's more. The cops don't seem to have talked to any of the people who might have witnessed this. So since Nick was the first on the scene, that could mean—and I hate to say this—that he was there, that he saw Anabel fall in, but for some reason failed to help her or to phone it in in time."

"You think Nick killed her?"

"I can't believe that. But he could have mismanaged the whole thing. He might not have figured out how to save her or, being Nick, even that she needed saving. Living with that might explain why Nick has been acting so crazy lately. Pepper said he was afraid of something. Felt threatened. And if someone else knew he'd let Anabel die, they could be blackmailing him."

Margaret said, "Letting a girl drown? That's heavy stuff. Nick would be terrified of exposure. Losing his standing in the police."

"That's it. And in the end, maybe it all took a toll. Maybe it triggered some kind of psychotic break and that explains what happened to Pepper."

Margaret rubbed her forehead.

I added, "That's my thinking to date, but I could be wrong. It doesn't seem enough to account for his behavior. I wouldn't have thought Nick capable of any of this, but of course, it wouldn't be the first time I was wrong about a man. Maybe DeJong was right and he just snapped."

———

After Margaret left, I decided to check on Pepper in person before I tried to find Dean Oliver to get his spin on the whole tale. I needed to know that she was all right. And she needed to know that Little Nick was all right. I called Jack first. I also needed to know what he might like to eat when he got home and if he needed more baby food. "We'll be late. Business is booming," he said. "We had an excellent day. And we're good for dinner. Sally dropped off some jars of weird strained concoction for the little dude and people food for me. And I had that great chili for lunch. I think the dude can't wait to grow out of all that jarred grub and eat chili like a man. Anyway, don't worry about us getting dinner."

I called the hospital and once again, the nursing station staff was evasive. I fed the dogs, popped them out for a constitutional, promised them a nice long walk the next day, and tore off to Woodbridge General.

Pepper was not in her room. An unfamiliar police officer was guarding an empty space. He did not know where she was. The nurse in charge was unwilling to say where she was as I wasn't family. "I'm a lot closer than family," I protested, but it got me nowhere.

After an hour or so of frustration trying to find out where Pepper was, I was informed that visiting hours were over. The cop was still guarding the empty room, waiting for Pepper to return from wherever. Surgery? Tests? No one had told him, as he wasn't family, either. More to the point, he was told to stay put. I asked conversationally if Dean Oliver was on duty that night.

"Dean?" he said. "I think he's days this week."

I left and headed home. I called Sally from the parking lot and asked her if she could find out through Benjamin what had happened. Next I phoned Tierney and got, naturally, his voice mail. I mentioned I had something that might be a lead on Nick's whereabouts. Let *him* follow purple key cards all around town. See if people looked at him as if he had two heads. I added that I had an interesting tidbit from witnesses in the Friesen and Potter Street area, witnesses who had not *ever* been interviewed by the police, although far be it from me to criticize the pros. The voice mail cut me off before I said everything that was on my mind.

—‡—

The day seemed to be a hundred hours long so far even though it was just after nine o'clock. It didn't help that the weather had changed from sunny and warm to hot and humid as evening arrived. I felt sticky and exhausted and imagined we were in for another muggy, rainy night. Luckily Hannaford's was open late. I swung by and grabbed some eggs, cheese, bacon, frozen entrees, and the makings for stir-fries, as well as take-out barbecue chicken and potato wedges. If Jack was going to play poppa, the least I could do was make sure he didn't starve. I picked up a premixed salad in case I turned over a new leaf. And some ice cream in case I didn't. Hannaford's was beautifully air-conditioned.

I ate half the potato wedges in the car on the way home. There are times when plates are overrated. I was pleased to see that Jack was already home when I got there. As I eased the Matrix into my driveway next to Jack's dung-colored Mini, my head was still whirling with thoughts of Pepper, Nick, Anabel, Lorelei, cops, and keys. I got out of the car, juggling my briefcase and my haul from Hannaford's. For some reason the front door was open and the lights were ablaze on both floors. A small black shadow dashed in front of me. My jaw dropped along with the bag containing the eggs.

What was that? The familiar shape headed for the backyard. Truffle! A similar one dashed in the opposite direction. Sweet Marie heading straight for the road! I dropped everything and dashed after her, shrieking, "Treat! Cheese! Cookies!"

Five minutes later, I held the quivering little brown dog and trotted back to find Truffle. My terror was matched by my fury. What was Jack thinking leaving the front door open? He must have left my apartment door open, too. Was this the responsible daddy behavior? Truffle turned up in the backyard, hiding under a bush. He inched out when I lured him with a potato wedge.

I would have stomped up the stairs, but as annoyed as I was with Jack, I didn't want to take a chance and wake up the baby, if by any chance he was asleep. Jack's apartment door was open, the lights on. I headed up to my own open door. I let the dogs down, but they huddled against my ankles, whimpering. "What's wrong with you two?" I said.

I nudged them through the door, shut it, and headed back to salvage what I could of my food, currently scattered on the ground. Back at the top of the stairs, I managed to open the door, trip over the dogs, close it, and get the bags into the kitchen. "Jack," I whispered in what I hoped was a compelling voice. "Where the hell are you? And what were you thinking letting my dogs out? They could have been killed."

No answer from Jack. Probably hiding under the bed, I decided.

Little Nick's gear was clearly in evidence, but he was not. I knew that Jack was quite capable of taking his new obsession for a moonlight walk so I didn't panic. I planned to let him have an earful when he stumbled in. My darling naughty dogs might have been flattened. I showed my affection by giving them quite a bit of stuff that falls under the category of Not For Dogs. I slumped on the sofa and they joined me, snuggling, glad to be rescued or at least glad to be given cheese. As I sat there, still pondering what was going on and hoping that I'd get a call from Tierney, I became conscious of an unfamiliar noise. A groan? I got up, annoying the dogs, and followed the sound. The pooches stuck close to me. The sound seemed to be coming from my large lovely linen closet. I hesitated and then told myself not to be silly. I grabbed the door handle and opened it.

I shrieked.

Jack was curled almost double on the floor. He moaned. I pulled at his arm frantically. He was obviously alive, with blood flowing from his head wound.

"Jack!"

He moaned again. His eyes stayed closed. I grabbed the phone and dialed 911. Mona answered. "No jokes, Mona. Jack Reilly is injured, my apartment, linen closet."

Mona Pringle, who seemed to live at her job, said, "What—?"

"Head wound. Like Pepper's."

"Oh my God!"

"Send an ambulance fast. And police."

"Will do. And you should—"

"Mona? Listen to me."

"I have to advise you to—"

"Forget the advice and listen. Jack was looking after Pepper Monahan's baby. The baby's vanished. Make sure the cops know that."

*Keep a basket handy to your closet. Toss stained,
torn, or ruined items as soon as you notice them,
and then dispose of them quickly.*

24

Jack's pulse seemed strong to me. Although I begged him not to move, he dragged himself out of the closet, mumbling about the little dude. Had Nick taken the baby? But why? He never even looked after the child. Did he plan to use Little Nick as a bargaining chip? And if not Nick, who?

The EMTs arrived before the police. I'd been hoping Brad Dykstra would be one of them, and I was happy to see that he was. He and his partner checked out Jack. I'd never seen Jack panic, but he was shouting, "I can't go to the hospital. What about the little dude?"

I ached to go with Jack, but I knew I had to locate the baby. "Don't worry. I'll find him," I said as both the EMTs tried to calm him. I was glad Jack didn't realize the terror I felt for Little Nick.

Brad's face was grim when I explained about the baby.

"What's taking the cops so long?" I complained.

"Search me," he said. "This is pretty serious stuff. You ask me, these guys are real bozos."

"No argument here," I said.

I didn't want the pooches to escape again on this night of calamity. I leashed them and followed as Jack was taken down the steep stairs and loaded into the ambulance.

Our neighbors are all either pleasant, low-key middle-aged couples, or young families. Eight or nine people were gathered in nervous clumps watching the ambulance load up Jack and speed off. Still no police. I hurried over to the nearest group of murmuring watchers and whisperers. A flurry of questions about Jack followed. I asked, "Did anyone see anything? Did you notice anyone go into the house with Jack? It's very, very important. I am hoping the police will be here soon and we need to tell them."

My next-door neighbor, a pleasant young woman called Sarah, said, "But the police have already been here."

"What do you mean? The police haven't been here."

She nodded and her red curls bounced. "They were, and the officer carried the baby out. Jack had told me he was looking after the child of that injured police detective. The one whose husband tried to kill her. I guess they came to take the baby back."

"My God," I said. "I don't think so."

She stared at me. "Yes! He had the baby when I looked out the window to see what the noise was about. It's hard to miss a baby having a screaming fit."

It didn't make sense to me. Little Nick loved Nick. Pepper had said so. Wouldn't the child be excited to see his father? Not screaming his baby head off. Had he bonded with Jack? Or had he been traumatized when Nick injured Jack? How had I been so stupid as to give Nick the benefit of the doubt all this time, to defend him against accusations that he could have injured Pepper? Something very bad must have happened inside Nick Monahan's brain, and whatever it was, he had to be stopped. I tried not to imagine that he could hurt his child. But I'd never been able to imagine that he would attack Pepper, either.

A low rumble of thunder sounded. We both glanced up as a jagged slash of lightning lit the sky. I turned away from a lot of excited talk and called 911 again.

"Mona! Where are the police? The ambulance came, but there's not a single cop."

"But that was a hoax," Mona said. "You should know better, Charlotte Adams. What are you, addicted to 911?"

People backed away from me as I bellowed, "What do you mean a hoax? Jack has a head injury, a lot like Pepper's only not so severe. That's no hoax! Where did you get such a stupid idea?"

"Apparently it was a hoax."

"I was here. It's anything but a hoax."

"But the police are saying—"

"What police?"

"I don't know. We just got word."

"Wouldn't someone come by anyway? To verify? The EMTs are here, dealing with an injured man."

My mind was whirling. Did Nick still have the connections to call the station and tell them something was a hoax? Could he have still been able to delay the cops' arriving? I shook my head at my own question. I could have believed it of a more intelligent person, but Nick could never have carried off the subtle manipulation of the police communication system without a snag, especially now in the state he was in, with an APB out for him.

Mona said, "They know what they're doing, Charlotte."

"Not this time, they don't. Call it in again and tell them my apartment is a crime scene, attempted murder and kidnapping. I'm calling Todd Tyrell now with this. He'll be orgasmic to hear that the cops won't come out for something like this."

Mona said, "Wait, Charlotte!"

But I hung up and called the easy-to-remember number for WINY's eyewitness-news hotline. I described the injured man, the stolen baby, and the police decision not to show up. It wouldn't win me any friends in the police force, but it might get some action.

The rain started pounding down as I left a message for Tierney telling him what I thought of his so-called police force. I added that I was heading to check out the Bounty Inn, where I thought Nick might be. It was the last motel on my list and I was desperately hoping to find him and Little Nick. The dogs were too traumatized to leave at home. I put them in the car and sped off down the street. Still no sirens, but I passed a WINY media van whizzing toward my violated home.

I kept going toward the south end of town and the Bounty Inn. On the way, I called Sally to see if she could have Benjamin check up on Jack. I left a message for Margaret, asking her to let her lovely Frank know what had happened.

"I might need a lawyer again," I added. "If I get hauled in again, at least this time I won't be in my pajamas."

※

I pulled up in front of the Bounty Inn fifteen minutes later. It was a middle-grade motel, slipping into the lower ranks as the grubby vinyl siding and weedy driveway spoke of the need for an upgrade. I fished the photo of Nick out of my handbag, told the dogs to behave, and splashed through the driving rain to the front entrance, unable to avoid two giant puddles as I ran. I still had the purple key in my hand as I hurried across the worn red and green plaid carpet, trying not to breathe in the scent of too many cigarettes and spilled drinks from the bar off the lobby.

The beefy young man behind the desk half smiled a

weary welcome. I thought the smile faded a bit when he took in my drowned rat look. "How can I help you?"

"You can tell me if this man is a guest here," I said, placing the photo on the counter. The print was now damp around the edges, but there wasn't anything I could do about that. I could tell by the look on his face that he did recognize Nick, although I figured our boy was holed up in this spot under some other name.

"Is he here now?"

"I can't tell you that. Or even if he's a guest," he said, nervously loosening the collar of his shirt.

"I know you recognized him. This is a life-and-death matter. I need to talk to him."

"I can check with his room and see if he wants to speak to—who shall I say?"

"Charlotte." I waited to see if Nick would pick up.

He shook his head and his chin wobbled. "No answer in that room. Sorry."

I slumped against the counter. What now?

"Thank you," I said as a new plan formed. Nick might choose not to answer the phone if he was in as much trouble as I thought he was. But there was a good chance I had his spare door key. I thanked the young man and headed out, got in the car, and drove around to the back of the motel. I stared at the cars parked in the lot. There was a classic Mustang parked by room 116, precisely the type of car that Nick might want to buy, borrow, or possibly steal. The plates were strategically obscured by mud. I walked confidently up to the door and tried the key. Would it still work? But that didn't matter because the door wasn't even closed. I stood to the side and pushed it all the way open with my foot, one of the benefits of watching cop shows. I bent low and peeked. The room was obviously empty. The bathroom door was clearly visible from the entrance. It too was open and also empty. There was a jumble of take-out containers and some clothing that I thought I recognized as Nick's. Little Nick's monkey lay on the carpet. I gazed at the overturned furniture: a chair upside down, a spilt can of Bud, with a slow drip down the bedside table.

Where had Nick gone? What had he done with the baby? I got into the car as the desk clerk came around the corner with a person I figured must be the manager. I stepped out into the rain again. Truffle and Sweet Marie went into guard-dog mode and barked their heads off from inside the car.

"Did the police come for him? It's very important."

They exchanged glances, one of the sure signs that a question has hit home. The rain drenched their hair and clothing; mine, too.

I said, "Look, this involves a missing baby. It is going to be very serious, and if you don't cooperate, it won't look good for your motel when the media gets hold of it. I have been in touch with Todd Tyrell, and he'd love to get over here with his—"

"Don't threaten us," the manager blustered.

I shrugged and pressed the number for WINY. The manager held up his hand in defeat. I knew I was being a little bully, but I didn't care. The stakes were too high.

"A patrol car came by and an officer asked for him."

"Did you tell the officer to come back with a warrant?"

I could tell by their expressions that this hadn't happened. "What did the officer look like?"

They stared at me.

I said, "A uniformed officer? Male? Young? Bright? Not too tall?"

He shrugged. "A uniformed officer. I didn't see his face clearly. He wasn't exactly standing in the light."

"I bet he wasn't." No indeed. Officer Dean Oliver wouldn't want his face recognized this time any more than he would have when he ran into Anabel unexpectedly at the construction site. "Did he show you his badge?"

"He was a uniformed officer. What? Am I going to give him a hard time?"

He had a point, so I let that go. "Did you see them leave?"

That got one no and one yes. "Okay," I said, "maybe the television reporter will get it out of you."

The desk clerk blurted, "The guy you showed me was in the backseat. He's been staying here. He said his name was Mick Houlihan. I told the cop we didn't know it was the same guy. How could we?"

I said, "Where was the baby?"

"In the front seat with the cop."

The manager worked hard to be dignified, impossible with his hair flattened by the rain and his shirt and jacket soaked through. "They'll have a good reason for taking him in. I think he was the guy they've been looking for, the one who tried to kill his wife. If you want to know what happened, you'll have to go to the police station. It's nothing to do with us."

I had one last question. "When?"

The sodden clerk said, "A few minutes before you got here."

I jumped back into the Matrix and headed out at high speed. I wished I had my Miata as I knew how it handled in all conditions, including the now driving rain. I also wished I wasn't soaked to the bone.

One thing was sure: Dean Oliver would not be taking Nick to the station. Otherwise, he would have called for backup and for paramedics to check out Little Nick. The parking lot of the Bounty Inn should have been choked with police vehicles now. It wasn't. Not even the sound of a distant siren. Instead, Nick was in the backseat of the squad car, with no way to get out. I knew this was bad news for Nick. Dean must have a hell of a reason to take a risk like that. A person with nothing much to lose is a dangerous opponent.

I had nothing to go on but what I already knew. Where could this officer be taking them and why? Was Dean Oliver was using Little Nick to compel Nick to do something? But what? I couldn't imagine, but I knew this guy was capable of anything. The image of Pepper's face flashed through my mind. I imagined the screaming baby being carried away and poor foolish Nick trapped. Except for the why, it was beginning to fall into place. Dean Oliver was pleasant and smart enough to have tricked Nick to going to the storage area in the old industrial park. Easy enough to fool Nick with a text from his "wife." Oliver knew Pepper, too, of course. How hard would it have been to take Nick's baton, cell phone, keys, and squad car and head to Bakker Beach, having first texted Pepper to meet him there? My Miata was found not far from the same industrial park, probably close to where Dean Oliver had left his own squad car. If he'd burned rubber, he would have been back at the beach, but one of the late arrivals. He'd been watching the Monahan house, too, and getting paid to do it. I was betting it was Dean Oliver's own image that would have shown up on the security tape as he kicked in the Monahan's door, hoping to find Nick before the other cops did. What's more, he knew exactly where I lived and that Jack was taking care of Little Nick. Everything made sense, except the why.

I felt that this was all somehow connected with Anabel's death, as Nick's fear seemed to stem from that tragic event. Had Dean Oliver been the cop who entered the site from the Potter Street side? Had he been in a meeting that was best kept secret? Dean Oliver, golden boy, would have been perfectly positioned to keep the cops from interfering with criminal operations in that neighborhood. Had

Anabel, dressed for her simple City Hall wedding, stepped behind the gate and seen something she shouldn't have? Is that why she died? If Nick Monahan had any clue about that, it would be worth Dean Oliver's efforts to threaten his family. Had he turned the tables by attacking Pepper and turning Nick into a monster in the eyes of the cops and the community? Nick could accuse Dean of anything at this point and no one in their right mind would believe him. Except me. Not that the cops would believe me, either.

So where would they be now? I thought hard. On a night like this, the rough dirt road to Bakker Beach would be a sea of mud. Even a squad car could get stuck. So I doubted he'd pick that spot. The storage units were on the opposite side of town on the outskirts, about a twenty-minute drive. That was possible but less likely.

Aside from his home and Pepper's hospital room, both under police guard, the one other place that had a feature role in this series of events was the construction site. I was out of ideas, so it was worth a try. I tore off in that direction. The dogs huddled in the backseat, catching my anxiety, whining softly. I called Tierney again and told him where I was going. I told him to send a car to Bakker Beach and another to the industrial park to be sure. Then in case he didn't pick up or didn't believe me, I called Margaret and told her that Nick and the baby might have been kidnapped by Officer Dean Oliver. "I'm heading for the construction site. I'm not far now."

"Don't go there, Charlotte," she shouted.

"Tell Frank," I shouted back as I careened onto Friesen Street. "Tell him to get people out there, in case. But I'm here now."

"Stay in the car," Margaret yelled.

"I will. Get off the phone and call Frank."

I would have stayed in the car, too, if I hadn't seen a shadow move past the viewing slot in the fence. I moved the

Matrix as close as I could and got Sally on the line. "Sally, stay on the line. I need to see who has taken Nick and the baby. I believe it's Officer Dean Oliver. I'll try to identify him if I can and get a shot of him with my phone."

"Are you insane?"

"Sally, it's the baby, too. No, wait. I have a better idea."

I hung up on Sally and called Thalia. She was surprised to hear from me. "Remember you said there wasn't much excitement around here and you'd like some? There's going to be plenty tonight. Please call your friend on Potter Street and tell her to keep an eye on the construction site from her window. Can you do that, too?"

"We can go down there," Thalia said.

I yelped, "Please don't. The person has hostages already. Tell your friend Jane not to come out."

"Surely there's safety in numbers. We could get everyone in our buildings—"

"There's no safety in numbers if someone starts shooting at witnesses. Please stay inside, but keep watch to see if anyone comes or goes. I have to go. Thank you, Thalia."

Thalia said, "I can see a red car parked outside it."

"That's me. Please keep watching. And call 911. Tell them you think someone is being attacked on the site. But whatever you do, don't mention my name."

I snapped the phone closed and told the dogs to be good. With luck Margaret would have called Frank, and Tierney would listen to his voice mail. My hands were shaking so much that I dropped the phone. It slipped down the side of the driver's seat and landed on the floor underneath, out of reach. With fumbling fingers, I felt for the lever to let the seat slide all the way back. I grabbed the phone and picked it up. I wondered if it would be better to move the car to another spot, to keep the dogs safe. I was panicky, not thinking too clearly. Without pushing the seat back into place, I gripped the steering wheel. Of course, my feet didn't come anywhere near the pedals. Like the squad car, this vehicle could accommodate a very tall person. That's when the last piece of the puzzle slipped into place.

When I'd tried to drive Nick's squad car at Bakker Beach, the seat had been adjusted for a person taller than Nick. And much taller than Dean Oliver, who was probably no more than five seven. I'd liked not having to strain my neck looking up at Oliver. I'd accused the wrong cop. But if not Dean, then who?

By now, I figured the guilty party had been interrupted by my arrival. He hadn't intended to leave that car at Bakker Beach. And there was only one person it could have been. Not Dean Oliver at all, but the same officer who'd been on duty when Pepper supposedly fell in the hospital. With mounting horror I could see that he'd probably taken her by surprise and knocked her down, sparing him the danger that she would remember who really attacked her with his baton at Bakker Beach. Roger DeJong. The guy who got the Joe jobs and got chewed out by his superiors. He'd been the last uniformed officer to arrive back at Bakker Beach, and now I knew why. He'd had to ditch Miata in town and retrieve his own police car, left behind when he took Nick's to Bakker Beach. I was pretty sure the plan had been to kill Pepper and frame Nick.

He knew from guarding Pepper that Jack was looking after the baby. Easy for him to find out that Jack and I lived in the same house. He was a cop, after all. Roger DeJong had neatly fingered Dean Oliver. Roger DeJong knew that I was nosing around and talking to Dimitri. He'd have figured it was a matter of time until I talked to people on Friesen or Potter Street and found a witness to the fact he'd been there on the day of Anabel's death. I dashed from the car, scrambled along the sidewalk, and peeked through the slot in the fence. A convenient flash of lightning lit the sky. Sure enough. This time, I'd figured it out. In the darkened

area I saw Nick, on all fours, pleading with Officer Roger
DeJong. Another person lay crumpled in a dark heap. I
could see enough of his face to identify my smart young officer, Dean Oliver. I thought I could see dark blood pooled
around his head and a long gash marring his forehead.
DeJong really liked that baton. Had DeJong killed Dean
Oliver? Was he now setting Nick up to take the rap? I'd
been too stupid to see what was happening. DeJong had
his weapon trained on Nick and was holding the squirming
Little Nick in the crook of the other arm.

My cell phone trilled. I flipped it open, trying to keep
the noise from distracting DeJong. I ducked to the right,
hoping I was out of his earshot.

Thalia said, "Jane tells me there are already two police
cars on Potter Street by the site."

A shot rang out. I was pretty sure it would have gotten
me if I hadn't moved. I said, "It's not official police business for sure. The dispatcher won't know that they're there.
Tell them officer down."

Thalia said, "That will bring the cavalry."

I moved away from the Friesen Street entrance and
crept down the alley and out onto Potter Street. I scrambled
along by the two police cars, pausing to let the air out of the
tires, something that Pepper and I had amused ourselves
doing once or twice as preteens. Of course, we hadn't chosen squad cars for our pranks. The sight of a little yellow
toy duck lying in a puddle reminded me how deadly serious this was.

I stood on Potter Street and looked up. Faces showed in
the lit windows behind me.

I moved off to the side, shielded by the wall of the attached building, in case he decided to fire another shot.
"Roger," I shouted. "Give it up. The cops know what you've
done. Don't make it any worse. This time it would be pre-
meditated, not an accident. Let Nick and the baby go."

"Nobody knows." Roger DeJong's voice. Finally, I'd gotten something right.

My heart was thundering, because I knew that in my subsequent bluff, I could easily go wrong again and blow it. If so, Nick and the baby and Dean Oliver would pay the price. I hoped none of my lies were too obvious.

"Listen, Roger. They know that you tricked Nick into going to the storage area, where you knocked him out, and then you took his cruiser to meet Pepper at Bakker Beach. They've got forensic evidence to link you to that and to the attack on Pepper. It was all to frame Nick, wasn't it, so he wouldn't finger you for Anabel Beauchamp's death. I'm sure you can make the case that was an accident. No one will take Nick seriously. You can minimize the damage."

"You don't know what you're talking about."

More bluffing. "You have Dean Oliver back there, injured or possibly dead. And once again you plan to frame Nick."

Nick's voice, high and panicked, shot back, "Don't make things worse. He'll hurt Little Nick. He's been threatening me since just after that girl died. It took me a while to figure it all out, but he was already here on the site at the time. I was just on patrol and I happened by right as the 911 call came in. I guess he could tell by looking at me afterward that I knew what that meant. He told me he'd have Pepper and Little Nick killed if I accused him. And he said he had stuff on me, and I guess he did, and he swore he'd make sure my word was worthless. I had to keep quiet, but, Charley, I kept seeing that girl drowned and knowing he did it. I dream about it. And look, he did try to kill Pepper and make it look like it was me."

This was no time to suggest that if Nick had confided in his wife—who was ten times smarter than he was—none of this would have happened, except for Anabel's death.

"Nick, listen to me!"

"No. I'll do what he wants. I'm the problem. It has to look like I'm a killer. He'll let Little Nick go, but he'll kill me and claim that it was to protect Dean. Dean's toast, too. He's bleeding out, so he won't be able to talk. And DeJong is a hero, saving the baby. He'll come after you, too, and Pepper."

"I don't think he will shoot you, Nick. At this point there are many, many witnesses and not just me. Keeping you two alive is the only chance he has to save himself now. Trust me, he can't get away. Roger, I need you to listen to me. There must be a hundred eyes on you here. Every resident of this area has a light on and is watching. People have cell phone cameras and video cameras. You can't shoot them all. You won't be able to leave without plenty of witnesses. It's over. Give the baby to Nick. You can explain the rest, but not if something happens to Nick or the baby."

There was no freakin' chance this creep could explain his way out of his crimes, but I was on a roll.

"Do it!" I yelled. "I can hear the sirens. It's all over, Roger."

The next sound I heard was a sharp scream from Nick, then a splash. Was that a second splash? I wasn't sure. The gate to the site swung inward and DeJong emerged, firing his weapon in a seemingly random arc. He leaped into the first squad car and rocketed away. Sirens were coming closer. I didn't figure he'd get far with flat tires. I dashed through the gate to find Nick floating facedown in the watery foundation. The baby was nowhere to be seen. In a moment of horror, I realized what the second splash had meant. I had no choice but to jump into the water. I struggled to turn Nick over, get his face out of the water, and prop him against the slippery wooden wall. He was unconscious. The blood streaming from his forehead told me why. I bent down and crawled through the filthy murk, feeling around for the baby, splashing and shouting for help as I did. Seconds felt like hours until I made contact with something round and soft and moving. Little Nick! I lifted him up. He didn't cry. A bad sign. At the edge of the foundation, a head appeared. A smart young head with a gash on it. Dean Oliver.

At the same moment, I watched as the unconscious Nick flopped forward face-first into the water.

I shouted, "Mouth-to-mouth to the baby, fast, while I help Nick."

Turned out that was a good move. I could apologize to him later.

The WINY media van had a field day with me. I looked like what my mother would call the Creature from the Black Lagoon. Gripping footage that. But who gave a hoot? Little Nick, his father, and Dean Oliver were all alive. Even though we didn't yet know that Roger DeJong had been stopped at the end of Potter Street by a pair of squad cars, it was already a good news story.

Frustrated by fumbling for clothes in the dark confines of your closet? Install an inexpensive stick-on LED light inside the closet and make your life a lot easier.

25

I rang the Beauchamps' doorbell three days later. Harry was gracious, although he did say, "Well Charlotte honey, you sure do look a lot prettier today than you did the other night on television."

"The story of my life, Harry. I'm used to it now."

"It was pretty shocking news we heard. A policeman killing our little girl."

"Yes. They've arrested him, and I believe they'll make those charges stick. And of course, he was the officer who was supposed to talk to the neighborhood witnesses after her death. No wonder the police appeared not to follow up. Luckily some of the folks on the street will make good witnesses."

"Well, I guess it turned out Lorelei was right after all. I'll be making amends for that. I feel sorry I doubted her mother's intuition."

"If it's any consolation, I didn't believe it, either. I was only trying to prove that it had been an accident. If my friends hadn't been involved, I would have left it at that. Do you mind if I speak to her alone for a minute?"

"Sure thing. She's in the living room. Champagne cocktail for you? It's June Sparkle today."

"No thanks, Harry. Nothing for me."

I found Lorelei at the vast window gazing at the Hudson River. I stood beside her for a couple of minutes. I could only imagine how she was feeling. Finally I reached out and up and gave her a hug. "You didn't cause Anabel's death, Lorelei. I believe it was a fluke of timing that she went behind the gate and spotted DeJong talking to one of the criminals he dealt with. Anabel would have recognized him and she would have been well aware of who his cozy criminal contact was, although DeJong hasn't revealed that. He's probably afraid for his own life, now that he's in jail. Anabel must have concluded he was on the take. Perhaps she saw money changing hands, although I can't prove that. DeJong knew Anabel was fierce enough to make sure it would all come out. He knew she was fearless. She would have gone to the police, to the media, whatever it would take. She was a brave and splendid woman, a daughter to be proud of."

Naturally, I didn't talk about the specifics of my theory that DeJong must have struggled with Anabel, while his criminal contact left the scene. I had a horrible image of him knocking her out before pushing her from the slippery walkway into the brackish water to drown, solving his problem until Nick blundered in. I knew the police believed this was what happened, but no mother needed to envision that dreadful scene.

I'd never seen tears in Lorelei's eyes before. "I did cause her death, though. She chose to duck behind that fence so I wouldn't see her. She didn't want me to interfere in her wedding. And I couldn't let it alone. I had to go down there to plead the case for a long white gown and rose petals and violins. It was because I loved her. I thought I knew what was best."

And perhaps you wanted a more suitable groom, I thought. I kept my mouth shut, though. Whatever else I'd believed in the past, I knew that Lorelei had loved Anabel, not in the totally accepting way that Harry did, but it was love anyway. I wondered if she could ever share with Harry her part in the tragedy. I was glad it wasn't up to me.

"It wasn't your fault, Lorelei," I said again. Even though I knew she'd never believe me. "If you hadn't pushed the point, I never would have followed up and DeJong would have gotten away with murder."

I did take a moment to talk to Harry on my way out. "This boy Dimitri was very special for Anabel. I hope you will spend some time with him and support the work that Anabel was doing with Hope for Youth at Risk. Maybe in time Lorelei will take part, too."

"Of course, Charlotte darlin'," he said. "That will be Anabel's legacy."

I didn't stay long. I had a delivery to make. I had two boxes of black-and-white fudge, one for Thalia Waverman and one for Jane Cantley. They truly deserved a reward.

The Hudson was flowing fast as I stood alone on the shores by Bakker Beach. The June rains meant high, roiling water. I can always understand the fascination of the river. It's a good place to think. I had lots on my mind, mostly questions. Pepper was on the mend, although it would take a while. She and Nick were working on what she called "trust issues." Little Nick showed no negative effect from his minute or two under the filthy water, although Sally and Benjamin were keeping experienced eyes on him. I wondered if Nick's idiotic behavior attempting to evade Roger DeJong would mean the end of his career in the police. He was still going through interviews. Three generations of

Monahans on the Woodbridge force might not be enough to salvage his job.

— ❧ —

Sally and Margaret were planning a misfit party as soon as Pepper was out of the hospital. Negotiations were underway to see if spouses would be included. The fun never ends.

In the meantime, I had plenty to do to make up for a practically workless week. Lilith and I had a date with Wendy to show her the altered yellow skirt and take some "after" photos of the closet project. I imagined Seth would be around, tripping over his feet.

I had three messages from Tierney asking for a truce and suggesting dinner. I had already decided not to say "yes" to truce and "no" to dinner. In the hospital I had managed to apologize to Dean Oliver for falling for DeJong's trickery and for believing he could be a villain. He'd said we were even, as I'd saved his life. Like Jack he had a head injury that wasn't expected to do any lasting damage.

Jack was already back at CYCotics taking care of business; the stitches in his forehead seemed to go well with the swaying palms on the latest Hawaiian shirt. I'd never mentioned his secret stash of photos in his closet, but I thought I'd figured out what it meant.

I reached into my pocket and pulled out the small silk-covered box with the secret I'd kept in my own closet for the past two years. It was time to let the past go and start trusting again. Ready to stop looking to the wrong kind of man. More important, I was prepared to see what was right in front of my eyes. This time, I really, actually, truly did toss that square-cut diamond solitaire into the Hudson. Two years earlier, I'd tossed a stone into the Hudson, pretended it was the ring, and enjoyed the dramatic impact on my lying hound of an ex-fiancé. It had felt good at the time, but I hadn't done myself any favors hanging on to it. Now it felt a whole lot better to get it out of my life.

Half an hour later, I was sporting a wide grin as I used my foot to push open the door to CYCotics. I was juggling a tray of jumbo lattes and three sandwiches from Ciao! Ciao! Mozzarella, roasted red peppers, and Genoa salami on Tuscan bread.

Disaster usually improves Jack's appetite. He met me at the door. "Only three sandwiches? Is that all?"

"Actually," I said, "it isn't."

Mary Jane Maffini is a lapsed librarian, a former mystery bookstore owner, a previous president of Crime Writers of Canada, and a lifelong lover of mysteries. In addition to the Charlotte Adams books, she is the author of the Camilla MacPhee series, the Fiona Silk adventures, and nearly two dozen short stories. She has won two Arthur Ellis awards for best mystery short story as well as the Crime Writers of Canada Derrick Murdoch Award. She is currently at work on the next Charlotte Adams adventure and is grateful for all the tips she gets from Charlotte. Mary Jane lives and plots in Ottawa, Ontario, along with her long-suffering husband and two princessy dachshunds. Visit her website at www.maryjanemaffini.com.